EASY COME EASY GO

ALASKA GOLD FEVER

Ron Walden

Alaskan True to Life Crime Writer

ISBN 978-1-95-726314-4
eBook ISBN 978-1-95-726316-8

Library of Congress Catalog Card Number: 2014935812

Manufactured in the United States of America.

Acknowledgement

The Forelands Bar is a real place. It has been serving Nikiski residents for more years than most can remember. The past owners have been a checkered group: some reputable and some not. The current owner is a wonderful lady by the name of Chrystal Shoenrock. She rules from behind the bar with wit and humor. Her reputation for being a good and helpful neighbor is respected throughout the Kenai Peninsula. An import from Kalispell, Montana, Chrystal has made Nikiski her home and plans to remain in Alaska.

If you are in Nikiski, Alaska and want to enjoy a strong beverage or cold beer I encourage you to stop and meet this wonderful and friendly lady.

I thank her for allowing me to use the name and location of her bar in this book. I strive for realism in my novels and she has contributed to this effort with a willing gusto. Thank you, Chrystal.

I also want to thank my new editor, Diann Elyse Enderby. We had never worked together previously, but she has proved her worth. I thank her for making this book interesting and readable. She has a sharp eye for detail and the ability to make my story sound professional. Thanks a million, Diann.

Chapter 1

The rig tender service boat, *Champion*, had been off-loading supplies and goods for the ongoing upgrades to the Steelhead oil platform in Cook Inlet, Alaska. The delivery was completed and the *Champion* was backing away from the platform. Crane operator Dan Goodson was preparing to lock his crane into place and climb down from his lofty perch to the deck below. When he turned the boom parallel to the west side of the platform, he saw an airplane approaching. Normally they passed overhead at 3,500 feet or more, but this one was low and headed directly for the Steelhead oil drilling platform. He studied it a moment before speaking by radio with the skipper of the *Champion*.

"Gus, can you still hear me?" he asked.

"Yeah, I hear you, Danny. What's up?"

"Look south. That plane is coming right toward us, and I don't think his engine is running."

There was a short pause. "I see it. I think you're right. It looks like his engine quit. I'm going to point the bow toward the south and watch him. I don't want him to hit me."

Using the engines and the bow thrusters to maneuver made the huge boat look surprisingly nimble. The crane operator had his own field glasses trained on the descending aircraft now. It was getting lower and only a quarter of a mile to the south. Goodson judged the plane would hit the water less than 200 yards to the west. As he watched, the plane continued to lose altitude.

Goodson could see three men on the deck of the *Champion* preparing for a rescue attempt of the pilot. One of the men had donned a harness and another attached a safety line to the webbing. The third man had brought a large yellow lifting strap to the back deck. Now a fourth man appeared, moving toward a small hydraulic hoist mounted to the starboard side of the vessel.

All the while the small craft continued to lose altitude. It was only about fifty yards to the left of the boat when the fat tundra tires kissed the water. Spray flew from under the wheels and the aircraft slowed dramatically. Everything was looking good until the plane lost the lift created by airflow over the wings. When that occurred, the tires sank deeper into the water. They were about half submerged when the nose pitched forward, biting into the salt water. Now Goodson could see the pilot inside, fighting to control the craft. It was hopeless. The plane was in the water, nose first, and sinking, slowly.

The *Champion* quickly edged close to the sinking plane. One crewman on the back deck opened a small gate in the side rail. Gus inched the rear of the boat under and as close as possible to the sinking airplane. The crewman wearing the safety harness took one end of the lifting strap and passed it around the fuselage of the airplane. He gave it a pull and made another wrap while the crewman operating the small hydraulic hoist swung the boom around and dropped the cable. The man in the harness motioned for more cable, then snapped the hook into the triangular ring on the ends of the lifting strap.

As he was pulled back onto the aft deck, the hoist operator began to lift the airplane. The arm of the hoist was small and had just enough reach to lift the little Piper onto the deck. The three crewmen on deck manhandled the plane to its wheels and motioned for the operator to begin lowering the tail of the airplane to the metal deck.

As soon as the tail wheel hit the deck the men opened the door and released the seatbelt from the pilot. They quickly pulled him from the plane and checked for breathing and pulse. He was obviously beyond help, but they checked anyway. He had severe head injuries, though there was little damage to the plane. He had not been equipped with a shoulder harness and the violent pitching of the nose had caused him to lurch forward and be bludgeoned by the instrument panel.

Dan Goodson was still in the cab of his crane aboard the Steelhead when one of the men on the deck of the *Champion* gave him a thumbs-down signal. Goodson was on the cell phone with Alaska State Trooper Dispatch when he got the word. He reported the incident to the troopers with as much detail as he could accurately relate. After reporting the aircraft identification numbers, he signed off. He radioed Gus to call 911 and talk to the dispatcher. Gus said he would do that, as he pointed the *Champion* toward the Arness Dock in North Kenai.

Dan Goodson was shaken and trembling when he climbed down the long ladder to the open deck of the Steelhead platform. The shift foreman, Leon Pete, was waiting for him.

"Are you OK?" Leon asked.

"Yeah, I'm fine." He wiped his face with a handkerchief from his hip pocket. "I have to call the troopers again. I forgot to tell them I took a video with my cell phone. I think I have the crash on my phone. I haven't looked at it yet, but it should be there."

Leon Pete was stunned by Goodson's presence of mind in the crisis. "You took pictures of the crash?"

"I think so, if the camera did its job." He wiped his face again. "Can we go to the galley to look at it? I need some coffee."

The two men went inside and down the steps to the small galley. Pete poured two cups of coffee and brought them to the table where Goodson was sitting. He was pressing buttons on his cell phone. Suddenly he was excited, "Here it is. Come take a look."

The two men stared at the small screen. The video began at the point when the wheels touched the water and continued until the crew was affixing the lifting strap to the craft. Some detail was lacking due to the quality of the camera and the shaking of its operator, but it clearly showed the entire crash incident.

Pete was the first to speak. "Let's download this to my computer right now. We have to keep a copy of this. You did an amazing job, Dan."

"I don't know about amazing. I hardly remember taking the pictures, but I agree with you about making a copy. I'll get my cable out of my room and call the troopers to let them know about this. I'll send it to Gus, too. He'll want a copy for his reports."

"Come to my office when you finish your coffee and get the cable and the troopers called. I'll meet you there." Leon Pete picked up his cup and headed out of the galley while Dan took another few sips of his and collected his thoughts.

Goodson keyed his radio, which was still on the channel he used to talk with the *Champion*. "Gus, are you still listening?"

There was a short pause, "I'm here, Dan, what's up?" Gus replied.

"I just wanted to tell you that I got video of the crash on my cell phone. I just looked at it and it's pretty good. We're going to download it to the foreman's computer, and I'll email you a copy. "

"Wow! That's almost too good to be true. I'd really appreciate that. Thanks, Dan."

"You guys did all the work. I just sat up there in the cab of my little toy and watched. It doesn't have all the rescue on the tape, but it shows your crew in action and getting the strap on the plane. They did an outstanding job, Gus. The company should give them a bonus for this one."

"I think you're right about them. Thanks." The *Champion* was approaching the dock where a trooper was waiting. The afternoon light was beginning to fade and large work lights were turned on at the Arness Dock. The tide, which had been almost slack high tide when the rescue was attempted, was now running hard and going to get worse. The day's high tide was 19.9 feet and the low would be a minus 3.8 feet. "I have to go, Dan. We're about to tie up at the dock. I'll talk with you later."

Goodson set the radio aside and dialed the phone. He called to notify the trooper dispatch of the video he had taken. She said she would relay the message to the investigator, who was at the dock in Nikiski, and she gave him the investigator's email address to send the video to.

Dan finished his coffee and picked up his phone. He felt weak and tired as he descended the stairs to the office of the foreman. He made a mental note to never again wish for a little excitement on the job. Boredom had suddenly become pleasant.

Trooper sergeant and head investigator for this detachment, Bob Seaton, was standing on the edge of the Arness Dock as the *Champion* approached. Arness Dock is comprised of several old World War II Liberty ships. They were grounded here and filled with dirt and gravel. It was inexpensive and quick and has filled the purpose since the early Cook Inlet oil exploration days. Seaton watched as Gus brought the boat to a halt and the crew tied lines to the dock. Once the engines were back to an idle, Gus came to the back deck to welcome the trooper.

"Hello there, Gus. It's been a long time." Seaton greeted the captain.

"I'm glad to see you, Bob. Come aboard."

Seaton asked, "Can I have a look at the body of the pilot?"

"Sure. Is someone coming to pick him up?" asked Gus.

"As soon as I finish with my preliminary notes and pictures, I'll call someone. I have a body bag in my car. Also, when I finish with the body I would like to lift the plane to the dock. The National Transportation and Safety Board will be sending an investigator in the morning from Anchorage. They will want to look at it before we take the wings off and truck it to a safe place. Could I use one of your men to help me with my pictures?"

"How long will you be, Bob?" asked Gus.

"It's only a guess, but I think it will take about an hour. After that we will be able to move the plane and you can have your boat back."

"I'll give you two men. The one who attached the lines to the plane is in the galley--getting warmed up. When you finish here, come inside. After the plane is lifted off I'm going out to my buoy and tie up for the night. Let me know when you finish."

Seaton judged the time about right. It was just an hour before he came inside to report he was finished for tonight, and the wrecked plane could be hoisted off the deck. Gus immediately lifted his radio to notify the crane operator on the dock to begin. Arrangements had been made to set the little Piper on the dirt in an open area away from any loading activity.

Once the plane was on dry ground, the sergeant sealed it with evidence tape to prevent any entry before the NTSB investigator had a chance to inspect it. Security of the site was done by a local guard service with an officer to watch over things tonight. It was near midnight when Seaton sent the body bag containing the pilot to the hospital for safekeeping, until the state medical examiner could look at the body. That was scheduled for 10 AM tomorrow.

Seaton was sitting in his car making final notes and checking the time. It had been several hours, but the time had passed quickly. The real work would start tomorrow when the cause of the wreck was determined and the body was examined. He was going back to the office to put the camera with its recorded photos, along with his notes, in the evidence locker. Tomorrow he would retrieve the cell phone video he had been notified of. Today had been a very long day.

Chapter 2

At 6:30 the following morning Bob Seaton came into the office. He poured a cup of fresh coffee and went to his desk. His task was to review his notes from the night before and look at the crash video that Dan Goodson had captured. Everything that Bob had learned from interviews and firsthand inspection of the airplane indicated this was an accident. The NTSB investigator would be here this morning to verify that verdict. Seaton checked the time. He was to pick up the federal agent at the airport; his flight was scheduled to arrive at 7:45 in Kenai. He would take him to the Arness Dock, where the wrecked airplane had remained overnight, and then back to the office to view the crash video.

The sergeant finished his coffee, made his morning equipment check, and headed for the Kenai airport. It was still dark at this time of day with only a light dusting of frost. The stars overhead were bright indicating it would be another sunny day. Somehow, that thought made the day look brighter. The scheduled flight was taxiing to the terminal when Seaton arrived. He parked in a restricted zone and went inside to meet the agent.

A tall man in his mid-50s, the federal man had spotted Seaton's uniform as he entered the small terminal. "I'm Carl Dewayne with the NTSB. Are you here for me?" he said, extending his hand in greeting.

Seaton grasped his hand and shook it strongly, "If you're here about the crash in the Inlet last night, I am." Dewayne nodded. "I'm Bob Seaton; I'm the investigator assigned to this incident--pleased to meet you Carl."

"I'm your guy. Can we go directly to the aircraft? I'd like to see the plane as soon as possible." Carl Dewayne exuded confidence and a polite poise.

"Sure. We can get some coffee in the café at the end of the terminal if you'd like to take some with you."

"That won't be necessary. I seldom drink it."

Carl carried a small athletic bag he had with him out to Seaton's vehicle. The trooper investigator gave him a stiff new manila folder and Carl began to read the crash report, He was quiet most of the way to Nikiski. "My office called this morning and said there was a video of the crash. Is that true?"

"Yes it is. The crane operator took it with his cell phone. He had been off-loading a boat and was just stowing his crane when he spotted the plane coming toward him and descending. He said when it was obvious there was going to be a crash, he picked up his cell phone and took the video. He was high above the action and got some great shots of the plane hitting the water and of the crew of the *Champion* hooking the plane before it sank in the Inlet. Pretty impressive work, in my mind."

"It sure sounds like it." Dewayne went back to reading.

The trooper car left the Kenai Spur Highway and drove slowly down the side road to the Arness Dock, a distance of about two miles. They drove through the gate and stopped near the small airplane.

Dewayne pulled a small recorder from his jacket pocket and began to speak into it: "The aircraft, a Piper PA-11 bearing the identification number N5591D, looks to be dry from last night's dunking in Cook Inlet. The aircraft is being secured by the Arness Dock security people. Evidence tape is visible and undamaged." He put down the recorder and turned to Seaton. "Did you seal the plane with evidence tape?" He asked.

"Yes. I tried to seal the cockpit and engine to prevent contaminating any evidence that might be inside," Bob Seaton explained.

"Good thinking. It looks great, but for your future information, you didn't seal the fuel tanks. Do you think I can get a stepladder? A 6- or 8-foot will do. I want to check the fuel tanks."

Seaton turned to the security guard. "See what you can do, will you?"

The guard walked away shaking his head. He returned a few minutes later with a 6-foot stepladder under his arm. He opened the legs and stood the ladder in front of the wing.

Dewayne thanked him and climbed up, carrying a small glass tube and his recorder. He removed the tank cap and shined a small flashlight inside. He spoke into the recorder, but neither the guard nor Seaton could hear what he was saying. They saw the agent stick the glass tube inside the tank and withdraw it again. He studied the end of the tube and again shined the flashlight inside the tank. Again he spoke into the recorder and began to climb down the ladder. Once on the ground he moved the ladder to the other wing. The previous ritual was repeated. Again he climbed down, returning the glass tube to his small bag.

"I need to open the cowling. Is it OK if I remove the tapes?" Dewayne asked politely.

Seaton pulled a shiny Spyderco Police Model knife from his pocket. "Yeah, it's OK. Let me give you a hand with the tapes." Bob Seaton was determined to make this as professional as possible, but it was plain this man had no intention of making friends.

Once the cowling was opened Dewayne seemed to study every line, wire, fitting and part. All the while he spoke into his recorder. After studying the small Lycoming engine from the right side for several minutes he made his way to the left, opened the cowling, and began the same routine as before—with one exception. On the left side of the firewall where the fuel lines came to the engine compartment, there was a small filtering device with a drain on its underside. Dewayne took a small glass jar from his bag, placed it under the drain, and opened it. Only four or five drops of fluid came out. He closed the drain, stepped back, and held the glass up to the light to inspect the drops inside.

"Just a couple of drops of water. The tanks are empty and there is no fuel at this point in the system. In my opinion he ran out of fuel, causing the crash. That isn't the final verdict, but the evidence points to it as the cause." He didn't wait for a comment but placed the small glass jar inside an evidence bag and marked it. He dropped it inside his small bag and, again, spoke into his recorder.

"Can we get inside the cabin of the plane now?" he asked politely but somehow indicated it was an order.

Bob Seaton cut the evidence tape from the only entrance door. It was located under the wing on the right side of the fuselage. Once the tape was removed Dewayne stepped up and said, "I'll take it from here."

Seaton and the guard stepped back and let the NTSB agent do his work. They watched as Dewayne took several items from inside and placed them on the ground beside the plane. He could identify a sleeping bag, a rifle, a small plastic tool box, and a small bag with, what looked like, emergency supplies. Dewayne also removed what appeared to be a small collapsible sluice, a folding shovel, a gold pan, and a couple of other tools.

"The pilot must have been gold mining," thought Seaton.

Dewayne inspected the inside of the plane for nearly an hour before stepping out from under the wing to answer his phone. He made a note in his notebook, said thanks to the caller, and closed the phone. "That was my office. They say the plane is registered to a man from Nikiski, Alaska by the name of Otis Fairfax. Have you ever heard of him?"

"As a matter of fact I have. I busted him about a year ago for DUI. As I recall he was sort of a nice guy. He wasn't on the highway but on a side street heading home from the Forelands Bar. I can't remember seeing him again since." Seaton did remember that he didn't impound the vehicle: he let

Fairfax's neighbor drive it the quarter mile to the owner's house. The sergeant got chewed out for doing that.

"The registration and other papers in the plane indicate he was the owner. You might want to load these personal items to take with you. You can conduct your investigation now. I think I'm finished here. When you finish with your look-see you can take me to your office and we'll watch the video." Dewayne again spoke into the recorder, and when he finished he made notes in his book.

Seaton judged the NTSB agent to be extremely efficient, albeit without much of a personality. He began to load the items from the airplane into the trunk of his patrol car. The rifle and sleeping bag were first in. When he reached for the small plastic toolbox he was surprised by the weight of it, for its size. He could not imagine what kind of tools would weigh this much and still fit in this box. It was about 14 by 6 inches and 5 inches high. He judged the weight of the box to be 25 or 30 pounds. It was secured with a padlock, which stopped the trooper from looking inside. Once he finished loading everything, he called to Dewayne to get in and they drove back to the office. The trip took almost a half hour; there was little conversation.

Back in the office, Bob poured a fresh cup of coffee and brought Dewayne a bottle of water. Seaton had put the crash footage on a flash drive for the agent. He took it from his desk drawer file and placed it in his computer. He moved a chair and turned the computer to allow the NTSB agent a view of the screen. When the short video began to play both men were amazed at what they saw. It began when the plane was nearly touching the water. It clearly showed a skilled pilot making a water landing in a wheel-equipped airplane. Everything seemed to be going fine until the plane slowed and the tires began to sink. The plane slowed quickly, then the tail of the plane rose quickly, and the nose dipped into the water. The Piper pitched quickly and violently and stopped with the nose beginning to sink deeper into the water. The boat was seen maneuvering close to the tail and a crewman, secured with a harness and a rope, leaned over the side to secure a yellow lifting strap around the fuselage just below the horizontal stabilizer. The crewman snapped the cable from the small hoist to the strap and the hoist operator began to lift the plane. He lifted slowly to allow water to drain from the plane, reducing the weight enough for the small hydraulic hoist to lift and swing it over the rear deck of the *Champion*. Because of the wing, there were no views of the crew removing the pilot from the plane; however, only a moment later, a crewman stepped out and gave a thumbs-down signal to Goodson, who was filming the scene. The video ended there.

Dewayne was impressed. "I don't recall ever, in my career, when I had a video of a crash. This is a first. That crane operator did a great job. You can clearly see the engine was not running when it touched the water. That sort of confirms the fuel starvation theory."

"I agree," said Seaton. He would have commented more, but the phone rang just then. It was the medical examiner.

"Hi, Bob. I missed you at the proceedings this morning. I just called to let you know I finished the autopsy: the pilot died of head trauma. It looks like he was thrown into the instrument panel, fracturing the right side of the skull and breaking the eye socket. He died instantly. There was no water in his lungs. I didn't find anything unusual, but you can read it all in my report." Seaton had attended many autopsies done by Dr. Dean Winston.

"Thanks, Doc. Do you have a positive ID on the victim?" Seaton asked.

"I bagged his personal effects for you. There was a wallet with his driver's license. The picture matched the victim. His name is Otis F. Fairfax. He has a Nikiski address."

"Thanks again, Doc. I'm going to the Kenai Airport in a few minutes to take the NTSB agent back. Would you like a ride?"

"That would be great. Just give me time to clean up."

Seaton turned back to Dewayne. "That was the ME. He confirms the victim is Otis Fairfax. He said the cause of death is trauma to the head. Fractured skull. I'll send you a copy of the autopsy as soon as I get it."

The sergeant gave pulled the flash drive out of the computer and gave it to Dewayne, who placed it in his small bag he had carried all day. The men left the trooper office and made a stop at the hospital to pick up Dr. Winston. Seaton dropped the two men at the terminal without getting out and drove away as the two walked inside. Seaton was not sad about sending the NTSB agent away without thanking him. It seemed to Bob that the agent had an arrogant attitude that went beyond professional norms.

Be that as it may, Sergeant Seaton now had to drive back to North Kenai in an attempt to locate any relatives of Otis Fairfax.

Chapter 3

In the early days of the oil boom, the Forelands Bar and Hotel was the center of much of the rowdy behavior in North Kenai. There was a large camp, owned by the oil company, located almost next door to the Forelands Hotel. In those days fighting, shooting, gambling, prostitution, and any other form of illegal activity were common, off of oil company land—much of it at the Forelands Bar and Hotel. The hotel suffered a suspicious fire some years ago and was since demolished. The bar has seen several owners, but the reports of illegal deeds declined in recent years. The current owner is a retired hooker who goes by the name of Cuddles.

Cuddles, whose real name is Claudia Morris, worked the streets in Anchorage many years ago. In those days she was a petite, cute little thing who did a lot of business. One evening she had a client pick her up in his new sports car: he was drunk, but he paid well. His father was a well-known politician in the city. The son took Cuddles to a motel near Merrill Field, an airport on the east side of town. When he finished he was even more intoxicated than before. He drove her back to the pick-up site and threw her out of the car without paying her. She jumped in front of the car to prevent him from driving away, but he put the little car in gear and gave it the gas. She fell to the curb with her legs in the street. He accelerated over her legs, breaking both. She spent many weeks in the hospital and several years in rehab learning to walk again. The medical expenses were paid by the father, as well as a large settlement to compensate for her loss of work.

After her injury she never returned to the streets. She did nothing for a couple of years but eat, drink, and feel sorry for herself. Eventually she invested her settlement in the Forelands Bar. She now weighed in at nearly 300 pounds and at five feet three inches could only shuffle back and forth behind the bar on her wounded legs. She was as wide as she was tall and sported a huge tattoo of an eagle that spanned from shoulder to shoulder on her back. The artwork was impressive and she delighted in showing it to every newcomer who entered. She was loud and encouraged her customers to join in. The customers were mostly regulars who lived in the neighborhood, many of whom owed her for large, unpaid bar tabs.

As a road trooper Bob Seaton had made many bar checks in the Forelands and was well acquainted with Cuddles. She recognized him the moment he came through the door. She waddled out from behind the bar to hug the tall trooper.

"Where have you been, Honey? I ain't seen you in more than a year." She hugged him again.

"Good to see you, Cuddles," he greeted her. "How have you been?"

"Gettin' bigger and better every day, honey. What brings you out to my neighborhood?"

"I arrested one of your patrons about a year ago. Otis Fairfax. Does he still come in here?" asked Seaton.

"Yeah, when he gets a little cash. Haven't seen him in a few days, though. What's he done now?"

"I hate to be the one to tell you this, but he landed his plane in the inlet last night and died in the crash. I need to find his house and check it out. Do you know if he had any relatives?" asked Bob Seaton.

"He didn't have none that I ever heard about. His place is about a mile up Industrial Street, out front here. Go up to the turn and he owns the first big trailer on the right. Crappy looking place. Can't miss it." Cuddles added, "Damn I'm sorry to hear about Otis. Nice guy. All's he ever talked about was gold mining and striking it rich. I'll miss him."

"Well, thanks anyway, Cuddles. I'll be seeing you," he said as he turned to leave.

"See ya 'round, trooper," she called after him.

Before getting into his car he opened the trunk to get the bag of personal items Doc Winston had given him. He hoped there would be a key to the house among the items. In the bag, under the wallet was a small ring of keys. One looked like the key to an old Ford. One looked like the door key to the home. There were several he could not identify, but one looked like it was to a padlock. He made a mental note to try it in the lock on the plastic tool box when he returned to the office. For now he returned the bag to the trunk of his car, keeping the key ring in his hand. He followed Cuddle's instructions and found the mobile home. It had seen better days and was adorned with a porch that looked unsafe to walk on. At the back was a shed constructed of random types of material. There was a padlock on the shed door.

Seaton stepped up on the porch and knocked on the door. There was no answer. He tried again. Still no answer. He searched the key ring for the one he determined was the key to the door. It unlocked. He opened the door and shouted inside, "Trooper Seaton here. Is anyone home?" Still no answer. He punched the key on the radio attached to his lapel to notify dispatch he was entering the home.

The sergeant flipped the light switch as he entered; a single overhead bulb lit up. Surprisingly the place was clean and neat. There were few frivolous items to be found. This was the home of a person with little income and plenty of free time. Seaton walked through the place looking into each room. One room contained an old desk covered with books on mining and mining law. In a drawer he found an address book with only a few personal entries. Mostly it contained numbers of mining supply companies, an attorney, and numbers for BLM and other agencies dealing with mining claims. Finding nothing else, and no names of personal contacts, he turned out the light and locked the front door. This time he secured it with evidence tape.

He located the key to open the shed in back of the mobile home. Inside it was neat and orderly, like the house. There were some shovels, a pick, some ropes, and another small portable sluice. Bob made notes of the contents of the shed and locked the door, sealing it with evidence tape. It was getting late. He notified dispatch he was returning to the office.

On his way back to the office he stopped at Rediske Air Park. Seaton had met the mechanic who worked there and spotted him as soon as he turned into the airstrip. The mechanic had Rediske Air sewn on the back of his coveralls. Seaton checked for air traffic and drove to where the mechanic was working.

He still had his head inside the cowling of a Cessna 206. "Got a minute, Leo?" the trooper called.

Leo Westfal looked up to see Sgt. Bob Seaton. "I do for you," he said, stepping back and wiping his hands on a red rag. "What can I do for you?"

"I came to see if you can help me out. One of your locals put his plane in the inlet last night. We got it before it sank, but I have to get it to somewhere safe. It's on the Arness Dock right now and their security is keeping an eye on it."

"I heard there was a crash; who was it?" asked Leo.

"Otis Fairfax. He lives across the road from the Agrium plant. Do you know him?"

"Oh, wow! He keeps his plane here. His tie-down is over there," he said, pointing down the other side of the runway. I work on his plane for him. What happened? Do you know yet?" Leo fired off questions, still wiping his hands.

"The NTSB agent said it looked like he ran out of fuel. He knew he was crashing and landed the plane as close to the Steelhead Platform as he could. The plane flipped when it hit the water and he hit his head on the instrument panel. The crash killed him, but he would likely have drowned before they got the plane out. The rig tender boat, *Champion*, and its crew did an outstanding job of attempting to rescue him, Leo."

"I'm sorry to hear about Otis. What do you want me to do?"

"The plane has to be moved from the dock and stored somewhere safe until we sort out who owns it now. Is there some way you can move it back here?"

Leo thought a moment. "Sure, I have a trailer I can haul it on, and I can bring it back to his tie- down spot. I'll have to take the wings off to move it, but it should be done anyway. After that dunking in salt water it needs to be flushed out so the tubing doesn't rust. The engine should be flushed, too. I'll take care of that for old Otis. You know, most guys like to come here and talk about airplanes. Otis was different. He always wanted to talk about gold mining. He kept trying to get me to partner with him in a gold claim some-where. I think he had claims all over the state. I'm going to miss that old guy."

Trooper Seaton breathed a sigh of relief. "Thanks for helping, Leo. I didn't know exactly what to do with the plane. Will you need any help with it?"

"No, I know the crane operator down there and he'll help me load the plane on my trailer. The wings aren't heavy, but they're too big for one man to handle alone." Leo Westfal stared at the ground a few seconds and spoke again. "There won't be any charge for this, Sergeant. Otis was a friend and this is for him."

"I appreciate that, Leo. Call me if you need anything at all." Seaton handed a business card to the mechanic before leaving.

Back at the office Sergeant Seaton opened the trunk and took the per-sonal items inside the office for storage in the evidence locker. While there he remembered the key ring. He took the heavy plastic tool box from the locker and placed it on a small table in the room. He searched the key ring to find a key that fit the lock and opened the box. Inside, the toolbox held a surprise for him. There were no tools but personal papers and two leather pouches, each about three inches in diameter and eight inches tall. The small pouches were incredibly heavy. He untied the leather thong securing the top of the fullest of the pouches to find another surprise. The pouch contained gold nuggets, all of which were a quarter- to a half-inch in diameter. He checked the other pouch: it also contained gold, of smaller size but more densely packed. Bob re-tied the pouches and, after weighing them, returned them to the box.

The personal papers in the box were in a gallon-size, water-tight freezer bag. There were several legal documents—mostly mining claim registrations—and a handwritten will. The will was notarized by a court clerk in Kenai on October 1, 2005. That was eight years ago. The will was crude but straightfor-ward. It explained he had no living relatives to claim his property, but he had a friend who helped him many times over the years. The friend's name was

Larry Williams, better known as Skip. Seaton had heard of Skip Williams. He was a drug dealer and had been busted for manufacturing methamphetamines. Otis had left his entire estate, consisting of his property real and personal, to Skip Williams, the helpful neighbor.

Thumbing through the other papers he found a deed to the property on Industrial Street and title to his pick-up, which was parked at his tie-down on Rediske Airpark. There were also seven registered gold claims with locations scattered all over the state. Seaton placed the papers back in the plastic bag and locked them in the box. He returned them to the evidence locker.

At his desk he looked in the computer for the name, address, and possible phone number for Larry "Skip" Williams. He dialed and was surprised to get an answer on the third ring.

"Yeah, what?" came the gruff voice.

"Is this Larry Williams?" Seaton asked.

"Yeah, who wants to know?"

"This is Trooper Sergeant Bob Seaton."

Before he could explain further, an angry voice exploded on the other end: "I ain't done nothin', so just leave me alone!"

"Mr. Williams, please give me a chance to explain. I know you've done nothing wrong, that's not why I called."

Again the angry voice interrupted. "Then why are you callin'? I ain't telling you nothin'."

"Mr. Williams, if you will give me a chance to explain, we can come to an understanding. Your neighbor, Otis Fairfax, has been killed in an airplane crash. He has named you in his will. I want to know if you can come to the trooper office tomorrow to claim his personal items."

"Otis got killed? When?" The voice was now shocked.

"It happened last evening, but we only just now found his will. What time would you like to come into the office tomorrow?"

"Oh, man. I can't believe Otis is dead. Oh, man. How about I come there at ten in the morning, will that be OK?" A now calmed voice asked.

"That will be just fine. I'll be here at ten."

Seaton hung up and began to write his reports. The revelation of the find in the tool box would have to be discussed with his supervisor first thing in the morning.

Chapter 4

By 9:30 the following morning Sergeant Bob Seaton had finished his meeting with the captain. His report had been typed and copied. A fresh cup of hot coffee sat on his desk while he studied the papers in the file in front of him. The description of Otis Fairfax by Dr. Dean Winston gave his age as 63. The printout on the state ID sheet confirmed his date of birth. There was nothing startling on his rap sheet; he was not wanted anywhere, there were no warrants, and he had only one arrest with the date showing it was the arrest Seaton had made last year for DUI.

Larry "Skip" Williams, on the other hand, had a number of arrests and had served time in Alaska for several drug charges. He had been arrested once for possession of cocaine, once for possession of methamphetamines, and once for possession of marijuana for sale. He had served all his time and was no longer on probation. Either he had cleaned up his act in recent months or had not been caught. The intercom interrupted his thoughts. It was the receptionist announcing Larry Williams was at the front desk.

Seaton had never met Williams but picked him out as he opened the door to admit him. He had on a denim jacket, ragged and torn; blue jeans, also torn at the knees; and tennis shoes, unlaced. Not exactly a picture of neatness. Seaton opened the door wide to admit the visitor. "Come with me, Mr. Williams. I'm Sergeant Seaton."

Williams stepped through the door. Once inside he stopped long enough to say, "You can call me Skip. Everybody does."

"Ok, Skip, come with me to my office. I have some things to talk with you about. Can I get you some coffee or a soda?"

"No thanks, I'm going to have breakfast when I leave here."

The two men walked down the hall to Seaton's office. Inside, the sergeant pointed to a chair and stepped behind his desk. As he sat, he began to speak to the nervous guest.

"First of all I would like to offer my sympathy for the loss of your friend. I didn't know Otis well, but everyone I have talked with says he was a nice fellow. Everyone says he was obsessed with prospecting for gold," Seaton explained.

"Thanks. I liked old Otis. He lived next door to me. I used to do chores for him and help him on his place when he needed it. He was twenty years older than me, but our birthdays were only one day apart. He didn't have much but always bought me a birthday cake for my birthday. He bailed me out of jail a couple of times, and I borrowed some money from him to pay a fine once." Williams was speaking quietly now while staring at the floor. It was clear he had kind feelings for the victim.

"Like I said, I feel for your grief and I want to make this meeting as easy on you as possible. I have some things here I want to share with you." Seaton slid a file folder across the desk. "This is a copy of a legally registered will written by Mr. Fairfax. It is registered and notarized by the clerk of the superior court in Kenai. What it says is that he left all his possessions to you. What you have in that file is a copy of the will you can take to an attorney to satisfy any probate questions. The judge will have to grant final transfer of his goods and property."

Williams was wide-eyed now. "Are you saying he left me all his stuff? His trailer and land and his plane? All his stuff?"

"That's right, Skip. Everything. I can't give you the things we have in evidence until the court authorizes you to have it, but I think you'll be surprised to know there is quite a sum of gold included in his things." Seaton had brought the tool box out of the evidence locker and had it in his desk for this meeting. He took it out and opened it to reveal the plastic bag containing his papers. "You have copies of all these papers in the file I gave you. They're his will and several titles, registrations, and the paperwork to several mining claims registered in his name." Seaton lifted the papers out of the plastic box to reveal the two leather pouches.

"These two leather containers hold what we think is gold. We have no idea where it came from, only that it was in this tool box when we opened it. The larger bag contains approximately 15 pounds, 14 ounces of gold nuggets. The smaller bag contains approximately 12 pounds, 3 ounces in smaller nuggets and dust. These weights are in standard U.S. weight and not Troy weight. Troy weight will be about ten percent less than our scales have given you. Again, these are approximate weights because we weighed the bags with the gold. When you consider the value at $1,325 per ounce, which is today's quote, you are a very wealthy man. However, possession is dependent on final disposition by the court."

Skip Williams was looking at the trooper in disbelief. "Are you saying all that gold is mine along with his property and other stuff?"

"That's exactly what I'm saying, Mr. Williams. I'm not completely sure of the weight differences between U.S. and Troy weights, but at today's price of gold I estimate the value of the gold alone at $1.75 million. That is an estimate, but nonetheless a very large sum. I am telling you this because you need to find a lawyer and begin proceedings to claim this property."

Skip was stunned. "I can't believe it … I just can't believe it. I didn't think Otis had a dime and all the time he was a millionaire. I can't believe it."

"The property isn't yours yet, Skip. Hire an attorney and follow the rules to get it signed over to you, and you will be a wealthy man. The court will want you to advertise for creditors for a given amount of time but, at the end of the wait, it will legally be yours. Congratulations; just be careful to stay out of trouble until this is settled. You can't spend it if you're in jail. My advice is to take that file folder to a good attorney on your way home." Seaton was enjoying the new Skip Williams.

They said goodbye and Seaton showed him to the door. Williams walked out to the parking lot seemingly a taller, straighter man. Seaton went back to his office to return the property to the evidence locker.

Skip Williams didn't stop to find a lawyer but drove directly to the Forelands Bar to see Cuddles. He needed advice and she would know what to do. It didn't seem right to take the word of the trooper in such an important matter. His excitement made him press the accelerator and increase his speed to nearly eighty miles per hour when he neared home. Luckily for Skip he wasn't spotted by any troopers on the way to the Forelands. He skidded to a dusty stop in front of the bar. It wasn't open, but Cuddles was inside and the neon lights were on. Skip beat loudly on the locked door.

"We ain't open," came the voice from inside. "What do you want?" It was Cuddles, and she was not in a good mood.

"Cuddles, open up. It's Skip. I have to talk to you."

"Go away, Skip. Come back later when I get open."

"It can't wait. Open up, Cuddles."

"All right, all right. Hold your horses." It seemed like a long time before the door opened. "What's so damned important you can't wait until I get open?" Cuddles asked as she opened the door. She was still wearing her jacket and didn't wait for an answer but turned to walk back to the bar.

"Cuddles, Cuddles. Stop walking and listen to me. I just came from the trooper office. Otis is dead. He got killed in an airplane crash yesterday. He's dead."

"I know that, Skip. I already talked with the trooper."

"Yeah? Well, I bet you didn't know he left all his stuff to me in his will."

"I doubt you have enough money to pay the taxes on his place. It ain't much, and you already own one crappy place."

"That's why I'm here, Cuddles. Otis left all his stuff to me and one of the things I get is two bags of gold. The trooper says it's worth about $1.75 million."

"Come on, Skip. It's too early in the day to listen to this crap. Go home."

"No, Cuddles. It's true. I'll be a millionaire. I just came from the trooper office and that's what he said."

"You should quit smokin' your own stuff, Skip. Get out of here and come back when you can tell me the truth."

"Listen to me, Cuddles. I am telling the truth. I need your help to find a lawyer to help me get my hands on everything."

"Are you serious? You really need a lawyer?" she asked, still skeptical.

"Yes. That's why I'm here. You must know a good lawyer to help me. I need your help."

As she waddled to the other end of the bar she said, "You had better not be scammin' me, Skip Williams. If you are, I'll have Crusher break you into a million pieces." Crusher lived in a room over the bar. He was a professional wrestler until he had his bell rung one too many times. Now he did odd jobs and acted as security for Cuddles at the Forelands Bar. His name is Dennis Carson, but he wrestled under the name of Crusher Carson. He had met Cuddles when she worked the streets in Anchorage. When he couldn't wrestle any longer, she felt sorry for him and brought him with her to North Kenai.

"Honest, Cuddles, this is for real. I need your help."

She pulled her bulk onto a bar stool, retrieved a napkin, and began to write something she was reading in her address book. She kept the book under the telephone at the end of the bar. When she finished writing she held the napkin out to her only patron. "Here, Skip. This is the name of a lawyer in Kenai. He ain't pretty, but he can do whatever you need."

"Thanks, Cuddles. I won't forget this. Thanks. Can I call him from here? I need to get hold of him right away."

"Sure, Skip. Just leave me alone so I can open this joint." With that she shuffled to the other end of the bar and resumed he morning duties.

Skip Williams was consumed by his excitement. He dialed the number on the napkin and waited. The phone rang and rang on the other end. When Skip had nearly given up hope, a voice answered. "Law office," it said.

"Is this Grant Cummings, the attorney?"

"Yeah, what can I do for you?"

"My friend Claudia Morris recommended you. I have a legal matter to discuss with you. I need to see you today. Are you available for an appointment?"

"I'm pretty busy, but if it's an emergency I can try to work you in this afternoon about two. Will that work for you?"

"Yes, it will. Where are you located?" asked Skip.

It wasn't an office at all, just an old house off Princess Street in Kenai. Skip Williams knocked on the door after finding the bell was out of order. He heard footsteps inside and finally the door opened. The man at the door was tall, 6 feet 3 inches, and heavy, maybe 290 ponds. His hair was dirty blond with a beard nearly as long and unkempt as his hair; both needed trimming and washing. The inside of the house had a stale odor that nearly made Skip wretch.

"Are you Williams?" asked the man at the door.

"Yes, Cuddles sent me." Skip began to wonder if he had made a mistake coming here. This "lawyer" wore a ragged flannel shirt and threadbare blue jeans. He looked far from professional.

"Come on in," he said, stepping aside to allow Skip to pass.

The living room he entered was a clutter of books, magazines, and newspapers. Cummings escorted him to the kitchen, which was in slightly better condition. The two men sat at the kitchen table.

"Now, why do you need a lawyer? If Claudia sent you here, you must be in deep trouble." Cummings pulled a new yellow legal pad close and took a pen from his shirt pocket.

"First of all, I'm not in any trouble. I have inherited a small estate and I need someone to represent me in the court. The trooper said I had to have the judge give me the property before he would release it to me. I have a copy of the will giving the stuff to me, and it was notarized by the clerk of the court. The trooper said the will was registered with the Kenai court. I need someone to represent me at the court. I'm not too popular over there. I've done my time and paid my fines and I'm not wanted, but they know me and I'm afraid they might not treat me right." Skip tried to explain with- out going into detail.

"Is the will in the folder you have there?"

"Yes, along with some titles and registration for his trailer and truck and his little airplane. He was killed when he ran out of gas and crashed the plane in the inlet a couple of days ago."

Cummings took the folder and began to read its contents. When he finished he looked up at Skip. "This should be pretty easy. We will need a death certificate. The mortuary will apply for that for you. Get about twenty copies. In these cases everybody wants one. I don't see much value in the total estate. The court may use a simple probate and give everything to you right away if you assure them you will pay the debts and taxes. There shouldn't be any estate tax, given the size of this estate. I can do this for a flat fee of $2,000. I don't take credit cards or checks. How do you want to pay for my services?"

"I don't know. I'll try to get the cash from Cuddles. She knows I'm good for it." Skip didn't want to mention the gold in the plastic tool box held by the troopers.

"You do that. If she says you're good for it, I'll start today. In any case we can't hurry the court, and the probate will take several weeks, at best. If there are complications, the cost could go up. That will depend on the judge and the court." Cummings suspected the client had not been forthcoming and was concealing important information. He wanted to leave the door open for a larger fee if he could get it.

Skip left his name, phone number, and mailing address with the lawyer. "Call me as soon as you hear anything. I'm going out to see Cuddles right now."

"I'll be here working on your case. Let me know as soon as you have made arrangements for payment." Cummings reminded his new client.

Skip was still excited as he drove back to the Forelands Bar to make a deal with Cuddles. His mind kept returning to the 1.75 million reasons to make sure this deal worked.

Chapter 5

Skip sauntered into the Forelands Bar, smug with himself about his good fortune. His goal now was to convince Cuddles to finance his legal case. He wasn't sure how to go about it but was sure Cuddles would think of something. He walked to the far end of the bar and sat on a stool. Cuddles sat on the next stool working on the financial books for the business. She paid no attention to Skip and never acknowledged his presence. She just kept to her accounting.

"I need your help, Cuddles," he said.

She finished her column of figures before answering. "What do you need now, Mr. Millionaire?"

"Aw, come on, Cuddles. I want to do some business with you. I'll have money soon and you will make a profit. Just take a minute to listen."

"OK, Mr. Rich Man. What is it you want and what's in it for me?" She asked in a sarcastic tone.

"The lawyer, Cummings, is going to take my case, but he wants $2000. You already know I'll get a lot of gold when the case is settled. All I want is the money for the lawyer. You've known me a long time and that I'm good for it." He tried not to sound as if he were begging.

"I have bailed you out of jail and paid your fines before, but I never loaned you cash. How do I know you'll pay me?"

"How about I sign a paper saying I owe you the money and give you my deed to my trailer for security? Would that be enough for you?"

She didn't answer right away. She wanted him to squirm and wait. "I'll do it for a return of $2,500. I can't hand out money without a profit. How long did he say it would be before you get your payoff?"

"Yeah, I can do that. He said it would take a little time. I think a couple of months. Give me a piece of paper and I'll write a note agreeing to the deal." Skip breathed a sigh of relief.

"One other thing," Cuddles added, "if this takes more than two months I want another $500. I would make more than that if I invested it in whiskey. I don't want you coming in here and begging for more. Just do the deal as we agreed. You got that?"

"Oh, I got it all right," Skip admitted.

The next hour was used to write the agreement. She counted the cash out of her cash box and handed it to him. Skip thanked her and walked back to his truck to drive back to the lawyer's office. Cummings had him sign some papers he didn't fully understand but was convinced they were for the judge.

There were several more visits to the lawyer in the next week. Then the waiting set in. Skip was becoming anxious and irritable about the amount of time without any word from his attorney. Finally, six weeks after the initial meeting, he had a call from Cummings.

"I just got the disposition from the court. Come down and sign the papers and you can claim your estate. You have to agree to pay all debts, taxes, and costs associated with the estate. Since you are the only heir there was no one to contest the document. The mortuary put pressure on the judge to settle in order for them to get their payment for the funeral. Due to the amount of time I had invested in this case I will need for you to pay an additional $1,000 in legal fees. I will expect payment within 30 days. If you agree to all this we can sign the paperwork today and you will be able to claim your property."

"That's great news, Mr. Cummings. I'll be there within an hour. It will take me a few days to settle all the debts and arrange to pay you. Thanks for doing this for me. See you in a few minutes."

Skip hung up the phone and slipped into his jacket. He was excited and wanted to get to the trooper office to claim his property. Before leaving the trailer he found a card with the phone number for Sergeant Bob Seaton. The receptionist answered and relayed that Seaton was out of the office, but he would return after lunch. He made an appointment to meet with the trooper at 1:30 that afternoon.

Skip had made up his mind to drive to Anchorage and sell a small amount of the gold to satisfy his debt to Cummings and the loan payment to Cuddles. He might even keep a few dollars for himself, for immediate living expenses. It suddenly struck him that he could dismantle the meth lab behind his trailer. He would no longer need the income he derived from illegal enterprises. That thought pleased him.

He knocked on the lawyer's door. The same disheveled slob answered. Cummings invited him in and they sat at the kitchen table. Cummings spread the papers on the tabletop and began to explain each one before asking for his signature. When they finished, Cummings handed Skip a folder with copies of all the documents. He kept the originals and a copy. The originals would be filed, with all the signatures, at the court today. The copy was for his files.

"You do understand you still owe me $1,000, which is due in two weeks," Cummings reminded Skip.

"I'll be out of town tomorrow, but I'll be here to pay you the following day," Skip remarked. "I had my doubts about you in the beginning and took it from Cuddles that you would do a good job. She was right. Thanks. If I ever need a lawyer again, I'll call you."

"I appreciate it," Cummings said, "I'll see you in a couple of days."

Skip went to a local restaurant, Louie's, for lunch. He seldom ate out, but this was a special occasion. After lunch he would have possession of a fortune.

At 1:20 in the afternoon, Skip parked his old truck in front of the trooper office. He was the opposite of apprehensive this time; he was almost euphoric. Armed with the writ authorizing him to accept ownership of all property previously owned by Otis Fairfax, he entered the office. The girl behind the glass asked him to wait for the trooper to come out to get him.

At the click of 1:30, the scheduled appointment time, the door opened and Sergeant Bob Seaton greeted him. Skip was ushered back to the same office he had been in before. Seaton's desk was clean except for a manila file folder on the pad. The sergeant motioned for Skip to take a seat in front of the desk.

"I hear you have all the papers from the court. Congratulations, Skip. This will make you a very wealthy man." He opened the folder on his desk. "I will need your signature on several documents in order to complete our business. They list the items in our possession and your signature signifies you accept possession of the item and relieve us of all responsibility. Is that clear to you?"

"Yes," said Skip, as he opened his own file and handed a copy of the top sheet to the trooper. "This is the paper from the court authorizing me to accept ownership of the property, which is not specifically listed on the paper. My lawyer said that is customary."

"Yes it is." Seaton took the paper and read the short document. "It seems all in order." He handed Skip a copy of the top sheet in his folder. "This is a release form for the airplane, a PA-11 located at Rediske Air in North Kenai. Do you know where that is?"

Yeah, sure, I almost forgot about the airplane. Thanks for reminding me. I guess I can sell that now, can't I?"

"Once you sign this form you will be able to do whatever you want with the plane."

Skip signed the form: two copies—one for him and one for the trooper. The next form was for titles to the mobile home and truck as well as the deed to the land and vehicle registrations for the truck and mobile home. Skip read these and signed both copies. The next form was the one he had waited for. It was for the plastic tool box and the pouches of gold inside. Included on this form was a list of the registered mining claims, which were now his. He happily signed the form and the trooper took the box from his desk drawer and slid it across the desk.

Seaton took all the forms and separated them into two stacks, giving one stack to Larry "Skip" Williams. "It's not my business to lecture or advise you, Skip, but you will be able to live comfortably for the rest of your life on what you have here. I would suggest you change your lifestyle and stay away from your past illegal activities. You don't need that life any longer. Good luck to you."

"Thank you, Sergeant. I intend to do just that. Before I sell this gold and use the cash I'm going to hire a financial agent. I want to invest this so I will always have an income and not have to resort to selling drugs like I used to." Skip was gathering his new possessions, but looked back at Seaton, "I want to thank you for being so nice to me. I didn't expect to be treated like this. Thank you."

"My pleasure, Skip. Can I help you out to your car with this stuff?"

"No thanks, I'm good. Thanks again." He picked up his new belongings and Seaton ushered him to the door where they said goodbye.

Skip sat in his pickup for a few minutes deciding what to do next. He still had a few dollars in his pocket and decided to stop at Sweeney's to buy some new clothes to help him with his new image. The stop didn't take him long. As he loaded the sacks in the front seat, he realized he had left all his fortune lying on the seat of his unlocked truck. He would have to learn to be more careful.

On his way home he swung his truck into the Rediske Air Park. At the office he was told where to find Leo Westfal. He drove down the side of the runway to a small twin-engine plane where Westfal was working. He got out and introduced himself to the mechanic. They discussed the plane and what should be done with it. Westfal made Larry an offer for the little Piper. It wasn't much because it needed quite a bit of work after the dunking in salt-water. Skip said he would think about it and get back to him.

His next stop was the Forelands Bar to see Cuddles. His lesson learned earlier prompted him to bring the plastic tool box into the bar when he arrived. Dennis Carson was cleaning up inside. He did all the manual labor at the bar. In return he had a place to live and a few dollars to spend. Everyone called him Crusher, which was his name when he wrestled. The general consensus was that he was an idiot. Skip knew this wasn't true. His mental processes were extremely slow due to his wrestling injuries, but he kept clear thoughts and could comprehend most things, given a little time.

"Hi, Crusher. Is Cuddles here?" asked Skip.

"Yeah, she just went to her room for a minute. She'll be right back. Do you want something to drink?"

"Give me a cup of coffee. I'll wait at the end of the bar." He sat at the end stool and picked up a newspaper while Crusher retrieved the coffee. Skip was on the sports page when Cuddles returned. She pulled her large rump to the top of the next stool, huffing and puffing from the effort.

"Well, Mr. Millionaire, what's up?" She asked sarcastically.

Skip quickly scanned the room and opened the tool box. He took out the larger of the two pouches inside and undid the leather thong at the top. Carefully holding his hand under the bag he poured a handful of nuggets into his palm. Her eyebrows went up and a look of amazement overtook her.

"Do you believe me now, Cuddles?" Skip said as he loaded the nuggets back into the bag.

"Skip, I'll never doubt you again. I've never seen that much gold. What are you going to do with it?" She stretched her neck to watch the nuggets falling back into the leather pouch.

"First thing tomorrow I'm going to Anchorage to the Oxford Mint and sell some it. I owe you some money and some to the lawyer. I have to pay the mortuary, and I need a little to live on. I have to find someone to help me invest the rest. The folks at the Oxford Mint should be able to tell me where to go for that help. I plan to be back tomorrow night to pay you."

"That's wonderful, Skip." She said.

Skip tossed back the remainder of his coffee, picked up his tool box, and strode to the door. He was clearly a proud and happy man.

Chapter 6

Skip Williams was at home, trying on his new wardrobe, and feeling particularly good about himself when there was a knock on the door. He slipped on a bathrobe and slippers and went to answer the knock. Opening the door he was surprised to see Crusher Carson.

"Hi there, Crusher. What can I do for you?"

"I don't mean to be a pest, but Cuddles said you had a lot of gold nuggets in a bag. I just wondered if you would show them to me. I ain't never seen no gold nuggets before, except on the end of a chain." Crusher said quietly, "I thought you might show them to me if I asked."

"Sure, Crusher. Come on in. Would you like some coffee or a Coke?"

Skip backed away from the door and Crusher entered. "No, I'm good," said Carson.

Skip pointed to a chair at the kitchen table. "Have a seat. I'll get the bag."

He returned to the kitchen with the little tool box in hand. He placed it on the table and opened the lid. Taking out the larger bag he untied the thong and poured several nuggets into his open hand. Crusher seemed in awe.

"Wow! Ain't them purty?" He was staring at the fist full of gold. "How much do you think one of them nuggets is worth?" he asked.

"Gold is worth a little over \$1300 an ounce right now. This nugget," he picked up one nice-sized nugget up with two fingers and held it up for his guest to admire, "this nugget is about a half ounce, so it's worth about \$600 or \$700." Skip didn't know much more about the value than his guest, but he thought he had given a close estimate.

Crusher was staring at the nuggets in Skip's hand, admiring them. "Could I have that Coke now?" he asked politely.

Skip nodded and poured the nuggets back into the leather bag. He set the bag on the table and stepped over to the refrigerator to get his guest a Coke. When he came back to the table Crusher was standing.

"Can I have a glass?" Carson asked.

"Sure, Crusher. Anything else?"

"Nah, that's all."

As Skip turned to get the glass from the cupboard, Crusher stepped up behind him and reached around his neck with a strong arm. He put his other arm against the back of Skip's neck and tightened the pressure. Skip attempted to struggle but the wrestler had lifted him slightly and he was unable to get any leverage to resist. He tried to twist his body out of the hold, but it was no use. It felt like his head would explode and his vision was fading. In less than a minute Skip was unconscious; two minutes later he was dead. Crusher laid the body on the floor and began to gather the contents of the tool box. He re-tied the top of the leather bag full of nuggets and dropped it into the box. He opened the back door, which opened into the add-on shed where the meth lab was located. It was full of toxic and volatile fluids. He picked up a gallon can of something that smelled like it was flammable and began to pour the contents around the inside of the trailer. He opened another can of the same fluid and dropped it on the floor of the shed. He found matches in the kitchen and struck several all at once tossing them into the shed, igniting the fluids on the floor. He struck two matches and dropped them into the fluids he had spilled around the inside of the trailer. He picked up the plastic tool box and quickly exited, closing the door behind him. He walked quickly down the road to where his old car was parked, got in, and drove away.

He parked behind the Forelands Bar and entered the back door carrying the plastic box. He left the box in the back room of the bar, picked up a case of Molson Canadian beer and carried it into the bar where he began putting the bottles in the cooler. The bartender, Lil Danby, stepped around him to serve a beer to a customer at the other end of the bar.

Cuddles sat on the end stool near where Crusher was stocking the cooler. "How did it go?" she asked quietly.

"Done," was the quiet reply.

"Did you get everything?"

"It's all in the box in the back room. I'll bring it to your room in a little while." Crusher seemed calm and unfazed by tonight's actions.

As Crusher finished his chore a new customer arrived and announced there was a fire behind the bar. Cuddles slid him the phone.

"You had better dial the fire department and report it," she said.

Several patrons stepped out the front door to see where the fire was. It was up the road a little way, maybe a mile. While this excitement was going on,

Crusher returned to the back room to retrieve the plastic tool box. He wrapped it in a stack of dirty bar towels and carried it upstairs. He took the box to the rooms Cuddles called home and dropped the soiled towels in the hamper at the end of the hall. By the time he returned to the bar he could hear the sirens of the fire trucks belonging to the Nikiski Fire Department. In the distance he heard more sirens coming from the other of the two stations. He tried not to be too interested in the fire, but continued to fill the beer cooler. Patrons were holding the front door open and the lights of the trucks could be seen from the bar. Cuddles looked into the eyes of her hired man and gave him a wink and a smile.

When the fire department arrived, the building was fully involved. Flames were coming from every window and door as well as vents and chimneys. It was extremely hot. The fire captain called his other units from the Salamatof Station to report he would need another tanker. By the time it arrived the first tanker was running low on water, but the fire was partially controlled. The second tanker connected to the hoses and firemen began to enter the trailer. The captain was familiar with the homes in this area and had ordered his men to wear airpacks in case fumes from a meth lab were present. It was a wise order. Once the second tanker was on the job, it only took a couple of minutes to cool the trailer down so the crew could enter and spray the interior. By the time the second fireman entered, there was a call to the captain: they had discovered a body inside.

The captain radioed his dispatcher to notify the troopers of the body. At the trooper office, Sergeant Seaton was about to go off shift when the call came in. He quickly started his car, and with lights and siren on he sped to the scene. He immediately knew the owner of the property. It was Skip Williams who had been in his office only this morning. He found the fire captain to get a report.

"Hi Kelley, what have you got for me?" Seaton asked as he approached the captain with his pad and pen in hand.

Captain Pat Kelley turned and recognized Bob Seaton. "I know this place. It belongs to a guy named Skip Williams. He was a local meth manufacturer. We haven't identified the body yet, though. Off the top it looks like he was cooking a batch and caught the place on fire and it spread to the trailer. You might as well take five. I think it will be an hour before you'll be able to get inside. When you do, wear an air pack; those chemicals are nasty." Kelley held his hand to his ear, listening. "10-4," he said into his radio, then turned to Seaton: "One of my guys knows Williams and says it's him. They still have several hot spots in the building, so like I said, it'll be an hour until you get inside. Are you staying here or coming back?"

"I guess I'll come back in a little while. Call me on the radio if anything changes. I have some questions about the origin of the fire. Try to find what caused it, if you can."

"OK, Bob. Our fire marshal will be here to go in with you. He's good; if anyone can tell you how it started, he will."

Seaton waved and returned to his car. He thought it strange that Williams would try to make one more batch of meth when he had nearly $2 million dollars in gold in his hand. It didn't make any sense. He decided he would use the time to visit with Claudia Morris to see if she knew anything about the fire. Nothing he had learned so far made any sense.

He drove the short mile to the Forelands Bar, parked in front, and entered. Cuddles was sitting at the far end of the bar working a crossword puzzle. Lil Danby, the skinny bartender, was leaning over the bar talking with two customers—the only ones in the place. Seaton walked slowly to the end of the bar to where the owner sat.

"Hello, Cuddles. I understand the call about the fire came from here. Who called it in, do you know?" He checked the time as he asked the question.

"Hell, yeah. It was Cliff Beidermann. That's him at the far end of the bar, the one with the hat on. Don't be harassing my customers, Bob."

"Would you prefer I took him outside to talk to him?" asked Seaton.

"Nah, do it in here. At least he can keep drinking."

"Thanks, Cuddles." With that he moved to the other end of the bar. Lil moved away as he came near.

He faced the man in the hat. "Are you Cliff Beidermann?"

"That's me." Beidermann slurred. "And I ain't driving."

"Now that you mention it, I think you should call someone to drive you home from here. In fact, I'll be happy to drive you myself. What I want to talk to you about is the fire. I understand you were the one to report it." Seaton placed his note pad on the bar.

"Yup, that was me. I saw it when I pulled into the parking lot here. I used the phone on the bar down there," he said, waving a finger toward the other end of the bar.

"Do you remember what time it was?"

"Nope. I was in a hurry to get a beer. Got one, too."

"Mr. Beidermann, I'm going to leave my card with you. I want you to come to the trooper office tomorrow and make a report for me. Will you do that?"

"Sure, Trooper. I'm not driving over there tonight. Ha, ha," he chuckled. "It wouldn't be legal, would it?"

"Don't forget. Come to the office tomorrow." Seaton took a card from his shirt pocket and handed it to good ol' Cliff.

He returned to Cuddles at the end of the bar. As he approached her, the bartender walked back to the other end of the bar again. "Tell me, Cuddles, do you remember what time Cliff made the call to the fire department?"

"Sure, it was 7:30. Crusher was stocking the beer cooler. He does that every night at 7:30."

"One more question, Cuddles. Have you seen Skip Williams this evening?" he asked.

"He was in early this afternoon, but not tonight. I haven't seen him since about 4. Was it his place where the fire was?"

"Yes. It's a total loss. Thanks for the information. I'll be seeing you." Seaton watched the bartender as he walked to the door, trying to remember where he had seen her before. It just wouldn't come to him.

The fire captain contacted him by radio as he sat in his car making notes about his visit to the Forelands Bar. He said the fire marshal was on the scene and that they could get inside now. Seaton drove back to the scene to meet Eustes Burns, Fire marshal. The name always inspired a joke.

Both men strapped on air packs for safety. Seaton pulled a pair of white hazmat coveralls from the trunk of his car and tugged them on. He followed Burns inside. Two firemen with hoses were inside checking for any last hot spots. Burns asked the men if it was safe for them to look around. They agreed it was. The body lay uncovered on the floor near the kitchen table. It was badly burned, but Seaton recognized Larry Williams. He was studying the body when the fire marshal spoke to him.

"This fire was deliberate. I'd bet money on it. See the streak on the floor?" He pointed to where the floor was scorched unevenly. "It looks like this was set intentionally with some kind of accelerant. We won't know what kind until we have a sample tested. Come over here." He motioned for the sergeant to come to the back door. "This looks like a meth lab, but the fire here was set just like the other part of the building. Do you have any ideas as to why?"

"I think I do. I have to look around. I'm looking for a small plastic tool box. It probably melted in the fire, but inside were two leather pouches. Their contents wouldn't burn or melt. There were some legal papers in the box, but I wouldn't expect them to survive. Can we look around a bit?"

"Yeah, I'll help you look." He turned to one of the firemen: "Get us some light in here, will you guys?"

Three minutes later large banks of lights were hauled in and set up in different rooms making the search much easier. After an hour of searching and finding nothing and with the temperature dropping inside the trailer, he called to have the body removed. He had taken still and video pictures of everything in the place, including the body and the spots on the floor where the accelerant was used.

Seaton called to the fire marshal. "Is there anything I missed, Burns?"

"I don't think so, Bob. I think we covered it pretty well. My crew will be back in the morning to complete the investigation, but I still hold with what I said before—only now I'm not saying suspicious. I'm saying arson and possibly murder."

"I agree with you, but for different reasons. Call me tomorrow after you finish up and we'll get together and compare notes." Seaton needed to get home and take a shower.

Chapter 7

The body of Skip Williams had been sent to the coroner in Anchorage. Samples of the ash and debris from the burned trailer had been sent to the crime lab in Anchorage. The investigation was at a standstill until reports came back verifying the cause of death and the cause of the fire. Both the fire marshal and the trooper sergeant had been occupied with other items in their regular schedule. This was just one more case for each of them.

Crusher continued to do his work as if nothing had happened. Cuddles found that curious. A normal person would have some remorse or guilt, but Crusher showed neither. She thought perhaps his violent wrestling career hardened his emotions so that he was able to deal with it. Even so, it didn't seem normal to her.

The owner and operator of the Forelands Bar had been busy herself. After confirming the existence of all that gold and checking out the mining claims, she realized she needed professional help to find the source of the nuggets. If there was this much gold on Otis when he returned from one of his prospecting trips, then it stood to reason he had found a rich claim somewhere. An old acquaintance of hers, and his business partner, lived in Fairbanks. They would be perfect for the job. She had contacted them the day after the fire to come down and now, two days later, they still had not arrived. She had tried calling them at a cell phone number she had been given, but there was no answer. She was desperate to find her hired miners. She knew the troopers would be investigating and she wanted her two new employees in and out of here by the time troopers started nosing around asking questions. Trooper Bob Seaton was too good and too thorough to have these men hanging around and available to talk. Cuddles tended her business and in private moments and tried to make sense of the locations of the mining claim registrations she now had in her possession. They were scattered all over Alaska. There were claims in Galena, Fox—near Fairbanks, two in Chicken, two near Copper Center, and four in the Lake Clark/Lake Iliamna area. The last claim covered a great deal of distance and was now being surveyed for the proposed Pebble Mine project, which was being touted as the largest gold find in recent times. If proven, it would be the largest gold mine in the world. There was a lot of opposition to the proposed Pebble Mine from Native groups and commercial fishermen, as well as the environmental lobby.

Cuddles had studied the topographical maps of each area and decided the most likely place to start looking was in the Iliamna area. It was the closest out of all the claims, and since Otis had run out of gas returning from a mining expedition, she figured he had miscalculated his fuel supply by just a few minutes. Otis had claims registered in the upper Stuyahok River drainage, as well as on the Mulchatna River. This was a possibility, but she judged it a low priority because of the added distance to the area. There was another possibility in the upper Knutson River, near Pile Bay on Lake Iliamna. She would discuss all these possibilities with her two mining experts, Buddy Phelps, mining engineer and geologist, and Gene De Sylva, miner and pilot. Both these men had been in trouble with the law in the past and Cuddles knew she could count on them to do what was necessary to accomplish her goal: finding the gold source.

The two men finally arrived late in the afternoon. Someone at the Rediske Airpark gave them a ride to the Forelands Bar. They walked in, each found a barstool, and ordered a couple Alaska Amber beers. They were making conversation with Lil Danby when Cuddles came back to the bar. She recognized the pair the instant she entered the barroom. She placed her newspaper, open to the crossword, on the bar and pulled her bulk onto the end stool. She asked Lil for a cup of coffee.

"About time you two showed up. Where have you been? I've been wasting time here waiting for you." She finally said to the men.

"Good to see you, too, Cuddles." They each picked up their beer and walked to the end of the bar where their new boss was sitting. The place was empty except for the three of them and the bartender.

"Finish your beers and we'll go to my place upstairs. We can talk there." Without further explanation she crawled off the barstool and exited through the door in the back of the room.

The two miners finished their beer and ordered another. This one they took with them as they went to find where Claudia Morris had gone. When they opened the door she had disappeared through, they were met by a very large man with a mean scowl on his lined face. His presence stopped them cold.

"Cuddles wants to meet with us," explained Phelps.

"I know," said Crusher. "Come with me." He led the men up the stairway to the second floor and the home of Claudia Morris. When they reached the doorway at the end of the hall, he tapped on it once and opened it. This was the office and Cuddles was sitting at the desk. "They're here," Crusher announced, and without another word returned to his duties in the bar, closing the door behind him.

"Where'd you find the giant?" asked Phelps.

"He's a friend. Have a seat. We have a lot to discuss." Cuddles was all business and didn't want to pass the time in small talk with these men. She knew they would do anything she asked, but she didn't trust them. She was not going to tell them any more than they needed to know in order to complete the job she had in mind. She had topographical maps laid out on the table she had set up in her office. The two men stood over the maps while Cuddles moved her office chair around to the table. She brought with her a leather bag. She untied the top of the bag and poured a few of the nuggets on the table. "This is what we're looking for."

Buddy Phelps picked up several of the gold pieces and looked at them closely. He reached into his pocket and found a small loupe. He held the loupe in one hand and the nuggets in the other. "There's a lot of quartz in the gold, but these nuggets definitely came from a stream somewhere." He looked up at Cuddles. "I suppose if you knew where they came from you wouldn't have had to call us." He looked at De Sylva and nodded.

"OK, Cuddles. You have our attention. Now give us the story." De Sylva wanted to get to it.

"All right. The short version is that the man who found these nuggets died in a plane crash a few days ago. He crashed into the inlet. He was out of gas. That fact should help you pinpoint the location of the source. That's what we're after—the source."

"What kind of plane was it?" De Sylva asked.

"They said it was a Piper PA-11, whatever that is." She was only giving the information they were asking for.

"Did they find any empty gas cans in the plane?" Again it was De Sylva asking.

"I don't know, but the plane is at the Rediske Airpark. The mechanic there, Leo Westfal, took it there from the Arness Dock after the crash. He'll be able to tell you more about that. I just don't know." Cuddles thought a moment and decided to introduce these men to Otis Fairfax. She gave them a fairly accurate narrative of Otis and his lifestyle. She told them of his obsession with finding the mother lode.

"It looks like he may well have done just that," Phelps commented.

Cuddles nodded in agreement. She drew closer to the maps on the table. "You two will know more about where to look than I do, but I have some maps here of the area he was coming from. It'll be your job to figure out how far he could have gone and to look inside that range for the location of his mining operation. Of course you guys know about the Pebble Mine proposal and all the controversy about it. I think he was somewhere in the same general location, maybe on their land. His friend told me he had a small aluminum sluice in the plane. He had a folding shovel and a small rock pick, like you geologists use. He had a sleeping bag and emergency gear. He didn't have any food or camp gear on him when he crashed. I think he may have stashed that stuff at the site. It could be a clue for you."

"You're asking us to search a huge area, Cuddles. It will take time and at ten dollars a gallon it will take a lot of money. We will need cash for expenses and gear. I have a sluice in the plane along with some camping gear and some tools. I think we have everything we need to look for the location, but these maps include a lot of area." Phelps knew what he was up against.

Cuddles rolled her chair back to her desk and opened the center drawer. She rolled back to the table and placed a large, fat envelope on the table. "I'll pay your expenses, buy the gas for the plane, and pay for any other things needed for the search. I don't expect it to be quick or easy. But I do expect results."

"Is there any way to narrow this down a little?" asked De Sylva.

"Maybe. You will know more about that than me." Again she rolled her chair to her desk and returned with a file folder. "Here are some mine claims registered to Otis. If you can plot them on these maps you might be able to have a starting point. There is no guarantee he found this gold on his registered claims, but it will give you an idea of where to look. It might also indicate what kind of places he liked to look. I don't know. That's your job."

De Sylva answered. "We have a Cessna 185. It burns about 15 gallons an hour. At ten dollars a gallon out there, it is going to be expensive. We fly twice the speed of a Super Cub and can land most places that the PA-11 was able to get into. Win or lose, I want $2,000 a week and expenses for each of us. You can pay it when the job is finished, like I said, win or lose."

"Agreed. I know you two and I know you will do the job. If you find the site and it's what we expect, I'll add a nice bonus or, if you prefer, a piece of the action. After all, I'm not going out there and operate a damn mine." She was being very generous with the two men and from past dealings knew they would treat her fairly and honestly—honesty among thieves, you might say.

"We'll talk to the mechanic tomorrow. We also have to go into Kenai and get some sectional maps from the FAA. They're more detailed and accurate than the ones you're using. Can I take the claim registrations? I want to plot the locations on the sectionals."

"Sure, but bring them back before you take off for the Alaska Peninsula." She paused a moment. "Have you got a place to stay?"

"Not yet, maybe in Kenai." Said Phelps.

"I have an empty room at the other end of the hall if you want to use it. Room number 22, last one on the right. It's across the hall from Crusher," she offered.

"Thanks, Cuddles, we can use it."

"I have to go back downstairs and keep an eye on things. You two can stay here and use the office if you want. I'll leave the maps here. Nobody but me or Crusher should come in here." She rolled her chair back to the desk and put the pouch of gold in a drawer and locked it. "I'll tell Lil, the bartender, to put your drinks on a tab and I'll take care of it."

Cuddles stood and shuffled out the door, closing it behind her.

"Well, Partner, whatdaya think?" Phelps asked his partner.

"It's something to do and someone else is buying the gas. You can't beat a deal like that," De Sylva laughed. "Let's go down and get another beer." he said.

Chapter 8

The following morning, two hangovers emerged from the room at the end of the hall. Both had showered and put on clean clothing. The free drinks had inspired the men to overindulge and they were paying the price. The bartender, Lil, had refused to accompany the men to their room last night. By closing time they were the only patrons in the bar. Lil had been pleasant and conversational all evening, but wanted nothing to do with the two drunks after closing time.

Cuddles had agreed to loan them her SUV to run errands this morning. She suggested they find a laundry and wash their clothing. She didn't know how the men could stand the smell of each other. Though neither would admit it, both felt terrible. Secretly, they vowed to not let the lure of free liquor cloud their judgment again. They were off to a slow start today. Before giving them her car keys, Cuddles asked if they were able to drive. Both men admitted they were not feeling the best but could drive or fly without problems.

The first stop was a laundry in Kenai. They left their clothes and said they would pick them up in the afternoon. Next was breakfast. Louie's was an easy choice and looked as if it had a regular clientele. They found a booth and ordered coffee. The waitress—a short, thin lady with a single braid hanging down her back—brought it without delay. After they ordered and the waitress was out of earshot, they began to plan their day. They needed maps from the FAA. That would be their first order of business. They would need to stock up on food and decided a two-week supply would suffice. If the trip took longer, they would come back to restock. They decided to buy fuel at Rediske's and fill several plastic gas cans for spares. Water could be a problem on these excursions, so they decided to take ten gallons with them. De Sylva wanted a new camp stove: propane fired and compact, with extra fuel bottles. Their breakfast arrived and the writing stopped.

Two blocks from Louie's Restaurant was a wholesale grocery and sporting goods outlet. After buying maps at the FAA building near the airport, they drove to Three Bears Wholesale store. The back of the SUV was beginning to fill up with their purchases. They decided to drive to North Kenai and load some of the items in the plane. It would be an excellent time to contact the mechanic who worked on the wrecked PA-11.

It was mid-afternoon when the pair began to load the Cessna 185 with their purchases. They taxied to the gas pump and filled the tanks on their plane. The tanks were topped off and the spare cans filled and stored in the plane. De Sylva taxied back to the tie-down space he had rented, tied the airplane down and met with Buddy Phelps. Together the two walked to where Leo Westfal was working near the PA-11 that Otis Fairfax had crashed in the inlet.

Leo saw the men coming and stopped working. As they approached he said, "Howdy, what can I do for you?"

"Hi," said Phelps. "Is this the plane that went into the water a few months ago?"

"Yes, it is. I've cleaned it up, you know, washed the salt water out of everything. Who are you fellas?"

"I'm Buddy Phelps and this is my partner Gene De Sylva. We thought the plane might come up for sale and wanted to take a look at it. We might want to buy it for speculation. Do you think it might be for sale?"

"It's hard to say right now. The guy who inherited it was killed in a house fire the other night. Too bad, too; the plane is in pretty good shape. There was a little damage to the tail when they lifted it out of the water, but the engine was shut down and there wasn't much damage to that. The radio and other electronics were junk anyway and needed to be replaced. I was thinking if the price was right I might buy it myself, fix it up and sell it again."

"Do you mind if we take a look, anyway?"

"Go ahead, I don't mind. I need a cup of coffee anyway," Leo said.

"Did you know the pilot?" asked De Sylva.

"Yeah, I did. He was always asking me to get into the mining business with him. He was a nice guy, but the only thing he was interested in was gold mining."

"Is that what he was doing when he crashed, coming from a gold mining trip?"

"Yeah, at least that's what the troopers think." Leo looked sad.

"Did he ever say where he was mining?" asked Phelps, trying to dig for a little information without arousing suspicion.

"Otis never said. He was pretty secretive about his mining trips. I used to tell him he should confide in someone in case he came up missing. That way we could come and look for him, but he always just laughed and said, 'Don't worry about me'."

"Well, thanks. We'll take a quick look at the plane and get out of your hair." De Sylva and Phelps hadn't learned much, but it was worth a try.

It was now late afternoon and the men returned to the Forelands Bar. They took a bag of Cheetos and a bag of potato chips to the room with the maps and two Cokes. Cuddles sat at the end of the bar and had grunted an unfriendly hello when they came inside. They returned her car keys and said thanks before going up the stairs to the room they occupied. Spreading the maps on the table, they began searching for likely locations to begin the hunt for Otis Fairfax's mine.

Phelps sat quietly, studying the maps and making notes on a small notepad. De Sylva, too, was silent, studying the same maps for different reasons. He was looking for landing sites, calculating fuel supply, and noting where the federal land boundaries were located. Finally he spoke to Phelps: "I think we should start looking as soon as we get to the other side of the inlet. There are nearly one hundred places to land a plane in Lake Clark Pass. The whole pass is one huge creek bottom. The old glacier that blocked the east end of the pass—you remember, we used to have to climb to about 800 feet to get over it?"

"Yeah, I remember. It was bad when the weather was low," Phelps replied.

"That's the one. There's nothing left of it. The whole thing has melted away. The glacier used to come down both sides of the canyon and meet in the middle of the pass making a huge dam, backing the water from the river and creating a lake full of icebergs. It sure was pretty."

"Think 'pretty' if you want, but I only remember how the winds used to kick our butts right over the glacier. I hated that place." Phelps didn't know how to fly but had been accompanying De Sylva on hunting, fishing, and mining adventure trips for nearly thirty years.

De Sylva laughed, "It did get exciting a couple of times when we passed the glacier."

Phelps responded, "Call it 'exciting' if you want, but it was just plain scary to me."

"Well, you don't have to worry any longer, my scaredy-cat friend. The glacier is gone, but I can't vouch for the winds. The whole point is that I think we should get low and slow all the way through the pass. I think we should start looking for places someone has tried mining in the pass. You said yourself that you figured the nuggets came out of a stream somewhere. Well, that stream runs the full length of the pass. I think we need to look at that 50 or 60 miles as a possibility."

Phelps pulled the map around to get a better look at the Lake Clark Pass area. "It hurts me to say this, Gene, but I think you're right. We have to start looking as soon as we enter the pass. There's no point in flying over a possible site without even looking." He ran his finger over the route, finally looking at his partner and grinning. "Remember that big, blue, hanging glacier that was on the right side when you first enter the pass? Man that thing was pretty."

Gene De Sylva chuckled, "Don't go getting all teary-eyed and sentimental on me, Buddy. I couldn't stand it if you suddenly became nice." With that he tossed his empty Cheetos bag into the trash. "My ham and eggs are wearing thin; how about yours?"

"There's a pizza joint up the road. How about we order a pizza and get some beer. We need to talk with Cuddles about tomorrow." Buddy had already forgotten the hangover he had earned the night before. Gene called the pizza place and ordered their supreme.

Buddy went downstairs to meet with Cuddles and get some beer to go with the pizza. He smiled and invited Lil Danby to join them, but she politely refused. Phelps asked her to call him when the pizza arrived, and he returned to the room to await the slow-moving Cuddles.

When she arrived they gave her a thumbnail sketch of their plan. They began with using her car to go into town for breakfast, then back here to have Crusher drive them to the airstrip. Daylight was getting later this time of year and sunrise was not until nearly nine in the morning. The night air was not so bad as to need to pre-heat the engine, but it would take a few minutes to warm it enough to make a safe takeoff. De Sylva explained their strategy of beginning the search as soon as they entered the pass. She agreed it was a good idea.

"I don't know how much cell phone coverage there is out there, but you can try to contact me at this number. The airplane number is on there in case we don't make it back. I'll try to contact you once a week. If there's no cell service, I'll try to fly into a town with phone service every Saturday afternoon."

"OK, that sounds like a good plan. If you need anything, just let me know and I'll have it shipped out to you as soon as possible. If you do find something, I want to know as soon as you can get word to me." Cuddles wanted them out of there and on the search.

There was a knock on the door. It was Crusher with the pizza. He passed it to Gene and went back down stairs. Gene set the box on the end of the bed and returned to the immediate business.

"I don't know what to add," Cuddles said. "Just stay in touch as best you can and find that gold mine. Is there anything else you need?"

"Yes, there is. I need two cases of beer for the plane in the morning. I plan to stop and see an old friend in Nondalton at the other end of Lake Clark. He used to prospect this area and may be able to give us some tips. Beer makes a good bargaining chip in the village." Phelps had, in fact, prospected with Richard Onarak in the area of Chicken, Alaska, many years in the past.

Cuddles struggled out of her chair and moved to the door. "OK, boys, it's all up to you now." With that she opened the door and shuffled down the hall to the stairway.

When she was gone, Gene asked, "Are you hungry?"

"Yeah, and we need more beer." Phelps had his doubts about this venture, but it would pay well whether they found the mother lode or not. It would pay better if they found it.

The following morning the two men drove into Kenai and had breakfast at Louie's Restaurant for the second time in as many days. The same little waitress took their order and brought their coffee. Gene and Buddy discussed the trip they were about to undertake and agreed they were ready. After breakfast they drove back to the bar to meet with Crusher Carson. He drove them to the airport, helped them load the last of their gear, and drove back to the Forelands Bar without waiting for the men to take off.

Gene did his pre-flight check and drained the water from his fuel tanks. Daylight was breaking when he started the engine. He sat, idling the engine until the oil temperature began to climb. He switched on the navigation lights, just for safety, and began to taxi to the end of the runway. The windsock was limp and the runway long, making it easy to determine the direction of takeoff. He had decided to take off to the north since that was the direction of the east forelands, the narrowest place to cross the inlet. He would climb to 5,500 feet for safety, but once on the other side he would begin his descent to a cruising altitude of 300 feet. Once inside the pass he would slow to seventy-five miles per hour, making it easy to inspect the valley floor. He had the intercom switched on and asked Buddy if he was ready. Buddy nodded affirmative and Gene released the brakes. To Gene, there was no better feeling than when the wheels left the runway.

Minutes later they reached altitude, quietly cruising a couple of minutes before pushing the nose over for a long descent. They followed a track directly toward the entrance to Lake Clark Pass. Buddy pointed out several brown bears as they flew toward the pass. At Big River Lakes, Gene began to slow the Cessna; time to go to work.

Once past the first S turn in the pass Buddy bent low, looking up to see the hanging glacier he remembered. It was still there, though not as large as before. He nudged the pilot and pointed. "It's still pretty," he said into the intercom mic.

Hours passed as the two men scanned the river bottom for signs of someone landing and mining. There were several sites where they turned the plane around and made another pass to get a better look. Several sandbars had aircraft wreckage strewn on them, evidence of the hazards of flying this pass in bad weather. There were animals everywhere. Land otters were plentiful, playing in the stream and paying no attention to the noisy airplane. Many black bears were foraging along the stream, several with cubs. Eagles were feasting on dead and dying salmon along the banks. Further into the pass there were many brown bears migrating back to the mountains after gorging themselves on salmon in the lower reaches of the pass.

Chapter 9

It would have been easy for the men to forget the purpose of their flight, given the beauty of the surroundings and abundance of wildlife they were viewing. But this was a mission paid for by someone else; they had to keep that in mind. Nearly three hours of flying brought them to the west end of the pass with nothing to show for the effort. Gene asked his partner, "Which side of the lake do you want to check out first?"

"I think the south side. I was wondering about Little Lake Clark Pass. Do you think we should check that one out?" asked Buddy.

"We'll have to get fuel first if we do. I've been through there a number of times and I never was comfortable with it because there aren't many places to land in there, to say nothing of nowhere to turn around at low altitude. I doubt he took his PA-11 through there, even though it's a little shorter." Gene was a savvy pilot giving a pilot's assessment of the idea. "I think we should fly the left side, like you said, and make a stop at Port Alsworth for fuel. By the time we do that we will be running short on daylight. Did you want to spend the night in Nondalton?"

"Yeah, I think that would be a good stop. Find a place to land, will you? I have to drain a bladder."

"Not a bad idea for me either," commented Gene who instantly began to look for a landing spot. It came just minutes later: a sandy beach on the shore of Lake Clark. There was a large brown bear sow with two cubs on the little beach when Gene buzzed the landing sight. She and the cubs ran as the noisy plane flew over. De Sylva made a smooth landing in the soft sand, using less than half the length of improvised runway. After doing their business, the two looked at the size of the tracks left by the bear. She was a big one. They each drank a cup of coffee from a thermos in the back seat. It tasted good.

The rest of the trip to Port Alsworth was pleasant, but non-productive. A few residents of the upper lake cabins stepped outside to see who the low-flying aircraft was and why they were cruising so low to the ground. As the men approached the smaller of the two airstrips, they notified local air traffic and landed straight in, spun around, and taxied to the only gas pump. A young girl came out to see what she could do for the men in the Cessna. She was Alaska Native, by her look, with a broad smile and raven black hair. She was pretty by any standard.

"Do you need gas?" she asked.

"Yes, fill it up while I check the oil." He unsnapped the latches on the engine cowling and lifted the cover. He pulled the dipstick and wiped it clean before putting it back in and pulling it again. He studied it and returned it to its place under the hood and closed it.

The girl found a ladder and toted the hose up to the top to begin filling the tanks. "Are you going hunting?" she asked.

"No, we're geologists looking at some mining claims," he hedged. "Have you ever met an old miner who came here a lot by the name of Otis Fairfax? He has some claims somewhere around here. We thought we might look him up and ask him about the mining prospects." Gene hoped he had been convincing.

The tank full, she replaced the cap and moved the ladder to the other side of the plane. "I don't recognize the name," she said as she climbed the ladder with the hose over her shoulder. "What kind of plane does he have?"

"He owned a PA-11, a pretty nice one, in fact."

"Is he a short guy about 60 or 65 years old, always talking about mining?"

"That's him, nice old guy. Do you know him?"

"Not really, but he comes here sometimes and talks to my granddad. He buys oil sometime, but he has his own gas with him." She looked into the tank and drained the hose before replacing the cap.

"Do you have any idea where his camp is located? We sure would like to talk to him."

"He doesn't come here much, only stops to talk with Granddad." She pulled the fuel hose to the pump and hung it up. "Come inside and I will figure up your bill."

Buddy waited at the plane while Gene followed the girl inside. She stepped behind the little counter and punched the keys on a calculator. She wrote the amount on a billing pad and gave him a copy. The number shocked Gene, but he tried hard not to show it. He dug into his pocket and pulled out a wad of hundred dollar bills. He gave her a ten dollar tip and turned to leave. At the door he turned and asked, "Is your granddad here now? I'd like to talk to him. Maybe he knows where I can find Otis."

"No, sorry, he went to Anchorage today. He has a doctor's appointment."

Back at the plane he met Buddy. "I'm glad we're not paying for the gas out here!"

"They aren't getting rich, even at these prices. They have to fly all that gas out here from Kenai or Anchorage. That costs a lot," Buddy commented. "Did you find out where Otis had his camp?"

"She said he came here sometimes but only came to talk to her granddad. He isn't here today." Gene stared at the ground, deep in thought. "We are going to be out of daylight pretty soon. I think we should go to Nondalton and find your friend. I can fly in the dark, but we can't do our looking then."

"Yeah," said Buddy, "I was thinking the same thing. It's been a long day already and we did cover a large piece of the map. I hate to bring this up, Pal, but we haven't got much time. The weather is going to shut us down soon. Once we get snow it will be over until spring. And, the weather out here on the peninsula is notoriously bad this time of year. We could get up to 100 mile per hour winds tomorrow. I want to see Richard and ask him about Otis, but we'll have to get back at the hunt in the morning, as soon as we have light."

"I like the way you think, Partner. Let's go to Nondalton."

They flew down the south shore of the lake to the west end where they crossed over to land at the Native village of Nondalton. Gene had spotted the tie-down area and taxied to a good spot. He was giving Buddy one of the ropes to attach to the tie-down when an older, green pickup drove up. A Native man, with blue jeans and a uniform shirt bearing a police badge, stepped out. It was Richard Onarak.

"You two are under arrest for not saying 'Mother, may I?' before landing." Richard grinned; he had recognized Buddy Phelps as he drove up.

"Richard, you old scalp-hunter, how the heck are you?" He shook the hand of the policeman. "What's with the badge?"

"I've been appointed VPSO for Nondalton," explained the Village Public Safety Officer. "It doesn't pay much, but I don't work hard either. How about you? What brings you to my town?"

"That will take a little time to explain. Is there somewhere we can talk?"

"If you're staying the night, bring your gear and you can stay at my place."

"Thanks, Richard, we appreciate that. By the way, let me introduce my partner, Gene De Sylva." Buddy returned to tying up the airplane while Richard and Gene shook hands.

Buddy opened the door and handed Gene two small duffle bags to be placed in the truck while he off-loaded the two cases of beer. "We'd better take these to the house, too," he said, carrying them to the pickup.

"You can visit again, Buddy," Richard said laughing, as he spotted the cargo.

The house was small and easy to heat—a short distance up the hill from the large airport. There are no roads out here and everything must be brought into the village by air, necessitating the commercial-size airstrip. The three men went into the house, carrying their bags and beer. Richard turned on a single light over the kitchen table before showing them the only spare bedroom, with a double bed.

"The bathroom is across the hall. We have lots of hot water, so feel free to shower if you want. Come back to the kitchen when you get settled. I'll go and start some dinner."

By the time the men had washed up and found their maps, Richard had caribou steaks frying on the stove. Hash-brown potatoes were cooking in another pan, toast was in the toaster, and eggs ready for the pan once the steaks neared perfect. Richard was drinking one of the beers but had made a pot of coffee, which both the guests opted for. Dinner not only smelled delicious but tasted as good as it smelled. Richard was a single man who loved the out of doors. Now in his mid-forties he had tasted the civilized life and returned to the village without regret. Buddy had met him in Fairbanks several years ago, during a bar fight. Someone pulled a knife on Buddy and Richard intervened by kicking the man in the face, knocking him out cold.

"Richard, we're looking to find a mining claim being worked by a man named Otis Fairfax. Have you ever heard of him?"

"Sure, he came here sometimes. I think his claim is up above Nikabuna Lakes. Not the little narrow valley, but the big flat one that goes way up the mountain. I saw his plane on that little cinder strip above the creek. It's a small strip, though, and I didn't want to go in there with his plane sitting in the middle of it. I thought he left his plane there so no one could land. I didn't see him around the plane; he must have walked down to the creek."

De Sylva asked, "Can you show me on the map where the cinder strip is located?"

Richard came to the table to look at the maps. He was carrying another beer, this one cold, and set it on the table while he studied the sectional map. With a weathered finger he pointed to a spot on the map where the concentric gradient lines of elevation were spaced rather far apart. This was a very wide valley with a small stream meandering up its middle. There were several small ridges jutting into the wide, open valley. "This is the first one you will come to. The big mining company has a camp up there on one of those little ridges. You can't miss it. There is a big steel tower up there. Go about five miles further, to the next creek coming from the mountains. This stream runs down to the Koktuli River. Be careful out there, those little canyons look a lot alike. You should keep some altitude until you think you have the right one. The hills aren't high, but they get steep in the upper ends of these valleys. If I had the time I would take you out there, but I have a fuel delivery coming tomorrow and I have to stay in town." He reached for his beer and took a big swig.

"I think we can find it," said De Sylva. "There are a couple of other sites we need to check out, too. One is at the upper end of the big lake. It's called Knutson River. I've never heard of it until we started looking for these claims. Do you know anything about the area?"

"Only a little," said Richard Onarak. "I hunted caribou up there a couple of times. I have a friend who lives in Pile Bay. We went together. It's not a nice place to fly. The canyon gets steep and the mountains are high. If you get too far up the Knutson River you won't be able to turn around. Be very careful if you go up there."

"Thanks, Richard, you've been a big help." Buddy was sincere in his statement. "We would like to have the option of coming back here tomorrow night, if you'll allow us."

"How can I refuse a man who brought me beer?" Richard laughed and took another drink.

"I guess we'd better turn in, then. We have a big day tomorrow and so do you. See you in the morning," said Phelps.

In the room, Buddy was pulling off his shirt and socks when Gene commented, "I like Richard. I think he gave us some good information. I suppose it would be too much to hope for to find what we are looking for on the first try."

"Dream on, old friend, dream on." The two men had to share the crowded bed but slept well.

<h1 style="text-align: center;">Chapter 10</h1>

Buddy and Gene awoke to the smell of toast, bacon, and eggs cooking in the kitchen. They washed up and went to the kitchen in search of coffee. Richard had been busy. The table was set and coffee made. The big cast-iron griddle was full of food about to be served.

"You two are just in time. Breakfast is ready and I have to leave here in a few minutes. I've been outside and it looks to me like you can relax for a while. It's foggy up the valley where you will need to fly, but it usually burns off when the sun comes up. There will be frost on the airplane this morning. The temperature is only twenty degrees. Take a coat, but you'll be able to shed it by 9:30 or so this morning. I have to go to the airport after breakfast to get ready for the fuel delivery this morning."

The two visitors were now sitting at the table sipping their coffee. Richard began to fill plates with hot food. Gene was the first to comment: "I like the five-star treatment we get here." He took another sip of his coffee.

Richard laughed. "I treat all my paying guests like this. I have to because I don't have a wife to do it for me."

Phelps politely asked a question: "Richard, I hate to impose on your hospitality, but can we stay here while we survey the valleys behind Nondalton? I don't know how long it will take to cover the area. We know you have a job and we don't want to make you change your routine. It would just be better for us to sleep in a bed each night than in a cold tent on some remote airstrip. And to return the favor, Gene will get up every day and cook your breakfast for you."

"You're not imposing, Buddy. I don't get many visitors, and to tell the truth I'm enjoying your company. Stay as long as you like. I don't usually have set working hours. If someone needs me to break up a fight or anything, they just come to the house and knock on the door. That's why I can't go out there with you; I have to be here and available when someone needs me." Richard had been the VPSO for three years and liked the job. He was related to most of the people in town, one way or another, and could usually calm any dispute.

"Thanks, Richard, we appreciate it. We're working out of Kenai right now, but if you ever get back to Fairbanks, give me a call and I'll see to it that your hospitality is repaid." Phelps still owed his friend for saving him in that bar fight several years ago.

Gene chimed in: "Go ahead and take care of your business with the fuel delivery. We can't fly for a while, so we'll take care of the dishes and drink the rest of the coffee." He grinned with appreciation at his host.

Richard Onarak went to work and the two visitors cleaned the kitchen. As it became light they found Richard's assessment of the weather to be accurate. They spent the next two hours studying the maps of the area and searching for other sites to investigate. Each new one was circled with a pencil and each one would be looked at, judged, and either investigated or crossed off the map. As the temperature rose, the men gathered their needs and hiked to the airport at the foot of the hill. Gene untied the Cessna and turned the wings to the rising sun to defrost them. He made a thorough preflight check and climbed into the cabin with Buddy. He primed and started the engine to warm the oil. Warm air was soon coming from the heater vents. Minutes later the oil temp gauge began to rise. The heater vents under the windscreen had melted the frost and it was clear enough to see well. Gene taxied to the other end of the runway where Richard was watching the DC-6 tanker plane unload stove fuel for the village of Nondalton. They waved to him as they passed and made a turn to align with the runway. Gene notified local traffic by radio of his intentions and pushed in the throttle. A Cessna 185 is extremely noisy on take-off, caused by the propeller tips breaking the sound barrier. For the benefit of Nondalton residents, he pulled back on the propeller control once the wheels broke free of the earth. He climbed the plane to 1,500 feet before turning west into the foothills of the low mountains to the left.

Buddy had the sectional map on his lap and followed their path with the eraser end of a yellow pencil. He pointed to the first of many tiny circles on the map and pointed out the windscreen. He indicated the target was to the right of the nose. Gene made a small course adjustment. As they approached the spot marked on the map it became apparent there was no place to land the plane. Gene circled the area once and was unable to find a place to set down. Buddy drew a small line through the first circle.

The next circle was a small ridge top with a small cinder strip located on its spine. These small airstrips were made by an historic event in 1912 when a mountain on the south shore of Lake Iliamna exploded. Mount Katmai was larger than Mount St. Helens in Oregon, and after the cataclysmic eruption there was only a valley. Mount Katmai was now The Valley of 10,000 Smokes. Kodiak, 100 miles south and east of the mountain, had been covered with five feet of ash and pumice. The entire Alaska Peninsula was covered with cinders from the size of a grain of sand to boulders the size of houses. For hundreds of miles in every direction, the ash came down. Amazingly no lives were lost in this event. Today pilots use these patches of cinders as landing strips for small, and sometimes large, aircraft.

Gene skillfully touched down and rolled to a stop. Both men stepped out and stretched their backs and legs. They walked back and forth on the little cinder strip looking for some hint of a trail leading to the stream somewhere in the alders below. De Sylva reached into his side of the plane and retrieved a shotgun with a shoulder sling. Buddy pulled his small backpack from the rear seat and pulled the straps into place. With Gene and his shotgun in the lead, they began to hike to the stream they heard running somewhere below. A hazy sun shone down into the little valley they were investigating.

The distance was deceiving. It took the two men nearly an hour to reach the stream. Making a trail through an alder thicket had taken much of the time. On the stream bank, Gene stood guard as Buddy pulled up the tops of his hip boots and snapped the straps to his belt. He pulled off the backpack and rummaged inside to find his gold pan. The stream was narrow and shallow with clear water running over the beige colored stones in the bottom. Buddy knew he would have to find somewhere with a different bottom before panning. Pumice is very light weight and can sometimes be seen floating down these streams. His first experience with the floating rocks had made him wonder what was in the water to make the stones float.

He began to wade upstream looking for some natural outcrop with granite base where he could get under the pumice easily. The two men walked up the stream for more than a mile, and the stream began to shrink in size. It was a mere trickle when they decided this was not what they were looking for. They stepped out of the streambed and began to make their way through the alders again when something within a few feet began to break the alders as it ran. Minutes later the wary pair emerged from the thicket to see a large bull Caribou standing on the barren hillside above them.

"I'm glad it wasn't a bear," commented Gene.

Forty-five minutes later they had returned to the plane, shared a bottle of water, and stowed their gear. With little to no wind, Gene had a choice of which way to take off. He opted for downhill.

"Let's go directly to that spot," Buddy pointed to the place on the map. "Richard said it had a decent landing strip, and we don't know how long it'll take to hike to the stream. We'd better use our daylight to investigate this one. I think, geologically speaking, this is our best bet. It's a large area, and if we don't finish it today we can come back here in the morning," he concluded, giving his professional opinion.

Gene banked the plane hard to the left and circled to the new heading. "You're the guide, pal. I'm just the mule."

Ten minutes of flying put them over the desired place. De Sylva buzzed the landing site, shaking his head. "It'll be tight. See that big rock in the center of the strip? I can't tell how high it is above ground. Landing will be OK, but we may have to improvise to get out."

"In that case, let's take a look at the area and especially the stream before we land. If the streambed is like the other one, we might not need to land."

Gene circled around the little valley beginning his descent at the upper reaches of the stream. He had dropped his flaps and slowed. He flew downstream with the creek on the right side of the plane in order for Buddy to assess the possibilities. He flew downhill only a few feet above the willows and alders.

"Hey, look! Go around, go around. Let's look at this spot again."

"What did you see?" asked the pilot as he added power and gained some speed before turning.

"There's a little outcrop of hard rock and a riffle in the stream. If we start panning there, and walking down the creek, we should be done here by dark."

De Sylva was slowing the Cessna again. "Give it a good look," he said.

When the riffle came into view again, Phelps glued his eye to the spot, turning in the seat as they passed. "That's it. That could be the place. Let's land." He spent the rest of the flight looking for a trail to the upper end of the creek.

Gene decided to land just uphill from the big rock in the runway. He slowed and let his wheels caress the cinders only a few feet above the obstacle. He taxied to the upper end of the little strip and swung the tail close to the willows at the end. He set the parking brake and jumped out to pile cinders against both tires.

"I'm going to walk off the distance. I'll be back in a minute," said the pilot.

"I'll have lunch ready when you get back." Phelps took out his backpack and opened it. Inside he found two energy bars and two bottles of water. While waiting, he walked to the edge of the little airstrip and gazed at the stream below. There was a distinct game trail paralleling the creek. He judged the walk to be less grueling by staying in the bare cinders above the brush until they arrived at the upper reaches of the stream.

"There are about twenty caribou off the right side of the ridge," remarked De Sylva as he returned. "Where's my lunch you promised?"

De Sylva sat on a fat tundra tire eating his energy bar while Phelps watched the willows below. Buddy reviewed his thoughts on the trek to where he had seen the riffle in the stream. Ten minutes later they were walking to the upper reaches of the canyon.

It was an easy walk and the game trails made it effortless to get to the stream. Again Gene stood guard while Buddy pulled up his boot tops and stepped into the water. Close to the shore, behind the small rock outcrop, there was a deep pool. The stream was only about six inches deep, but this pool measured nearly two feet. He took the folding shovel out of his pack and stepped into the water. He had removed his shirt and was not looking forward to reaching deep into the cold water.

With his small shovel he pulled debris and vegetation away from the bottom of the small pool, letting most of it float downstream with the current. With the submerged overburden removed, he dipped his gold pan into the deep, clear water. He came up with a pan laden with gravel and dirt which he began to wash at the edge of the riffle. He was a practiced and skilled gold panner who had the pan picked down to small flecks of black sand in only a few minutes. He waded to shore to show his partner the result. Among the grains of black sand were several small flakes of what looked like gold. "Hand me one of those little glass bottles, will you, Gene?"

With tweezers from his shirt pocket he took the small flakes out of the pan and dropped them into the small glass vial. They look nice, but I'll have to pan some more to know if there's anything worth bringing the sluice up here for."

Buddy stepped back into the stream and again, with his shovel and pan, scooped up another pan full of creek bottom. Minutes later he again waded ashore to show his prize to De Sylva. He took several small flakes from the pan to be dropped in the glass container.

"Do you want me to get the sluice?" asked De Sylva.

Buddy looked at his watch. "Not now, I'll pan a few more times and we'll go back. We're going to run out of daylight again and I don't want you to be taking off on this strip in the dark. We can come back tomorrow and start early. I wish we had a pump, but we can make do with the sluice. I'll get a long handle shovel from Richard.

Half an hour later the two were hiking back to the plane. Buoyed by the prospects of success, the trip back seemed shorter than it did on the way in. Take-off was less perilous than expected. Gene managed to keep the plane to the left of the large rock and the wing out of the alders and willows. The sun was getting low and had set behind the hills by the time they returned to Nondalton. Richard heard them coming and met the pair at the tie-down spot.

"Red Cap mister?" he shouted as the men climbed from the plane.

Chapter 11

F ire Marshal Eustes Burns called Bob Seaton Tuesday morning. It had been several days since the fire claimed the life of Larry "Skip" Williams. Neither he nor Seaton had counted on the result of the autopsy showing anything out of the ordinary. Seaton had yet to receive his copy of the report.

"Bob," Burns said when Seaton answered, "have you seen the autopsy report yet?"

"No, I haven't. If it's come in they haven't brought it to me this morning. You got a copy, I take it?"

"It just came in. There was one big surprise in the report. Do you remember I said the body didn't look right?"

"Yeah, you said something about it didn't look like he had made an attempt to get out." Seaton remembered the conversation.

"Yes, and I was right. The medical examiner says his windpipe was crushed. Someone hit him in the throat or choked him out. Now, what do you think about that?" Burns was asking.

"Interesting, to say the least," Seaton remarked. "Now, let me give you some private information. Williams had been in my office to pick up the property belonging to the airplane crash victim. One of the items he got was a small plastic tool box with some papers and two leather pouches inside. I've been to the fire scene twice to look for the box. I can't find any trace of it. There is no ash or melted plastic or remnants of the two leather pouches."

"The fire was pretty hot, it could have burned. The papers would surely have burned and the box could have melted and burned. What was in the leather pouches you mentioned? Could they have burned, too?"

"That's why I went back to look," Seaton confided. "The pouches contained gold. There were a lot of large nuggets and a sizable amount of small nuggets and dust. I weighed the pouches and estimated the value of the gold at $1.75

million dollars. Bear in mind that wasn't meant to be an accurate measure, but it would have been close to the true value. There should have been a pile of gold in the place even if the box and pouches burned up in the fire. If Williams was dead when the fire started, by someone choking him to death, that same person could have taken the box when he left the scene. He probably set the fire to cover the murder and the theft."

Burns was silent for a moment, "I've been investigating this as a suspicious fire, but I didn't think it was a murder. The lab said the accelerant used in the mobile home was the same compound found in the shed behind the place. They gave me a list of possibilities, but it looks like the same chemicals used to cook meth."

"We've suspected Williams of making meth, and we know he's dealt it in the past," Seaton confirmed. Then it was his turn to be quiet a moment. "How about we work together on this? I'll investigate the murder and you take the fire. If I find anything, I'll call you and vice versa."

"Good idea," Burns said. "In the meantime I'll have someone go out to the scene and do a thorough search for residue from the plastic box you described and to look for the gold in the ashes. Stay in touch, Bob."

Sergeant Bob Seaton sat at his desk for a long while trying to wrap his mind around the news he had just been given. If Skip William's death was a murder, who would have been motivated to kill him? Three possibilities came to mind: First, revenge; second, a bad drug deal; the third option seemed the most likely. He may have bragged about the gold he had just inherited and someone thought it was a large enough amount to risk killing him for it. Given William's checkered past, any of the three possibilities were logical. Seaton surmised that if it was a bad drug deal, the timing would have been coincidental. The same applied to revenge. He couldn't rule these out, but he decided to find out if Skip had confided in anyone about the gold. In the past he had called Cuddles when he was in trouble and it seemed likely, if he boasted to anyone, it would be her. He had to start somewhere and he decided to go to the Forelands Bar and question Claudia "Cuddles" Morris.

He stopped in the captain's office to discuss it with him before driving to North Kenai. It was a little early to find the retired hooker open for business, so he decided to stop at Rediske Air to see Leo Westfal. Leo had worked on the airplane and, given the recent turn of events, it seemed prudent to interview him again about the condition of the PA-11.

Seaton found the mechanic installing a wing on the small Piper. Leo was an experienced mechanic and had devised a 2x4 wood support for holding up the wing while he installed the new wing struts. He was slipping the bolts into the upper end of the strut when the trooper arrived.

"You're just in time to help," said Leo when Bob stepped out of his car. "Lift and shake the end of the wing for me, will you Sarge? These bolts are a little tight, and I'm having trouble getting them into the strut."

"Sure, Leo," he said. Lifting up on the wing, taking the weight off the punch Leo had in the hole, made it easy for the skilled mechanic to align the bolt and hole and push the bolt into place.

"Thanks. Sometimes working alone is good, but sometimes it's good to have a little help." Leo stepped out from under the wing. "What can I do for you, Bob?"

"I just received information that changed the complexion of this case and I wondered if, during your repairs, you'd come across anything that would suggest this wreck wasn't an accident?" asked Seaton.

"Nothing I can think of," said Leo. "Are you looking for anything in particular?"

"No," said the trooper, "just curious. Something has come up in another case related to this one, and I was just double-checking."

"There is one thing that puzzled me. It happened a few days ago. I was working on the plane when two guys showed up to look at it. They said they were interested in buying it, but they didn't look at the plane like buyers. The thing that made me question them at all was the fact they were driving a car I recognized. These guys were out-of-towners, but they were driving the SUV owned by the big old girl who owns the Forelands Bar." Leo was pouring a steaming cup of coffee from a thermos. "I don't know if that's what you're looking for, but it's the only thing unusual around here."

"What do you mean they didn't look at the plane like buyers?"

"Nothing, really. It just seemed to me they were more interested in Otis than the airplane. They kept asking about him and his gold mining. One guy looked the plane over, but they never asked about hours on the engine or when the annual was due. They just didn't ask the usual questions."

"Have you ever seen them before or know who they are?"

"No, but they came in here in a Cessna 185. A really nice one. They rented a tie-down for a few days. The day they asked about the PA-11 they loaded a bunch of provisions into the 185 like they were going camping. They left a while but came back with some more stuff later, loaded it, and flew away. They left the SUV parked at the tie-down and that big bruiser who works at the Forelands Bar took it out of here. I watched when they left and they flew across the inlet at the forelands. I thought they were headed for Lake Clark Pass."

"You say Crusher Carson took the SUV out of here?"

"Yeah. The two out-of-towners seemed to know him." Leo took a final drink of his coffee.

"Thanks, Leo," said Seaton, putting his notebook back in his jacket pocket. "If I need any other info I'll come back."

"It's none of my business, but you said something came up in another investigation. Can you tell me what it's about?" Leo asked out of curiosity.

"Keep it to yourself for a while, Leo, but Skip Williams died in a house fire a few days ago, and it's beginning to look as if it wasn't accidental. He may have been murdered." The news was about to become public anyway, so he thought it should be safe to tell Leo. He waved goodbye to the mechanic, "See you later, Leo."

The weather was warm for this time of year. The sky was gray, but the clouds were high and it didn't seem as though it was going to rain or snow. Sergeant Seaton was wearing his summer weight jacket and happy it wasn't raining or the wind blowing. Back in the car, he checked in with dispatch and let them know he was headed to the Forelands Bar.

The signs were lit and the front door open when he arrived. Inside he looked for the owner, but the bartender was the only one in the place. "Good morning, Lil," greeted Seaton. "Is Cuddles here?"

"No, but she'll be back soon. She just went into Kenai to go to the bank. You can wait if you want. Can I get you some coffee or something?" The two were well acquainted from an incident two years ago. Lil was driving her boyfriend's car one winter day and slid off the road. The car rolled over, pinning her inside. Seaton was the first trooper on the scene and helped the medics extract her from the wreckage. He had gone to the hospital to interview her in the emergency room but encountered her boyfriend beating her, with terrified nurses standing by. Seaton sprayed the man with pepper spray and put handcuffs on him, but he had broken two of Lil's ribs to add to the broken arm she had already suffered. He dragged the man out of the exam room and into the hall. At that moment, Soldotna City Police officers came rushing in to take custody of the screaming assailant. Lil felt Seaton had saved her from even more serious injury. She never forgot Bob Seaton and never stopped thanking him.

"If you think Cuddles will be back soon, I'll wait and have some coffee, thanks." Lil was homely as sin but a pleasant person. Seaton liked her. "There were two men in here from out of town a couple days ago. They flew in and used Cuddles' SUV while they were here. Did you see them?"

"Yeah," she said, "a pair of jerks. They stayed upstairs a couple of nights. Cuddles gave them a room and paid their bar bill. They all had several meetings while they were here, but I don't know what they were about. It was all secret. They left a few days ago. I don't know where they went. Are they wanted for something?" Lil asked.

"No, I don't know about anything. I was just curious about them. With all the strange happenings around here lately I thought I should find out who they were." Seaton was avoiding specifics.

"There's a lot of strange stuff, all right. Poor old Otis got killed. Then Skip died in the fire at his house," Lil lamented. "All that happened right here, close to the bar. They say things happen in threes, and that's only two. I don't want to be number three."

Seaton was about to ask another question when the back room door opened and a huffing and puffing Cuddles entered. She took off her coat and hung it over the back of a chair at the first table. She placed her purse and a bank bag on the bar. It took some effort, but she hauled her bulk onto the end stool and asked Lil for the telephone.

Bob Seaton stepped off the stool at the other end of the bar and walked to where Cuddles was seated. When he reached her she never looked up, just asked, "What do you want now?"

"Just want to talk with you a minute, Cuddles. I need some clarification on what you told me the other day."

"And what, exactly, did I tell you the other day you didn't understand?" she again spoke without looking up.

Seaton took his notebook from his pocket. "The night of the fire at Skip's place you said no one came in here and the patrons inside had been here all evening. It now looks as if the fire was arson, and I'm investigating it and the death of the resident, who has been identified as Larry Williams. Did anyone come in or did you see a vehicle or person on the road that night?"

"Hell, you know I don't get outside during business hours. I'm always here, inside." Cuddles didn't like the way this conversation was going.

"Arson is a serious charge. Both the fire marshal from Nikiski and I are investigating. There's another little thing, too, Cuddles." He paused to let the question develop along with her curiosity. "It seems the medical examiner found evidence Skip was murdered. He didn't die in the fire after all."

Now Cuddles looked him right in the eye with a shocked expression on her own face. "Someone killed Skip? Why would anyone do that?"

"You were his friend and neighbor, I thought you might be able to give me some insight into that very question," said Seaton, trying to have an innocent look about him.

"Bob—if you're accusing me of killing Skip, then you can just get out of my place and talk to my lawyer. I ain't no angel, but you know I couldn't have killed the man. He owed me money. Now I'll never collect! Besides, what makes you think someone killed him?"

Seaton could see her begin to squirm. "I didn't accuse you, Cuddles. I know you couldn't do it yourself. Maybe it was someone who owed him money for drugs. Or maybe he owed someone else for drugs. Or maybe someone was just mad at him. He wandered over the legal line quite often—you know that."

"I don't know nothin' about his drug dealing. He never did it in here. I wouldn't let him!" Cuddles was getting nervous, "I don't think I want to talk to you anymore. I think you should just leave."

"Just one other thing before I go. Who were the two men you loaned your car to a few days ago?"

"Get out of here! I ain't sayin' nothin' more to you." She was now very upset, to the point of shaking.

"Well, Cuddles, if you think of anything you want to tell me, just call." With that he walked back to where Lil was standing behind the bar. "Here's for the coffee and a tip. Thanks," he said to the bartender. Cuddles stared at his back as he left the bar.

Chapter 12

Sergeant Seaton was chuckling to himself as he left the Forelands Bar. Cuddles had panicked, which meant she wasn't telling everything. His previous suspicions were substantiated now. Not proven, but confirmed. In the car, he made some notes and sat a moment to make a plan. He had decided to drive up the road to Skip's burned-out mobile home to make one more short search for the lost pouches of gold.

A white pickup, with Nikiski Fire Department emblazoned on the door, was parked in the driveway. He stopped his patrol car behind it and stepped out. There was a young man working in the debris with a metal detector. He looked up when Seaton pulled into the yard. He wore a set of headphones attached to the machine. The fireman removed the big earmuffs as the sergeant approached.

"Hello there," called Seaton as he walked closer.

The fireman made his way out of the pile of rubble to meet the trooper. "Hello. Are you Sergeant Seaton?"

"Yes, but call me Bob. Are you working for Eustes Burns?" he asked.

"Yes, he wants me to go over the site carefully looking for gold. It sounds a little weird to me, but my detector can differentiate various types of metal. Gold is one of the types it can pick out. In all this other debris it would have to be a sizable amount for me to find it. But, that's what he wants and so I'll keep looking," said the fireman, his coveralls covered with ash and soot.

"I know it sounds silly, but keep looking. I came out to look myself. That's why I'm here. But if you're looking and using the detector, I guess I'll leave it up to you." Bob was pleased Burns had sent someone already. "Have you found anything at all?"

"No; Burns said it could be buried in melted plastic. If it is, I'll have to move slower to be thorough. Burns told me this could be a murder as well as an arson case. Is that true?"

"Yes, it is. The autopsy said the man they found sustained injuries indicating he'd been strangled. Burns suspected it the night of the fire—sharp guy. That night he said the body didn't look right; it was too neat and tidy. He claimed he never saw a fire victim lying peacefully on his back with his arms crossed," Seaton explained.

"What's the deal about the gold; can you tell me?" asked the curious fireman.

"I can't give you specifics, but the victim had picked up some property at my office that day. One of the items was some raw gold—quite a bit of it, actually. My thinking is that if he was murdered the motive could be the gold he had with him that day. So this search is important to both cases. Do a good job."

The fireman slipped the headphones back over his ears. "I'll keep looking," he said, as he flipped the switch to start the machine.

At the intersection with the Kenai Spur Highway, Seaton turned right toward Nikiski. He called the fire marshal on his cell. When Burns answered, Seaton asked, "Burns, do you like Pizza?"

"As long as it's free," was the answer.

"If you're going to be in your office, I'll stop and get a pizza to bring over. I'm hungry. We can share lunch."

"Good, Bob. See you in a few minutes." Eustes Burns was a large frame man who loved to eat rich food. After hanging up the phone he went out of his office to make a fresh pot of coffee.

A half hour later Seaton was in Burns' office opening the box containing a Chef's Mistake. Seaton didn't know what kind of pizza to order, so he bought one with everything on it. It smelled good and Bob was hungry. Burns had poured two cups of hot coffee and brought them to his office. Paper towels served as plates as the men dug into the feast. Each man ate two delicious pieces before relaxing with coffee.

"I met your man at the fire site. He was hard at work with his metal detector. It looked to me like he was doing a thorough search," Bob commented.

"He's a good man. I think he'll take my place as fire marshal when I retire. Had he found anything when you were there?"

"Not yet, but he was still at it when I left." Seaton sipped the coffee, thinking it was some special blend. "Have you come up with any answers about the fire?" he asked.

"Only some educated guesses," said Burns. "I think whoever set the fire knew the victim. If it had been a stranger they would have used gasoline or something else they had brought with them. This guy knew he could find volatile chemicals on the premises and used them. The lab report also confirms Larry Williams was running a meth lab in the shed at his back door. All the chemicals the lab found are used in the manufacture of methamphetamines. It appears to me that Williams wasn't a very nice person."

"You're probably right, Burns. He had a couple of other things on his sheet, too, but dealing meth was the worst. But between you and me, I still don't think the drugs were the reason they killed him." Bob was sipping his coffee again. "I think—and I don't have anything but gut feeling to go on—I think he showed that gold to someone who followed him home and killed him for it. I don't think he had enough time to do much bragging about his new fortune. That leaves me thinking if I find who he confided in about it I'll find the person responsible for his death."

"Just remember, Bob, you're in Nikiski and there's a sub-culture out here. They're a tight-knit group who deal drugs, live off the grid, and have little respect for the law or civilized society in general. Most of us are just like people anywhere—hard-working, dedicated family people—but that group who live in the shadows, who seldom work and always have cash, those who use and deal in drugs, they form an independent society out here. Skip Williams was one of those. He wasn't a big player, but he was a player. It's going to be difficult to get anyone to talk to you."

"Every investigation has to start somewhere. I don't know where it will lead, but evidence piles up little by little. If I do my job, I'll find the answer in the cumulative facts. The problem is, where do I start and where do I look?" Bob put his empty cup on the desk. "I think I'll go back and ask Leo Westfal about those two men who asked about Otis' PA-11. They were driving Claudia Morris' SUV. They might be involved, but it appears they never came to town until after Skip was killed. Maybe the person who killed Skip sent for the two strangers. I don't know. I just need to find some facts to justify the next question."

Burns, too, put his empty cup on the desk. "Well, good luck. If we learn anything at the site, I'll call you. But, if what you say is true, we won't find anything."

The two men said goodbye and Sergeant Seaton walked to his patrol car. He made a couple of notes about the lab report before driving back to the Rediske airport. Once there, he found Leo Westfal and, once again, stopped his work.

"Hello again, Leo, have you got time to talk a minute?"

"Sure, Sergeant, I need a break anyway." Leo wiped his greasy hands on a red rag and sat on the tailgate of his truck.

"I was thinking about the two men you said came to look at the PA-11. Can you tell me when they got here?" Seaton had his notebook in his hand.

"Sure, they flew in here in a Cessna 185. I rented them a tie-down. I don't know if they'll be back, but they rented the spot for a month. Just a minute, I'll get my book. I can tell you exactly when they got here." He walked to the cab of his truck and retrieved a small spiral notebook. He flipped through the pages until he came to the entry for the Cessna. He gave Seaton the date and time of the rental.

"Would you happen to have the aircraft numbers for that Cessna?" asked Seaton.

"Yeah," he gave them to the trooper.

Seaton asked a few more questions before driving back to his office. It was plain Westfal had nothing further to add. At the office he asked dispatch to check out the ownership of the Cessna and he provided her with the aircraft registration numbers. She said it would take a little while to get the information from the FAA.

Bob Seaton was sitting at his desk in the early afternoon when his telephone rang.

"Sergeant Seaton, this is Lil Danby. Can I talk with you?" she asked.

"Of course, Lil, what do you want to talk about?" asked Seaton.

"I have to talk on the phone, 'cause I don't want anyone to see me at your office. I could be in big trouble if someone sees me." The bartender from the Forelands Bar sounded frightened.

Seaton pulled a yellow legal pad in front of him in case he needed to take some notes. "That's fine; we can talk on the phone. Are you being threatened?"

"No, but if anyone sees me talking to you I might be in trouble."

"What's this about?" asked Seaton. He looked at the clock and made a note of the time.

"I think Cuddles may have had something to do with the fire at Skip Williams' place." She sounded even more nervous now.

"What makes you think she had anything to do with this?" asked Seaton, sitting forward. Lil had his attention.

"Well, the night of the fire she had talked with Skip. It was her who sent him to see her lawyer, and after Skip was done at the lawyer's office, the lawyer called Cuddles. A little later she took Crusher up to her room, and when she came back to the bar, he left for a while. After he came back is when all the fire trucks came. Then when you came in, she said she didn't know anything about it. Nobody asked about Crusher. He just stayed in the back room. There's just too much weird stuff going on at the Forelands. I want to quit, but if I do she might think I know something … and I might have an accident, too." Lil Danby was now crying.

"Try to calm down, Lil. Are you saying you think Cuddles sent Crusher to set fire to Skip's place?"

"I don't know for sure, but it could be." She was crying harder now. "And then a couple of days later those two men from Fairbanks showed up. They were creeps. They drank without paying for it, and Cuddles said she would take care of it. They tried to get me to come upstairs and stay with them, but I told them I didn't do that. They got nasty and Cuddles chased them away from the bar, then they went upstairs to their room and kept on drinking. Crusher kind of looks out for me at work, and I thought I would have to call him to stop these guys." She was sobbing again. "I hate working there. I'm afraid to go to work, and I'm afraid to quit. I don't know what to do."

Seaton thought for a moment before answering. "Are you afraid she might hurt you?"

"I don't know, but I'm worried it might happen. I'm scared, Sergeant Seaton. You helped me once before and I knew I could talk to you."

"What is it you want me to do, Lil?" Seaton asked.

"That's just it, I don't know." She was pleading and sobbing.

"At this point I don't know if anyone at the Forelands has committed a crime, but it sounds to me like there is something going on. If you can do it, I would like you to go back to work and keep an eye open for anything suspicious. I don't want you to snoop and I darn sure don't want you to get hurt. I just want you to report to me if you learn anything. I think they may have been involved in a crime, but I have no proof. If you decide to stay there and report to me, I want you to do it discreetly. If you think Cuddles is on to you, I want you to get out immediately. Can you do that?"

"I don't know, but I think so." Her sobbing had stopped. "Will you keep an eye out for me?"

"Yes, I will. I'll give you my cell phone number in case you have an emergency and need me right away." He gave her the number. "You can call me anytime. Don't take any chances, please."

"OK, Sergeant. If it will help you, I'll do it. But if I call you for help, you have to promise to come right away."

"I'll be there for you, Lil. Thanks."

After he hung up he knew this may be the break he needed, but he didn't feel good about Lil being left out on a limb, alone, like that. He would have to make it a point to check on her on a regular basis.

The intercom rang and brought him back to the present. It was dispatch with the information from the FAA about the Cessna.

"The aircraft is a white over blue 2011 model Cessna 185. It is owned by Yukon Leasing Company of Fairbanks, Alaska. The leasing company has a single owner: Eugene De Sylva, also of Fairbanks. He is a licensed commercial pilot. He has no violations on his flying record," the dispatcher ended the report.

"Thanks," said Seaton, as he hung up the phone.

His yellow legal pad was filling up. "I wonder who the other man in the plane is."

Chapter 13

After three frustrating days of trying, Cuddles finally got an answer when she called Grant Cummings. The lawyer said he had been out of town on business, but Cuddles knew he had been shacked up with a hooker from Juneau.

"It's about time you answered the phone. I've been trying to reach you for a week. I've got a problem and we need to talk," she said with a short-tempered tone.

"Don't get so excited, Cuddles. I have other clients, you know." He was lying and she knew it.

"I can't talk about this on the phone. You need to come out here and meet with me in the apartment." Cuddles didn't like his attitude. She was used to having people jump when she barked.

"Yeah, yeah, I'll be out there in a couple of days." The lawyer didn't like being told when or where to appear. It was one of the many faults degrading his law practice.

"You'll come today," she demanded. "I pay you enough money to get you to come when I call. Now, get out here this afternoon."

"I'll see how my calendar looks for later today." Cummings was not about to let her get the upper hand. "Can you tell me what this is about?"

"When you get here—not before, and not on the phone," she shouted into the handset. With that, she slammed down the receiver.

An hour later Grant Cummings came into the bar wearing his uniform, a sport coat and tie over bib overalls. His aim was to portray the country lawyer, sort of the Ben Matlock of the Kenai Peninsula. The façade wasn't working for him. Everyone knew it except him.

When Cuddles saw him come in, she began the task of climbing down from her perch at the end of the bar. She hadn't spoken to him, only motioned for him to follow. She exited through the storeroom door and went up the stairs to her apartment with him in tow. The mental sparring for supremacy was continuing. Inside the privacy of the apartment, she spoke curtly.

"I can find another lawyer," she began. "I'm not certain you can find another client who will pay as well as me. You work for me: don't forget it."

Cummings had lost and he knew it. "I'm your employee, not your slave. You need my expertise, and don't you forget that."

"We'll settle this later," she spat, "but right now there is a bigger problem. The troopers are nosing around the fire site. I haven't heard what they found, but they're spending a lot of time out there."

"Have they found the gold?"

"What makes you think they will? Perhaps Skip got rid of it before he died." She was speaking quietly, hoping he would believe her innocence.

"Come on, Cuddles. You and I have done too many of these deals to start cheating each other now. I'm convinced you had someone off that little drug dealer and steal his gold. I think he got the money to pay me from you, and in order for him to get it he had to show you some collateral. That would have been those pouches. You're not fooling me, old girl; now, out with it. You know I can help you—and I will—but only if you level with me." He was convinced he had her now: checkmate.

She became quiet, seething with anger. She had hoped to keep all this from him, but now the cat was out of the bag. "I've gone to a lot of trouble to get this deal going. I have other employees out there working hard to find where this gold came from. I don't need you or anyone else wrecking it now. What I need from you is to help me cover my tracks. I don't want anyone connecting me with Williams. I don't know how much the troopers know, but I don't want them to associate Williams with me or the bar. There is enough money at stake here to let me deal you in for a percentage, but only if you can mind your manners. I'll let you in if you'll remember who's running the show."

"Now you're beginning to make some sense. How much money are we talking about?" asked the greedy attorney.

"There's about a million and a half now. I've sent a team of miners to find out where it came from. Otis was only gone for a little over a week, so wherever it is, it has to be a rich find. Too bad for him he crashed and died before he could register the claim." Cuddles was now confiding in the lawyer.

Cummings thought, rubbing his chin, "Or maybe he was working one of his already registered claims."

"I never thought of that, Grant. You could be right. In any case, the men I have out there are working on it as we speak. I haven't heard from them, but they'll have to come home soon because of the weather."

"Who are these miners?" asked Cummings.

"At this time, you have no need to know. I'll keep you apprised of their finds, if any, but I'll keep them to myself for now. When they get back I want you to go over the registered mining claims he owned and see if we can take them over somehow. If you're going to be a part of this, it'll be up to you to take care of the business and legal matters." She had effectively set the ground rules for this venture.

"If that's the way you want it, but it is going to cost you. Not just a legal fee, but a good deal more. I'll do everything needed, and then some, but I want my standard legal fees *and* 20 percent of the gross." He knew she would promise to pay what he wanted, but staying alive to collect it may be another thing all together. He would have to devise a plan of his own to protect himself.

<<<.>>>

Meanwhile in Nondalton, the two miners were having hard days. The weather had been somewhat cooperative, and the men had only lost one after-noon because of wind. The spot they had thought was a good one had been productive, but it failed to yield anything but fine gold. Phelps and De Sylva had carried the cumbersome sluice box into the stream nearly a mile above the small cinder landing strip they had found. The sluice box was 14 inches wide by 3 feet long, made of aluminum to minimize weight, with metal riffle bars at the upper end and green AstroTurf on the lower end. Material to be run was placed on the upper end with water poured over it to wash unwanted material away. Gold is heavy and collected behind the riffles with the fines depositing in the AstroTurf.

After panning in the stream they decided it was good enough to use the metal sluice. Phelps set up the sluice in the stream near the first spot he had panned. He moved the little sluice upstream as far as practical, then turned and worked the waters downstream below the first location. Each spot gave a few flakes of gold and seemed to promise more, but it was a vacant promise. Moving down the little river, the water became too deep to work without snorkel equipment, Phelps decided this was not where any of the nuggets had come from.

Each day De Sylva flew the Cessna to a new spot where the process was repeated. Each day they came up with the same result: there was gold but nei-ther the size nor quantity needed to make a profitable operation. Nowhere did they find any nuggets. They covered all the accessible spots to the west of Nondalton. From there they investigated site after site on both sides of Lake Clark. As the weather worsened, the men moved toward Knutson Creek. They soon learned it contained quantities of gold, but they would have to investigate the river on foot. There were few landing strips on the little river. Day after day they carried their packs and rifle up the river. Panning for gold as they went was a time consuming process. Both men were getting very weary, near exhaustion. After a particularly tiring day, they decided it was useless to proceed further on Knutson Creek. It was late when they returned to Nondalton, but there was still a little daylight showing. When they landed they were met by Richard Onarak.

"What brings you back to camp so early?" he asked in a joking way.

"I think we're running out of possibilities, Richard. We're going to re-group, study the maps again."

"I have a favor to ask, if you would do it for me." Richard did not ask lightly.

"Anything for you, Richard, what's the favor?" asked Buddy Phelps.

"The community is having a potlatch tomorrow. That's a celebration of thanks for a good fishing and hunting season. We've invited some people from Iliamna and from Port Alsworth, but the elders say there isn't enough meat for all the guests. I was wondering if you would fly me out to shoot a caribou. If we leave now we can be back before the wind kicks up. It won't take long. I sort of know where to look." Richard was unsure about asking his guests for a favor.

"How large is the landing area, Richard?" asked De Sylva.

"More than a thousand feet and smooth, no hummocks. We could get one right at the plane if they're in the area."

"Let me throw some of our gear out on the tie-down to make room and we can go now. Do you have a rifle?" De Sylva was taking the sluice and mining gear out of the plane.

"Yes, in my truck; I'll go get it," said Richard. He came back with a rifle and a small backpack, which contained knives and a small saw. "I'm ready," he said.

The seats had been removed from the back of the Cessna to make room for mining gear. Buddy sat on the floor without a seatbelt, his back against the front seat. Richard was in the copilot seat, pointing directions through the windshield. Less than ten minutes later they were landing in the grassy tundra near a small round lake. There was a small herd of caribou on the other end of the lake, slowly feeding their way toward them. The herd scarcely looked their way when they landed. Richard picked out a small bull and squeezed the trigger. It never heard the shot. The others moved off as the bull fell to the ground.

The three hunters took Richard's small pack and walked the hundred yards to the carcass. In fifteen minutes the animal was dressed, skinned and cut into manageable pieces to carry back to the plane. When they landed back in Nondalton, young men from the village met the plane. They carried the caribou away in an old pickup truck.

Richard turned to his friends, grinning, "That was a nice piece of work; thanks a lot. The potlatch is tomorrow afternoon and the two of you are invited."

Buddy answered, "I don't know if we'll be back from the field by then, Richard."

"You may not even go," was the reply. "The wind will be blowing right down Lake Iliamna all day tomorrow. My guess is it will be blowing fifty miles an hour, gusting seventy. I don't think you'll be going out tomorrow."

"That doesn't sound good. OK, Richard, if we're in town we'll come. Thanks for the invitation."

"Think of it as a good send-off: There's a big front moving in; the day after tomorrow the wind will die down in the morning, but in the afternoon it will pick up again and it will be snowing. If I were you two, I'd be ready to leave here that morning at daylight. Otherwise you may be staying with me for a week or more." Richard had lived here most of his life and knew what the weather could do.

"We'll look at our maps tonight and make that decision then," said Buddy. "We can load the plane tomorrow if we decide to go. Gene has the last word on flying."

De Sylva came around the plane at that moment. "The plane is tied and the gear put back inside. I think we can quit for tonight," he said.

"Gene, Richard says we'll be stuck in town tomorrow because of wind. I told him we would come to the potlatch."

"Is there anything we can do to help?" asked De Sylva.

"No, the elders will do it all from here. Thanks for helping me get the meat for the feed. It wouldn't do to have the elders embarrassed by running out of food."

"Richard has more bad news, Gene," Buddy Phelps interjected. "He suggests we fly out of here the day after tomorrow at daylight. He says the weather is going to go bad and it will snow later in the day."

De Sylva blew out a big breath, "I don't want to be in the pass when the snow starts."

"If I were you guys, I'd go up the lake and over the mountain from Pile Bay to Iliamna Bay on the Pacific side. That way, if the wind is blowing over there you can get out over the inlet and the going will be smoother. I hate those rough rides to Kenai." Richard was giving the men good advice.

They slept well that night and enjoyed the festivities of the following day. The potlatch was fun and meeting the village elders was a new and moving experience. The day off was a welcome reprieve from the long hard days they had been enduring. It appeared it was over for now; they were going back to Nikiski.

Gene De Sylva followed the route mapped out by Richard Onarak with great relief. He stayed high, following the road through the hills to the Pacific side. He flew out over the inlet before heading north toward the west forelands and crossing over to the Kenai Peninsula. He had not been looking forward to a slow, rough, stressful trip through Lake Clark Pass. It was late afternoon when they arrived at Rediske Airpark. Both men were tired and in need of a bath and a drink. Leo Westfal offered to drive the men to the Forelands Bar.

Chapter 14

Buddy Phelps and Gene De Sylva each dropped their small bags against the wall and sat down at a table. Cuddles was out of the room when they arrived, but they knew she wasn't far away. "Hey, girl, bring us a couple of Alaska Ambers."

Lil was mortified to see them sitting in the bar. She removed the caps from the two beers and walked them to the table. "I haven't seen the two of you for a while." She really didn't want to start a conversation with the men, but it was her job to be friendly to the customers.

"We've been out of town for a few days. We missed you, though." Buddy Phelps did the talking.

"I can't say I missed you two. Is Cuddles paying your bar tab tonight?"

"You can pay it if you want, honey," Phelps quipped.

"No thanks. Last time you didn't leave a tip." She picked up her tray and brushed the long sandy hair from her face. Back at the bar she was starting a tab when Cuddles returned.

Cuddles came through the rear door and immediately saw the miners. Totally out of character she waddled to the table and sat down next to Gene De Sylva. "It's about time the two of you decided to come tell me what you found." She was as gruff and impolite as ever.

"Be nice to us, Cuddles. We've had a long day, besides we brought you a present." Buddy paused to retrieve a small glass vial from his bag. "Here, this is so you know we weren't just taking a fishing trip."

"What is it?" she asked.

"Hold it up to the light and you'll see what it is. It's gold. It's what you paid us for."

She held the vial up to the florescent light and saw the small flakes resting on the bottom. The layer was nearly a quarter of an inch deep. "How much is here?" she asked Phelps.

"We haven't had a chance to weigh it, but I'm guessing a little less than an ounce." Phelps took a deep drink of his beer. "We found gold: not the mother lode, but we found gold."

"I want to hear all about it. Was it rough camping out every night?" she asked.

"You can't imagine. We had bears coming to camp, rutting moose all around us, eating half-cooked food every day. It was tough." Buddy took a last drink from the bottle and both men laughed.

"OK, Buddy, OK, now give me the straight story."

Both men began to laugh again. De Sylva was the one to break the news. "Buddy had an old friend living in Nondalton and he let us stay at his place. We had a nice bed, hot food, hot and cold running water—all the comforts of home. We were even invited to a potlatch last night. I have never been to anything like that, but it was great. They fed us moose, caribou, beaver, lynx and porcupine. We had ptarmigan and grouse and some things I couldn't identify. All of it was good, but I had trouble with the fall fish soup. It tasted good, but I didn't like the soup looking back at me. The little old Native lady sitting beside me saw I was having trouble and poked me in the ribs, grinning. She spooned all the eyeballs out of my bowl and put them in hers."

"What the hell is fall fish?" Cuddles asked.

"It's the spawned out fish that float downstream; you know, the ones with the hide coming off." De Sylva knew this would stop her curiosity. It did the trick.

"How come you came home so early? Did you miss me?"

"Not hardly, Cuddles. The weather was going bad and a big snowstorm was moving in, so we left ahead of it," Phelps explained while he motioned for Lil to bring another round. Cuddles asked for a tequila, straight up.

"To tell the truth, I'm glad you boys are back. Things are heating up around here. There's trouble brewing with the troopers. I have a lawyer hired to keep them away from me, but they may come snooping anyway." She thought for a moment and said, "Why don't you boys rest up a couple of days and then go home to Fairbanks. We can continue the search in the spring. I don't want to talk about it down here. I'll get with you when you come upstairs." Lil brought the tray of drinks.

Cuddles picked up her drink and tossed it back in one gulp.

"I think we'll be going into Kenai for dinner, if you'll loan us your car." It was Phelps asking.

"Yeah, I'll get the keys. Don't drink any more while you're in town," she said, pulling herself upright. As she began to stand there was a din of engine noise loud enough it rattled the glasses on the back-bar.

She turned back to face the two miners: "Stay put for a while; there may be trouble." She called out to Lil, "Bring two more beers to these guys," she said. Immediately she shuffled to the rear exit door and disappeared, a moment later Dennis "Crusher" Carson appeared carrying a case of Alaska Amber.

As the motor noise faded, leather-clad bikers began to enter the bar. Lil brought the Ambers to the miners and hurried back to the bar.

The first biker to enter was tall, blond, bearded, and smelled of marijuana. "Hi there, lover," Tom Hagel greeted the frightened bartender. "Have you missed me?" he said, laughing loudly as six more black-clad bikers entered.

Two of the new customers dragged two small tables together and pulled chairs up to them. All the men were wearing Harley Davidson leather clothing. All were loud and reeked of freshly smoked marijuana. The leathers were of varying ages and condition, like the wearers.

The leader of the band of north-road-outlaws was a truck driver/biker by the name of Chuck Hagel, brother of the rowdy blond who came in first. The men were brothers but total opposites. Chuck worked regularly for a trucking company in North Kenai. His brother Tom never worked but supported himself selling drugs, mostly marijuana. Chuck was a very large man, both in height and girth, with dark complexion and bushy black beard. Brother Tom had a light complexion, with a scruffy stubble he liked to call a beard. Chuck, most of the time, was pleasant and congenial. Tom, on the other hand, was abusive and irritating.

Lil came to the table carrying a plastic tray and a pad to take orders. "OK, Hagel, keep your troops peaceful tonight. Now, what can I get for you?" she asked as pleasantly as she could muster. The bikers gave their orders in turn and Lil returned to the bar to get the drinks.

The weather forecast had prompted the ride today. Snow was expected for tonight and the men wanted to get one more ride in before they had to put their bikes away for the winter.

"Listen up, guys. This is the last ride of the season. I'm buying the first round. Try to stay out of jail tonight. Let's not have any trouble, OK?" Chuck Hagel had made his speech, which he expected them to ignore.

Lil brought the first round to the table and Chuck gave her a credit card. "Hang on to this until we get ready to leave. Charge everything to me on this card unless I say different." She was pleasantly surprised at his attitude, but then they were still sober.

Two rounds later the mood was changing, a fact not escaping notice. Crusher sat on the end stool, where Cuddles normally would have been, reading a newspaper. The two miners were watching closely, while sipping the second beer of the night.

"Skull" Bryant, a small man in leathers and a red Harley bandana tied about his head, pinched Lil on the rear as she put round three on the table. Instinctively, she swung the now-empty plastic tray and caught Skull alongside the head. Her instinctively defensive response sparked the abusive Tom Hagel. Instantly he was overcome with rage, jumped up and grabbed her by the throat, squeezing hard with a muscled hand. She could not make a sound, but Crusher saw her face turning red. He knew immediately what to do. He stepped off his stool and was quickly at the bikers' table. Two of the bikers, Eddie Stone and Sid Castillo, stood to intercept him. Crusher caught Stone across the bridge of the nose with a huge, and fast, forearm smash. As Castillo faced the wrestler he was hit in the face just under the left eye with the heel of a calloused hand. Crusher got to Lil and reached over the top of her head to grip the throat of Tom, who dropped his hold on Lil's throat to reach for the hand at his own. Crusher used his free hand for the flailing fist of the biker: he bent it double and snapped Tom's wrist.

The other bikers were now on their feet, ready to take on Crusher. Phelps and De Sylva sprang into action. Both miners were familiar with barroom brawls, but the odds were heavy against them. Crusher quickly helped even those odds, knocking out one and then the other of the untrained biker gang fighters. Lil was hiding behind the bar, calling 911. The troopers were on the way, she was told.

Tom and Chuck Hagel were back to back in the center of the floor. John Taskert stepped away from the men, circling to get behind the miners. Taskert ran behind Phelps, attempting to get him in a choke hold, but Phelps quickly spun to meet his challenger, holding his arm and pinning it behind him. With nothing to tie the arm behind the biker, Phelps sat on Taskert, holding him down for now.

Though already injured, Tom Hagel set himself to meet De Sylva who kicked the biker brother in the groin rendering him semi-conscious, writhing in pain on the floor. De Sylva stepped back while Crusher faced Chuck Hagel. The two seemed evenly matched, but it soon became evident that Crusher's ring experience was more than a match for the overweight, though motivated, biker. Crusher grabbed the man by his leather jacket and spun him around, off balance, driving his head into a metal ceiling support pipe. The fight was over.

At that moment the first of the troopers arrived. Phelps and De Sylva stepped back while the trooper snapped handcuffs on Taskert. The second trooper to arrive was Sergeant Seaton. He assessed the situation and ran to his car, opening the trunk. He returned with a modified leg-iron set. The chains between the cuffs had been shortened. He knelt behind Chuck Hagel, who was now moaning and coming around. Seaton snapped the irons on the big man's wrists. He had seen this man before and knew the regular handcuffs would not fit his meaty arms.

Two more troopers arrived in time to finish handcuffing the rest of the half-conscious brawlers. The three road troopers began to load the prisoners in cars for transport to the local Wildwood Pre-Trial Facility in Kenai.

Seaton asked the three men left standing if they were all right. They said they were. He then walked to the bar where Lil Danby stood, shaking.

"Are you OK?" he asked in a kindly voice.

"I think so. If it hadn't been for Crusher that biker might have killed me. I was scared—I'm still scared."

"What happened, Lil?"

She gave her account of the events leading up to the fight. "Those two men over there are the ones I told you about before, the ones from Fairbanks. They jumped in to help Crusher and me. You can see they did a good job of it."

"I'm going to talk with them now. This will give me a chance to check their ID's."

Seaton walked to where De Sylva and Phelps were sitting. "You boys have had a busy night," he said.

"I just love sitting in a strange bar, in a strange town, having a relaxing beer, and topping the evening off with a good bar fight. Of course we're from Fairbanks and our customs may be different from yours down here." De Sylva was being his usual flippant self.

"In any case, fellas, I want to thank you for doing my job for me and for saving the bartender from being seriously hurt." Seaton put out his hand to shake theirs. "I have to get some information from you before I can let you go. Can I see your driver's licenses?"

Both men handed over the plastic documents. Seaton went to his car to call in a check for wants and warrants. Both men came back clean. "Print all that and put it on my desk," he ordered.

Back inside he returned the identification cards and thanked the men again. He then turned to Dennis "Crusher" Carson, asking him for his ID also. This one, too, was checked and a printout ordered to be put on his desk with the others. Back inside he returned the ID. While he had the man this close he had to ask, "By the way, Mr. Carson, did you know the man who died in the fire out here?"

"You mean Skip Williams?" asked Crusher.

"Yes, that was his name. Did you know him?"

"Sure, he came in here on a regular basis. He was a nice enough guy. He never caused any trouble." Crusher answered all Seaton's questions without emotion.

Sergeant Seaton finished his notes and thanked the man. No one had mentioned Cuddles or said she was present during the altercation. Seaton was not ready to confront her and let the opportunity pass. There would be another day, soon, when he would have enough information to question her.

Right now it was late and it had been a long day. It would be longer by the time he finished his report.

De Sylva looked at Phelps, "Let's just order a pizza."

Chapter 15

In their room at the Forelands Bar, Phelps and De Sylva were drinking fresh beers and eating hot pizza. Cuddles knocked on the door. Buddy let her in and offered her a seat and some pizza. She refused the pizza but sat on the bed.

"I want to thank you boys for helping out downstairs. Crusher would have had a hard time if it weren't for you. Those bikers come in about twice a year and every time they come there's trouble. I think Lil used to buy drugs from Tom Hagel, but she's cleaned up and she's doing good. She's the most honest bartender I've ever had. I'd hate to have anything happen to her. I owe you guys for that."

"Nothing to it, Cuddles. Those bikers were interrupting our conversation about ordering a pizza." De Sylva was making light of the fight now that it was over.

"You kept my name out of it. I appreciate it," said the bar owner. "I came up here to see what I owe you for the expedition and to pay you. You didn't find the mother lode, but you did eliminate a lot of places to look," Cuddles explained. "I need to know how much I owe you for expenses while you were out there on the Alaska Peninsula. I don't need receipts. Just give me a horseback figure. I'll pay you your price and a few extra days as a bonus."

Buddy took a sheet of paper from his dresser and gave it to his boss. "This is an accounting of what we spent. It's pretty high because of the fuel prices out there. I've also added $500 to the total to send to Richard Onarak for room and board while we were in Nondalton."

She took the paper and ran her finger down the column of figures. "This looks OK to me. I expected it to be more."

"We won't cheat you if you don't cheat us," commented De Sylva. "There is one thing, though: Buddy and I talked it over and wondered if you would pay half of what you owe us in nuggets. The price may go up and we could make a little from the deal. The paper quoted gold at $1,329.40 today. We'll take that figure and reduce the weight by 20 percent to compensate for the quartz content of the nuggets. Buddy has a scale in his bag."

"Sure, if that's what you want. That way I can keep some of my cash." The gold had cost her nothing. It was a bonus for her. "I'd like you two to come back in the spring and start again. I'm convinced there's a lot of gold out there somewhere, and I want to find it."

"If we live through the winter, we'll talk about it in the spring," said Buddy while digging out his gold scale to weigh the nuggets.

"What are your plans for this winter?" asked Cuddles.

"I'm not sure," offered De Sylva. "My leasing business needs some attention; one of my twin engine planes needs work. I guess that will be my first order of business."

Buddy had his own plan. "I think I'll try to talk Gene into going to Las Vegas with me."

Cuddles got up to leave, "I'll be back in a minute with the cash and the nuggets. Figure up how much you get by weight." She waddled from the room and the miners returned to their pizza, which was now very cold but so was the beer washing it down.

Cuddles returned with a stack of $100 bills and the larger of the two leather pouches. Buddy began to weigh the nuggets, tallying the total weight and dropping the nuggets into a Crown Royal whiskey bag. It took a few minutes to get it right. When finished, Cuddles tossed in two medium-size nuggets for good measure.

"I'm not in the habit of giving away money, but you boys deserve a little bonus. I'll look to hear from you in the spring. Crusher will take you to your plane in the morning. And the $500 for your friend in Nondalton is in the envelope with your cash."

"Thanks, Cuddles, we'll see you in the spring." Both men waved to her as she turned to close the door behind her.

"That didn't seem like the Cuddles we know and love," said De Sylva. "She didn't argue the price or try to cut our take. Strange."

"Yeah, she must be desperate to get us back next year," agreed Buddy.

"Let's have another beer," suggested Gene.

The following morning Crusher came to their room to get them for the trip to the airport. It was still dark outside and the flyer had not yet checked the weather on the route to Fairbanks.

"I want to go into Kenai and eat breakfast, Crusher. I have to go by the FAA office and check out the weather before we go, anyway." De Sylva knew the wrestler had orders to take them wherever they needed to go. He led the way to the back door where the SUV was running.

It was daylight, but the sun had not yet come up, when they returned to the little airport to load the plane and top off the fuel. The office was open and they paid their bill. Crusher had gone and the two men were making a final check before takeoff. Windy Pass was forecast to be bumpy, but the rest of the trip was supposed to be smooth.

De Sylva crossed at the forelands and headed for the Susitna River, expecting a relaxing trip to Fairbanks.

<<<.>>>

There was fresh snow on the ground and the temperatures had dropped below freezing during the daytime. Winter was here and the pace of life had slowed. The slippery roads meant an increase in moose/car accidents. Burglaries had increased, too, adding to the workload for Sergeant Seaton. His investigation into the fire and death on the North Road had gone nowhere. There were no new leads and, as forensic evidence trickled in, no new clues were found. It seemed a dead end.

Seaton spent the day finishing reports and catching up on files. It was boring work, but it had to be done. In the old days, he would have had a secretary to do this kind of work for him; budget cuts had eliminated his helper and reduced his productive hours considerably. He had spent the entire day in the office and was about to sign out for the day when he got the call: a body had been found in a dumpster behind the Forelands Bar.

Icy roads and heavy traffic made his response time slow and agonizing. When he arrived at the bar, a road trooper was on scene along with an ambulance from Nikiski Fire Department. The fireman met him at the front door of the bar to show him where the body was. Seaton walked around the building to see the trooper busy keeping onlookers away. As he rounded the building, a white SUV pulled into the lot. It was Claudia Morris returning from an errand in town.

Dennis Carson stepped from the back door to meet her. "What's going on, Crusher?" she asked curtly.

"It's Lil. Someone killed her and put her in the dumpster. I'm sorry, Cuddles. I was working upstairs. I was fixing that plumbing leak you told me about. I didn't hear anything."

Sergeant Seaton was taking pictures and checking the body, which he had asked the on-scene trooper and the medic to remove from the dumpster. The medic brought a folding gurney and they laid out the body of Lil Danby. The road trooper then began to reel out a large amount of yellow police line tape, excluding onlookers from the immediate area. It was nearly an hour before

Seaton gave the order to remove the body from the scene. Cuddles had gone inside the bar along with Crusher Carson.

Bob Seaton took a final look at the body and determined the probable cause of death was strangulation. The neck was severely bruised. He hoped he could get forensic evidence from her fingernails—DNA—that would identify the assailant. As the ambulance drove away, taking Lil to the hospital to hold for the medical examiner, Seaton entered the back door of the bar looking to find the owner and her hired man. She was, sitting on her customary stool.

"Did anyone see this happen?" Seaton asked.

"I was in town, you saw me come back, and Crusher was upstairs working on the plumbing. You'll have to ask him if he knows anything. He's in the restroom, but he'll be right out." Cuddles seemed almost disinterested. "How soon can I open for business?" she asked.

"Not today, Cuddles. We'll have to check the place for fingerprints and other evidence. "

Just then the men's restroom door opened and Crusher walked slowly to where Seaton was conversing with Cuddles. "Have a seat over there at the table, Crusher; I want to talk to you about what happened." He turned to the owner, "You might as well go to your room, Cuddles. I will be a while here."

"I'll be upstairs if you need me." With that she climbed down from her tall perch. At the back door she stopped and turned. "Lock up and turn out the lights, Crusher," she said as she exited the storeroom door.

Sergeant Seaton parked his lean frame on a chair across from Dennis Carson. "OK, Crusher. Sorry I took so long to get to you. I know you liked Lil, so did I, but it will be my job to find out who killed her, and I need your help. Cuddles tells me you were the only one here when it happened."

"There had to be someone else. I didn't hurt Lil," he didn't look at the trooper, only stared at his hands on the table.

"Did you see anyone else come into the bar before you went upstairs to work?" asked Seaton as he opened his notebook.

"No I … wait a minute! I did see someone come in just as I was going out the back door to go to work. It was Tom Hagel. He was coming in when I left."

"Are you sure it was Hagel?"

"Yeah, I'm sure. I was face-to-face with him the other day when he tried to choke Lil, you remember."

"Yes, Crusher, I do remember. I thought Cuddles 86ed him after the fight."

"She did, but you know Cuddles, she let him back in after he promised to behave himself. I didn't think it was a good idea, but it's her place." Crusher looked sad.

"I need to see your ID again, Crusher." Seaton continued to write information on his pad. He had brought his briefcase with witness forms inside and gave one to the handyman. He sat with Dennis Carson for nearly an hour before telling him he could go.

An hour after he finished with Crusher he cleared the area, got into his car, and called dispatch for the address of Tom Hagel. As it turned out, Hagel was living with his brother, Chuck, a few miles north of the Forelands bar. The road trooper was still on the scene and Seaton pulled his patrol car up next to his.

"I'm going to interview Tom Hagel. He has a habit of becoming violent. I want you to follow me for a backup. Are you free to do it?" asked Seaton.

"Sure, just let me check in. How far is it?" he asked.

"Just three or four miles up the road. I know the place, follow me." The trooper nodded and the sergeant pulled away.

When the troopers arrived at the residence there was a snow-covered motorcycle in the driveway as well as two pickups: one old, registered to Tom Hagel; the other newer, registered to Chuck Hagel. It appeared both men were at home. The two troopers walked up onto the low porch and knocked. A large, hairy man answered.

"What do you want?" Chuck Hagel growled.

"Is your brother Tom in?" Seaton asked politely.

The big biker was about to say something, then changed his mind. "Tom, the troopers are here to see you," he shouted over his shoulder.

"Yeah?" came the response. "What do they want?"

"Come find out." With that Chuck Hagel walked out of the living room to the kitchen, leaving the troopers standing by the door.

A minute later a disheveled Tom Hagel entered, wearing sweat pants and a Harley Davidson tee shirt. "What do you two want?" he asked.

"We'd like to ask you a few questions about your whereabouts earlier this afternoon." Seaton remained polite.

"I was here all day," the younger Hagel lied. "Ask my brother."

"We will, but are you sure you didn't go to the Forelands Bar this afternoon?" Seaton asked again. "We have a witness who says he saw you going into the bar."

"Oh, yeah, I did go over there around three o'clock. I only stayed a minute. Lil refused to serve me a beer. I didn't argue with her 'cause she was mad at me for the fight we had the night you were there." Hagel seemed to be telling the truth. "Why? Did she say I robbed the place or something?"

Seaton ignored the question. "Then, you did go into the bar this afternoon and talk with Lil Danby—is that correct?"

"I said I did, didn't I?" Tom Hagel was becoming impatient.

"Are these the clothes you wore when you went to the bar?" asked the sergeant.

"No, I was wearing jeans and a flannel shirt and my leather jacket." Tom Hagel looked from one trooper to the other. "What's this all about, anyway?"

"I need to see the clothing you wore this afternoon, Tom. Where is it?"

"Back there," he pointed to a room in the back. "Why?"

"Let's go get them," Seaton issued the order.

"Why? You still haven't told me!" Hagel was becoming frantic. It sounded to him as if he were about to be arrested. Tom got the clothes from his room and the senior officer told Beeles to bag them up.

"I am placing you under arrest for the murder of Lil Danby." Sergeant Seaton took the handcuffs from his belt and motioned for the other trooper to watch the other Hagel. He turned Tom Hagel around and began to read him his rights.

When his brother heard what was going on, he rushed to the living room. As he entered, the other trooper held up his hand to stop him. "We are taking him to the pre-trial facility. You will be able to see him once he has completed the booking process. In the meantime, I suggest you back off and remain peaceful."

"OK, OK," he said to the trooper. "I'll call a lawyer, Tom. I'll see you at the jail."

Seaton and his backup took charge of the prisoner and walked him to the car. The road trooper drove Tom Hagel to the jail with Seaton following.

"This one has an end anyway," Seaton thought to himself. "Not like poor old Skip Williams. But, it seems as though these cases are related somehow." He couldn't make the thought go away.

Chapter 16

Seaton returned directly to the office to begin his report. Something about this whole thing bothered him. He just couldn't put his finger on what that something could be. Murder is an uncommon crime in the small local communities. Now he had two in a short period, both in the same neighborhood and both involving the same group of people. Somehow the outcome of this second case didn't smell right.

He had been in front of the computer for more than an hour when someone tapped on his office door. It was Jason Beeles, the trooper who had spent the day backing him during the investigation and responsible for seeing the prisoner booked into jail.

"Got a minute, Sarge?" asked the young trooper.

"Sure, come on in Jason. What can I do for you?"

"First of all I want to say I admired how you handled things today. I want to be an investigator someday and you taught me a good lesson today," Beeles began.

"What could you learn from me? I certainly didn't do anything spectacular today."

"It was how you handled the witnesses, Sarge. You got them to talk; even Tom Hagel was talking to you. I expected him to put up a fight, but you didn't give him a chance." The young trooper had, indeed, learned a valuable lesson. "But I have some questions about all this."

"So do I, Jason, let's hear yours." Seaton liked this young man.

"The biggest one is, we took Hagel into custody without any evidence whatsoever. Why did we do that?"

"You covered that question earlier. I did it to prevent a potential violent situation. We had evidence, albeit circumstantial. He was involved in an altercation at the bar a few days ago in which he was choking Lil, the victim—

meaning he was capable of the crime and had a motive. He was there this afternoon, meaning he had opportunity. She was strangled, meaning he easily had the means. But please don't ask if I believe he did it."

"So you don't think he's guilty either?" Jason asked, incredulously.

"I hate coincidence. This is the same location, same group of people and the same means of death with the same "innocent" bystanders. It just doesn't smell right to me," Bob Seaton confided in his newfound partner.

"Then why did we arrest Hagel?"

"You said it before, to prevent a more serious situation from developing. And, don't forget, he could be guilty."

Jason Beeles was confused, "I guess I don't understand. How can you arrest someone you don't believe is guilty? Doesn't that violate his constitutional rights?"

"I like the way you think, Jason. How long have you been a trooper?"

"Just over two years, Sarge. I'm still learning, but my goal is to be an investigator."

"How would you like to partner with me on this case? Help me with the investigation?" Seaton asked. "This isn't charity; I need someone right now. In truth, Lil Danby was a friend and informant for me. I'm not sure I'll be entirely objective if it turns out Hagel didn't commit this murder—and I don't think he did."

"Are you serious?" Beeles asked. "You really want me to work with you?"

"You're already asking the right questions. I can use someone who doesn't investigate with computer models. If you say yes, I'll clear it with the captain in the morning."

"Thank you, Sergeant Seaton. I won't let you down." Beeles was overjoyed at the opportunity.

"I'll see you in the morning after roll call."

When the young trooper had gone, Seaton picked up the bottle of water on his desk. He leaned back in his chair and relaxed a few moments. It would be good to have someone to discuss the case with, someone willing to look at options and discuss possibilities, he thought.

Early the next morning Seaton was in Captain Arnold's office. He explained the events of the previous day and suggested Beeles come on as his assistant. Normally a frugal and fiscally prudent man, the captain agreed. There had been two murders, one unsolved as yet. These cases must be closed.

After roll call, the sergeant pulled Beeles aside: "Grab a cup of coffee and meet me in my office." When the junior trooper came in, Bob gave him the good news that the captain had officially approved him to assist on the case. Seaton began to tutor his new protégé.

"We'll be working in uniform," explained Seaton. "At least for now we want everyone to know we are troopers investigating a homicide. With some witnesses we need the intimidation factor. However, don't get complacent. Some folks take offense at the sight of a uniform. Always be aware of your surroundings. You don't need to fear the people you are dealing with, but you must be ready for all threats. The result is the reward for a job well done. If we catch a bad guy and take him off the street, we have done our job. The problem comes when we get a case like this one." It was an indoctrination speech of sorts. "I want you to take the two files there on the desk and read them. I think a fresh pair of eyes may be what the arson/murder case needs. Let's get to work."

"I have to take the papers on Hagel to the district attorney this morning. I'll start as soon as I get back from Kenai," uttered the proud young trooper.

Seaton started a personnel file on Beeles. As sergeant he was responsible for certain routine tasks, one of which was evaluating his subordinates. It was getting late in the morning and he was about to go out on the road when his telephone rang. It was Cuddles.

"Mornin'," greeted the bar owner.

"Good morning, Cuddles. What can I do for you?"

"I heard you arrested Tom Hagel for killing my bartender, is that right?"

"Yes it is."

"Then I can relax and hire a new bartender?" she asked.

"Yes, but I still have to come out and see you about all this. I have some questions." Seaton's intent was to annoy the large lady. It worked.

"Why do you want to talk to me? I wasn't even here when it happened; I was in Kenai at the bank."

"I know, Cuddles, but I still have a few questions and will be out to see you this afternoon. I have a new assistant and I would like for you to meet him. He's a nice young man. His name is Jason. You'll like him."

"I doubt it. I don't like cops of any description, but I'll be here." She hung up.

Seaton chuckled about the conversation and was anxious to introduce Beeles to Claudia aka Cuddles Morris.

"How about you riding with me?" Seaton asked his new partner. "We'll be coming back here after the interview and it'll give us a chance to talk about the cases. I should preface this interview with what you should expect. Claudia Morris is a retired hooker. She is short, fat and coarse. She swears like a sailor and sometimes does her best to embarrass you, if there are other people around. She goes by the name of Cuddles. She is greedy and short tempered. She has a hired hand, Dennis Carson. He was a wrestler and used the name "Crusher." I hope I never have to arrest him. I saw what he did to the Hagels and their friends in a bar fight. He doesn't talk much, but he isn't dumb. My advice is, don't turn your back on him."

"You certainly have interesting friends, Sarge." Beeles was listening and learning. "What do you want me to do when we get there?"

"I'll handle the interview, but if I miss something I want you to speak up. By the way, did you get a chance to look over those files I gave you?"

"Yes, I did. I took them home with me last night. I found one question in them."

"What was that?"

"Did they ever find evidence of the lost gold in the fire remains?" Jason asked.

"I knew you were a thinker, Jason." Seaton was amused at the question. He was now convinced he had picked the right partner. "No, they haven't. I'm thinking they never will. My theory is that the gold was the motive for the fire and for killing Williams. I think Skip Williams told or showed someone the gold and they went to his place and killed him for it, then set fire to the mobile home to cover the murder."

"I think that's a pretty good theory. Do you have a list of suspects?"

"The top name on the list would be Cuddles. If Skip needed money he would have gone to her. I know there is no way she could have gone to his house and killed him by herself. But, that pet ape she keeps—Crusher—could have handled it easily. The trouble with it all is that there's no evidence. I think the only way to confirm my theory is to find the gold." Seaton hinted at his frustration.

"Did you bring a rubber hose? We could beat the truth out of her." Beeles had a sense of humor, too.

When the two reached the bar and went inside, Cuddles was at her usual spot at the end of the bar. A new girl was behind the bar, familiarizing herself with her new territory. Crusher was nowhere to be seen.

As they approached the bar owner Seaton said, "Hello, Cuddles. I'd like to introduce you to my new partner, Jason Beeles. He's a nice young man. Try not to corrupt him on the first visit."

Cuddles smiled and held out her hand, "Pleased to meet you Jason. Don't listen to this calloused old trooper. He lost his sense of humor a long time ago. Have a seat at that first table. I'll come over there."

The two troopers sat at the table and waited for her to climb down and take a seat at the table with them. Once she had parked her bulk she asked, "What can I do for you two?"

"I just have some questions bothering me, Cuddles," Seaton began.

"Like what, Bob? I already told you, I wasn't here when this happened. If I had been I would have stopped it."

"I'm just checking, since no one was here to see her strangled, could someone else have done it? Could someone else have come in after Tom Hagel left and done it?"

"I suppose they could have, but he was the only one seen here."

"There was one other person here, Cuddles: Crusher. He saw Hagel come into the bar and what he did next puzzles me. He knew Hagel was the one who had put her in a choke hold during the bar fight, and yet he left to go upstairs and fix the plumbing. He said he found her body when he went out to dispose of some old pipe and fixtures." Seaton was mapping out another scenario. "It just seems strange he left her alone with Hagel. I think Crusher liked Lil and seems unusual for him to leave when Hagel came in. Don't you find it unusual?"

"Hell no, I don't find it unusual! He got hit in the head and sometimes doesn't think straight. I don't like you suggesting Crusher had anything to do with her death. He was sweet on her," she said, making a case for her hired man.

"I'm not saying he did it, but I am saying it is possible someone besides Hagel could have done it."

"Well, think again cowboy. He didn't do it. Go find some other patsy for your fairy tale."

"Let me ask you this, Cuddles. He was here all night the night Skip Williams died in the fire, is that right?" asked the trooper sergeant.

"Of course he was. Everyone saw him here. He was stocking the beer cooler while customers were here. Lil talked to him that night. Hell, you were in here, you saw him yourself."

"Yes, that's true, but that was after the fire started."

"If you're going to sit here and talk like that, I'm going to call my lawyer. I pay him a lot of money to protect me from abuse by you troopers." With that she pulled herself erect. She turned to Jason, "You'd better find a different partner, young man. This one is senile." She turned and shuffled back to her seat at the end of the bar.

She watched as the two lawmen stood and walked out. She gave them about one second, picked up the telephone, and dialed Grant Cummings. The phone rang about ten times before a raspy voice answered. "What do you want?" he asked.

"It's noon, Grant. Get out of bed and get out here. Seaton and a new partner were here asking a lot of questions. I don't like the direction they were taking." Cuddles tried to sound calm.

"I'll be there in a little while. Keep your shirt on." He hung up on her.

Chapter 17

An hour and a half later, the lawyer sauntered into the Forelands Bar. When he took off his coat, Cuddles was appalled at his appearance: worn out blue jeans with no belt, a flannel shirt with the elbows out and filthy tennis shoes with untied laces. He wore no socks. "Can't you dress like a normal person? You look like a homeless person someone dragged out of a box."

"I'm glad you like it," the lawyer chided. "My dress is my cover. It lets me slip up on city lawyers who think I'm just a dumb hick." He parked himself on the stool next to his client. "I know you think I haven't done anything, but I've been very busy."

"Good! Impress me with your work," Cuddles snapped.

"Well, for starters, I've begun probate proceedings in the matter of the estate of Larry "Skip" Williams. I was able to do this under the statement he had hired me to represent him in matters of acquiring the properties the estate now owns. I assured the court he had no creditors other than you. I have filed the necessary advertising which will appear in the newspaper beginning Monday. I've filed a lien against the estate to recover the large sum of money owed to you by Mr. Williams. I've asked to grant you possession of the two pieces of property on Industrial Drive and the Piper PA-11, which is now at Rediske Airpark. The judge told me he considered the value of the estate negligible and after it was advertised he would sign off on the transfer of ownership, assuming no other creditors or relatives come forward."

"How much money have I loaned Mr. Williams?" the bar owner/loan shark wanted to know.

"How much does he really owe you?"

"I have a signed note for $3,000," she said.

"Good. Where is the note? Perhaps we can amend the amount above his signature by adding a figure in front of the amount he signed for."

"Congratulations, Grant! You do have a heart steeped with larceny," she smiled and narrowed her eyes at him, knowingly.

"Of course; isn't that why you hired me in the first place?" Grant Cummings was grinning now.

"Wait here and I'll go up to the safe and get the note." She slithered off the stool and made her way through the storeroom door.

Several minutes later Cuddles returned with the document. The lawyer was drinking a cup of coffee provided by the new bartender. She handed the note to the lawyer for evaluation. He studied it a minute and began to nod his head.

"I think we can add a "9" here," he pointed to the spot in front of the "3". When this was typed someone left a space between the dollar sign and the 3. This is perfect for our purpose. We won't have to forge or copy the signature."

"Isn't that illegal?" asked Cuddles.

"Do you want this done or not?" the lawyer snarled.

Cuddles blew out an exasperated breath, "Just get it done, and quickly. I want to own all the property including the mining claims when the snow melts in the spring. Gene and Buddy will be back in May, and I want to be able to search all the claims."

"My guess is it will take about three months to finalize the estate. As it stands right now, I don't see anything to stop the process and you attaining ownership. Of course there's the possibility of more creditors or a relative coming forward, but you assured me there weren't any of either." Cummings was pleased with himself for being one step ahead of Cuddles. "I'll take this note to the office and modify it to our purpose."

"OK, Grant, but I want that note back here. Don't try to get cute," Cuddles warned Cummings.

He put the note in his tattered briefcase and headed for the door. "Don't ever call me before 2 PM," he said, as he departed.

Cuddles sat a long time, thinking. Just when she was beginning to think things were getting better, the troopers had come asking questions and implying accusations. Just when she thought she would be able to walk in and take over the mining claims, Grant Cummings comes in with his legalese and stirs it all up again. It worried her that there was so much interest in the death of a drug dealer. And she couldn't understand why the troopers were so interested in the death of Lil Danby; they already had a suspect in jail for the crime. Most concerning of all, there was one loose end the troopers had not yet confronted: Dennis "Crusher" Carson.

She slid off her stool and started toward her office. Crusher was in the back room stacking cases of beer in the main cooler. She admired Crusher. He worked all the time. He never complained and never missed a day of work.

Crusher's main virtue was that he did any job, no matter what it was, without asking questions. He just did it.

"Come up to the office, Crusher. We need to talk." She spoke softly to him and kept walking to the stairs. She held the rail with both hands and pulled her great mass, step by step, up to the second floor. She rested at the top, panting and sweating. When she heard the cooler door close, she made her way to the office. She was sitting at her desk when Crusher came in.

"What do you want, Ma'am? Did I do something wrong?" he asked, respectfully.

"No, you haven't done anything wrong, Crusher. You are my dearest and most loyal friend. I do need to talk to you about something, though."

"Sure. What about?" Crusher said as he sat in the chair near the desk.

"The fire, for one thing. The troopers have been asking a lot of questions and keep coming back out here. Sooner or later they'll want to talk with you again. I think you need to take a little vacation. You should leave here for a while, until all this blows over. That trooper sergeant was here making noises like he didn't believe Tom Hagel had killed poor old Lil. I know you didn't have anything to do with that, but the troopers will be back and talk to you about it."

"Why would they want to talk to me about her dyin'? I don't know any more than I already told them. That Trooper Seaton isn't very nice to me. He thinks I'm dumb and can't figure stuff out, but I can." Crusher was becoming nervous, pulling at a loose thread on his shirtsleeve.

"I'm just worried about you, Crusher. I don't want anything to happen to you. You are the best helper I have around here. I couldn't run this place without you."

"I like working for you, Miss Cuddles. You know I'll do anything you say."

"I know, Crusher, that's why I asked you to come up here. I think you should take off for a few weeks, enjoy the holidays." Cuddles was making a suggestion but meant it as an order.

"Where would I go?" asked the wrestler.

"Don't you have any relatives or friends in the lower 48 you would like to see?" she asked.

"I only got one sister left and she lives in Kansas. I ain't seen her in a lot of years. I guess I could go visit her for Christmas... but I don't know if she'll let me come see her. We don't get along too well. Not since Ma and Pa died. She thought I should take care of them instead of her, but I was wrestling then and couldn't get away to do it. I like my sister, though, she's nice. She never got married, just lived out there on the farm by herself." He had never told Cuddles about his home life. She was shocked to realize he had a sister.

"I'll be happy to pay for the trip if you'll go away for a while. Take a vacation and enjoy yourself. How about it, Crusher, will you go?"

"I don't know. I'd have to call her and ask if I could come. I think she would let me; we only have each other now. We're the last of our clan. I'll have to think it over for a while, but I'll let you know what I can do." He was still tugging at the string on his shirt. "I sure don't want to talk to that trooper anymore."

"That's why I think you should leave for a while."

"Can I give you an answer later today?" asked Crusher.

"Sure you can. Think it over and let me know. Remember I'll give you the money for the trip." Cuddles was wiggling the carrot on a stick.

Dennis Carson nodded his huge head and made his way to the door. "I'll have an answer for you later today or by tomorrow," said the big man.

Crusher had a lot to think about. He checked the time and added three hours to get Central Standard Time. Back in his little office area in the storeroom he sat thinking about his conversation with his boss. If the troopers wanted to ask him questions he would rather not be here to answer. There were many things he didn't want the police to know. Because of his head injuries, his thought processes were not capable of solving more than one problem at a time. Usually he left that thinking to Cuddles. She wanted him to leave and that was probably best, but he had not been out of Alaska in many years. He had not seen his sister in that time. It would be good to see her and renew his family tie, especially at the holidays. Although he never let on, he was fearful of the trooper learning of his part in the fire at Skip Williams' place.

He checked the time again and reached for the telephone. He took a small piece of aged paper from his wallet with his sister's number written on it. He dialed the number and waited for an answer, apprehensive about the outcome of the call.

"Hello," answered the friendly voice on the other end.

"Hi, Darlene, it's Dennis."

"Well, for heaven sakes, is the world coming to an end?" She was truly shocked to hear from her brother.

"You know me, Darlene. I try not to bother you. I know it's been a long time, but since I got hurt in the ring I haven't been my old self. I was wondering, if I came down to Kansas would you let me come and visit you, stay for Christmas? I won't be a pest, I promise." Crusher waited while his sister paused, thinking.

"I'll let you come here, and you can have your old room, but I warn you: if you give me any trouble, I'll call the sheriff and have you arrested. You always caused trouble when you came, even when the folks were alive. I don't want to go through that again." She was giving him fair warning. She was two years younger than Dennis and had spent her life taking care of her parents. Dennis had run off and left the family without a man to do the hard work on the farm. She hated him for that.

"I know all that, Darlene, and I'm sorry. You have no idea how sorry I am. I'm sorry for leaving you to take care of the farm and the folks. I'm sorry for never sending money home when I was making good purses. I'm sorry for my whole life, but I can't change that now. I just want to get reacquainted and try to make amends for the things I've done. I won't cause you any trouble, I promise."

"As long as you stick to that, I'll be happy to see you. But be warned, if you act like you did in the old days, I'll have you thrown out of here." She was skeptical, but she, too, wanted him to rejoin the family. After all, they were the last ones and they weren't getting any younger. "When do you think you'll be coming?"

"Would it be OK if I came down this week?" he asked politely. "The weather is getting cold here and I ache all the time. I'd like to come down for a while. It would make my winter here a little shorter."

"I'll get your room ready, Dennis. It'll be good to see you again and enjoy the holidays together, like when we were young." She hoped that was true.

"I'll call and let you know when I will arrive. I think I'll fly into Topeka and rent a car. Thank you Darlene; I'll call you when I have a schedule."

He sat for a while wondering if he was doing the right thing. Finally he went into the bar and checked the coolers. It had been a slow night and they were fine. He walked back to the second floor and the office. Cuddles was still sitting at her desk.

"I've decided to take the trip, Boss. Will you get me a flight out of here to Topeka, Kansas?"

"Sure, Crusher. I'm glad you decided to go. I want you to stay in touch while you're gone. I'll keep you posted on happenings here. I'll call my travel agent in the morning and make your arrangements. You'd better take the rest of the night off and pack for the trip. I'll need to go to the bank and get you some money for the trip. We can do that on the way to the airport." Cuddles was now relieved.

Crusher Carson returned to the bar to instruct the new bartender about things that must taken care of in his absence. He was beginning to enjoy the thought of a winter vacation out of Alaska.

Chapter 18

Tom Hagel had spent Christmas in jail awaiting a trial date. There had been delay after delay and Hagel was becoming impatient. He hated being in jail. He hated his attorney, a public defender appointed by the court. He continued to claim he was innocent and no one seemed to want to listen.

Bob Seaton, too, was impatient. He had run out of leads and one key witness, Crusher Carson, was gone from the state. No one seemed to know when he would return. Claudia Morris said he had gone to visit relatives. She claimed she didn't know where, exactly, he was or when he would return. Somewhere in the Midwest is all she said.

It was now past the first of the year and Seaton had just been notified of a court date for the trial of Tom Hagel. He was reviewing the file when his phone rang. It was Alan Lewis, public defender, representing Hagel.

"Sergeant Seaton, this is Alan at the Public Defender's Office. I am representing Tom Hagel. I just came from the pre-trial building and he asked me to call you. He wants to talk with you. He said he doesn't want me to be there. I advised him against that, but he insisted."

"What does he want, do you know?"

"Yes, he told me. I can't tell you, but he will. You know—client-attorney privilege."

"Is this genuine or is he just wanting company?"

"Actually, I think it's genuine. I wish I could say more, but my hands are tied. He wants to talk with you."

"All right, I'll go out there this afternoon. Call the jail and tell them I'll be there to see him at 2. They'll want your permission. Thanks for the call."

He hung up the phone and wondered what this could be about. Hagel had shouted his innocence since the day of his arrest. Was he now willing to confess and make a deal? It was hard to say. Trooper Beeles was back on the road, but Seaton called him to meet up with him at the jail to talk to the prisoner. It could be a waste of time for both men, but you never know.

The two troopers met outside the pre-trial facility and went inside together. They were met at the door by the shift supervisor who knew both men. Seaton explained the situation to the corrections sergeant and asked to see Tom Hagel. They were taken to the secure portion of the jail and asked to wait in the attorney visiting room. Minutes later Hagel was brought to them and his handcuffs taken off. No one spoke until the door closed and they were alone.

"Man, am I glad to see you, Sergeant Seaton. I've been sitting in here trying to figure out who killed Lil, 'cause it sure wasn't me. I remember you said a witness saw me come into the bar. I couldn't figure who it was. Then it came to me. It had to be Crusher, the guy who works for Cuddles. I didn't see him, but it had to be him. I didn't know why he would say I killed her. Then the other day it came to me: He killed her! He had to of." Hagel was talking rapidly and excitedly.

"Why would he say you killed her, Tom?' asked Seaton.

"I couldn't figure it out for a long time; then I remembered something Lil said when she was shouting at me to leave." Hagel was still excited.

"What did she say?" asked trooper Beeles.

Hagel looked at Seaton, as if to ask if it was alright for him to talk.

"Go ahead, Tom. Spit it out," ordered Seaton.

"'That day, when I walked into the bar, Lil was mad when she saw me. She told me to get out, and said she didn't want me trying to kill her again. I tried to explain to her that I was there to apologize to her and really didn't want to hurt her. She said she didn't want to hear it. She said she couldn't trust men anymore, that Crusher had saved her but she couldn't trust him, so she wasn't gonna' trust me. I asked her what she was talking about and she said she knew Crusher wasn't in the bar at the time of the fire at Williams' place. I really didn't pay much attention to that at the time, but I've been thinking while I've been in here that maybe, just maybe, that dimwit overheard her say that. Maybe he killed her to keep her quiet."

Seaton was stunned and glanced quickly at Beeles. It was difficult for the young trooper to keep a straight face and not display emotion. This truly was information worth knowing. If Hagel was telling the truth, it meant Bob's suspicions about Crusher were confirmed. With Crusher out of the state he would have to find another way to confirm this statement by Hagel. The two troopers finished talking with Hagel, assuring him they would investigate his revelation. They called the corrections officer to take Hagel back to his cell.

Outside they met to discuss what they had just heard. Beeles was as amazed at the statement as Seaton. "If we can prove what he says, it will confirm what you told me from the start: you thought it was someone else connected to the fire and murder of Skip Williams." Beeles gave Seaton a concerned look, "Knowing is one thing, proving is another."

Beeles went back out on the road, but Seaton decided to drive to North Kenai and talk again with Claudia Morris.

"Hi there, Cuddles," he said as he entered the bar. She and the bartender were the only two in the place.

She looked up and frowned. "What do you want now?" she barked.

"Just a friendly visit, Claudia. With Crusher out of town I thought I should check on you and make sure you're doing OK. When do you expect him to come home, anyway?" He hoped the disarming conversation would mellow her a little. It didn't seem to do the trick.

"I don't know and wouldn't tell you if I did. Alls I know is he went to visit family. He didn't say when he was coming back, or if he was coming back, for that matter." As Seaton came closer to Cuddles, the bartender edged toward them in a protective manner.

"Is everything going OK for you these days?" Bob asked the defensive owner.

"What do you care?" She was continuing her bad attitude. "You still haven't caught the guy who killed poor old Skip, and the guy who killed Lil still ain't gone to trial. What good are you anyway?"

"I just investigate and arrest, the rest is up to the court. I'm still working on the death and fire at Skip's place. Have you heard anything that might help me out?"

"I ain't saying nothin'," she growled again.

"Sorry you feel that way, Cuddles. I want to talk with Crusher and came to find out when you expect him back. Please give me a call if you hear from him, will you?" he asked politely.

"Don't hold your breath," she snarled at his back as he walked to the door. The bartender now walked back to the other end of the bar.

<<<.>>>

Dennis Carson was enjoying his visit to the family farm. He had spent many happy hours reminiscing with his sister. She, too, was enjoying the visit. Carson helped the hired man repair the farm equipment. Farming was at a standstill, but the equipment had to be made ready for next season. The hired man, Lester Peterson, was young and energetic. He had come to work here right out of high school twelve years ago and learned the farming trade well. He had built a small cabin near the main house and lived in it year around.

Lester was friendly as well as skilled. It seemed his only interest was taking care of the farm, which was of considerable size. They had 2,300 acres in wheat and 2,000 acres of harvested land, which had to be tilled in the spring. A few miles from the home place, there was a 1,500-acre parcel, where they ran 200 head of Hereford cattle. They would be calving in a few weeks and the work would begin. Spring and summer months required Lester to hire a large crew of farm hands, so he acted as foreman.

Darlene had come to rely on the young man. In the past she would drive a tractor, ride a horse, help with the branding, and do any other chore on the ranch. This had become too much for her in recent years as her knees and back gave out and age slowed her down. Now she kept the books and managed the farm while Lester did the labor and managed the help.

It was an efficient process and Dennis Carson could see he was not needed on the ranch. His sister was patient with him and encouraged him to stay, but spring breakup in Alaska would be little more than two months away in Alaska and he would be needed there for the busy season. He dreaded the thought of going back to the turmoil he knew was awaiting him. It was time to give Cuddles a call and see if it was safe to come back.

Cuddles answered the phone on the second ring. She must have been at her perch at the end of the bar. "Hello, Cuddles, it's Dennis Carson."

"Well, for land sakes, Crusher. It sure is good to hear from you! How have you been?" she asked with genuine interest.

"I'm good. I've been helping out on the ranch, fixing equipment and stuff. How are things there? Has anyone come looking for me?"

"The troopers are still nosing around, but except for Sergeant Bob Seaton, no one's been asking for you. Seaton has been a real pain all winter." She didn't volunteer much information.

"What about Tom Hagel? How did his trial turn out?" asked the wrestler, with interest.

"He hasn't gone to trial yet, but I heard it was coming up soon. There hasn't been anything in the papers about it. Grant has been working on the other stuff and says I should be in possession of all the property soon. He says the time limits for creditors to come forward is about up. I haven't heard from Gene or Buddy since they left here. There isn't much to report, Crusher. Business is slow and I think you should stay and enjoy your family." She was in no hurry to see him come back to face Bob Seaton.

"I think I'll try to take Darlene to Las Vegas before I come back. I have some money in the bank and I can afford it. She doesn't get to do that sort of thing much. She's been really nice to me while I've been here. She deserves some time off." Carson was thinking aloud more than stating a plan. He didn't know if Darlene would be willing to leave the ranch or not.

"Just enjoy yourself for a while. After the Hagel trial, things should calm down. Stay in touch." Cuddles had no idea when Hagel would go to trial but assumed it would be soon. "Thanks for calling, Crusher."

The bar owner was sitting on her stool, thinking about her conversation with Crusher when Grant Cummings called.

"I've got some bad news for you, Cuddles," he began.

"Now what?" she responded.

"You remember I told you things were all going our way and we only had to wait to see if there were other creditors or relatives? Well, there's a relative. Williams had a sister back in Michigan. She didn't know he had died, but she made some calls trying to talk with him. One of his old drug buddies told her he was dead. She called the court and they asked her for verification of her relationship to Skip. The court clerk said she went to pieces while on the telephone. The result, at this time, is that she is on the list as a relative."

"I didn't know he had a sister. What's this going to do to our claim?!" Cuddles was furious at the news.

"If no creditors come forward, and so far none have, you'll have first claim on his property. You might want to make a list of the things you want and place a monetary value on them. That way when the judge decides to award property, you'll get what you want even if she gets the rest. So far there's no mention of the gold. That means the airplane and the land will be the big items. The mining claims will be a secondary issue. I suggest you place a value on the property and plane of, say, $60,000 and $3,000 on the mining claims. That way you will have recovered the amount owed you and she'll still receive the real property. That should satisfy her as well as the judge."

"Do you think this will work?" she inquired in a skeptical tone.

"You never know what a judge is going to say, but it will look like you're being fair with the relative." Cummings was clever and strongly suspected it would work.

"OK, Grant, put that together and submit it to the court. It had better work." She wasn't so sure it was going to satisfy the court, but she had no other plan in mind. "Keep me posted on what he says."

As it turned out, Cuddles learned the sister was a druggy and needed money. That was the reason for the calls to find her brother Skip. Cuddles began to think Cummings had been right: the value of the property would look like a lot of money to Skip's sister. She would probably sell it quick for the cash and run back to Michigan. Cuddles might make that cash offer herself. This plan might work after all.

Chapter 19

The following week Cuddles had a phone call from her favorite barrister. "Guess who just came to my office?" He liked guessing games, as well as tormenting his client.

"How should I know? I pay you to find out those things. I'm busy, spit it out." Cuddles was in a good mood today.

"It was Pamela Williams," again tormenting his client.

"I don't have time for your silly games, Grant."

Cummings snickered and told her, "It's Skip Williams' sister. She came into town and went to the court, where the clerk referred her to my office. She's looking for money. What do you want me to do with her?"

There was a long silence on the other end of the line. Finally Cuddles replied. "Bring her out here. I'll see if I can make a deal with her. I'm getting into this whole thing pretty deep, so I won't offer her much. Where is she now?"

"She's in the waiting room and I'm in my office," meaning she was in the living room and he was in the kitchen.

"Why don't…" she paused. "I was going to ask why you didn't get an office like any other self-respecting lawyer, but I remembered you have no self-respect."

"Ah, Cuddles, is that a nice thing to say?" Again he was chuckling to himself.

"Shut up and bring her out here."

"You'll enjoy meeting this nice young lady," he commented facetiously.

A half hour later he entered the Forelands Bar with Pamela Williams. He escorted her to the end of the bar where Cuddles was sitting and introduced the two.

"Let's you and I go to that table," Cuddles said pointing to the first table nearby. "Go get some coffee or something, Grant. Pamela and I can do this without your help."

Cuddles drug her frame from the barstool and waddled to a chair at the table. The frail, pitiful- looking woman followed her. The bar owner was never one to be sentimental, but this woman was a zombie—the walking dead. It broke the heart of Claudia Morris, who remembered how it was to be lost and without hope. And, like Claudia, this woman would be dead if someone didn't intervene.

"How do you do, Cuddles?" the sister spoke. "Please call me Pam."

"OK, Pam. What is it you want from me?" Cuddles answered.

"To tell you the truth, I don't know. I don't mean to sound like I'm begging, but I'm broke. I've been on meth for a long time and I want to quit, but I can't afford treatment. I just want to get some money and go back home." Tears were forming in her eyes.

This woman was about 5 feet 6 inches tall, and weighed about 90 pounds. Her teeth were all rotted to the gum-line and her skin was gray and lifeless. The pitiful sight of this woman struck a note in Claudia's heart. She knew, too well, how this creature felt.

"Are you serious about getting off the drugs, or are you just looking for cash to buy some more?" The question seemed cruel.

Pam held her clenched hands to her face, tears rolling down her cheeks. "I have to get off the stuff. Look at me. If I don't do it soon it's going to kill me. I'm desperate. Skip promised to help me when I wanted to stop, but now he's gone and I have nowhere to turn."

This younger woman was breaking Claudia's heart. She thought a few moments, then asked, "I can't make you get off the drugs. Only you can do that, but I have a proposition for you. I'll pay for your stay at a rehab center here in Kenai. You'll have to play by all the rules, no backsliding. If you do well for three months and stay on the program, I'll pay for you to have your teeth replaced. I'll pay for medical help if you need it. Remember: drop the ball, even once, and it's over. It will all be up to you. You can do it if you really want it. I've been there, honey, and it ain't easy."

"You don't even know me; why would you take the chance to help me?" she asked, crying.

"I know you better than you think. I ain't no angel, and I know you can't do this alone. Take my word for it, honey, I know you better than you know you." Cuddles hated to admit it, but this was the truth. "I think, without help, you'll be dead in six months. I think with a little help you can have a long and happy life. I'm not giving you anything. You have to do it yourself. All I'm doing is offering you a way to do it yourself. And if you make it, maybe someday you'll be able to help someone else. Now, do you want to get clean bad enough to take my offer? It won't be easy."

Pamela was sobbing uncontrollably now. "Oh, Miss Cuddles, how can I ever thank you?"

"Honey, before this is over you'll hate me. It's all up to you."

"I'll do whatever it takes," she said, sitting up straight and taking a deep breath.

Cuddles wrote a number on a piece of napkin and gave it to Pamela. "Keep this number. It's my personal number and you can call me anytime, day or night."

"Thank you." She was crying again now.

Cuddles called the lawyer over to the table. "Take Pamela to Serenity House and check her in. Tell them to send all the bills to you. Get her a physical and find her a doctor for any continuing treatments. This is going to be a long process. See to it that she has everything she needs: clothing, medications, counseling, anything. I gave her my number and she can call me any time. Make sure she has the help she needs."

"That's going to cost a lot of money, Cuddles. Are you sure you want to do this?" asked Grant Cummings.

"Look in the mirror, Grant. I take on charity cases from time to time." It was Cuddles' turn to poke at his ego.

The bartender had been busy checking on a Budweiser delivery in the back room and was not aware of the negotiations going on in the bar. When he returned to his station, Cuddles called him to the end of the bar. The new bartender was a second generation American. His father immigrated from Hungary during the Russian purge many years ago.

"Vito," she called. "Come down here." She was on her throne at the end of the bar.

"Yes, Ma'am," he said.

"Did you get the beer delivery put away?"

"Yes. It was a small delivery today."

"Do I pay you enough for the work I have you do here, Vito?" she asked.

"Oh, yes, plenty," was his reply.

"Then, why do you find it necessary to skim ten dollars a day for yourself?" she asked.

"Miss Cuddles—"

She cut him off. "Vito, I'm not asking *if* you were stealing, I asked *why* you were stealing."

He started to speak then stopped. "I'm sorry, all bartenders do it. I'm sorry."

"How can I trust you now, Vito?" she wanted to know.

"I guess there is nothing I can say that will make you trust me. I'll get my stuff and leave. I'm sorry. I like it here and I like working for you." He began to untie his apron. "I'm sorry," he said again.

"I'm not going to fire you, Vito. If you want to stay, I'll keep you on. I want you to understand, though. Nothing happens in this bar I don't know about. It's your job to look out for my interests. If you need more money, ask me. Don't take it on your own. There won't be another chance for you. This is it. Do you want to stay?"

"Yes, Ma'am, I'll do the right thing. I'll earn your trust back." He was re-tying his apron and walking to the other end of the bar.

Life was becoming complicated. She reached for the phone and dialed the number from her private phone book. It was the cell phone of Dennis Carson. He answered with a sleepy voice.

"Hello," Crusher said.

"Hello, Crusher. How are you?" she asked.

"Fine. The trip to Vegas was fun, but I'm getting a little bored with farm life. How are things in Alaska?"

"Good. Things are good. There's a lot going on right now and I think I should have you here. Can you come home soon?'

"Them is sweet words, Cuddles. How soon?" he asked.

"How soon can you come?" she inquired.

"Get me a ticket out of Topeka as soon as you can. Let me know the day and time. I have to check my rental car in at the Topeka Airport and I'm ready."

"I'll call you back." She hung up and called her travel agent who made the arrangements for the next morning. Crusher would be back in Kenai by late tomorrow night.

<<<.>>>

Dennis Carson had been back at the Forelands Bar for week when Bob Seaton came into the place looking for him. The new bartender had never officially met the trooper sergeant, but had seen enough of him. When Seaton reached the bar, Vito Hocker, introduced himself.

"Pleased to meet you, Vito, how do you like working here?"

"I like it here. I've been a bartender for a long time, mostly in warm climate beach resorts. This is my first winter in a cold climate, but I think I'll survive. Ms. Morris treats me great and the workload is pretty easy. I've heard horror stories about fights and shootings, but so far there haven't been any while I was on duty."

"The stories are probably true, but they don't happen often. Good luck to you." Seaton reached out to shake the man's hand. "Is Crusher back yet?" he asked Vito.

"Yes, he got back last week. He's a quiet sort of guy. He helps me out a lot. I like him."

"Is he working now?" asked the trooper.

"He's in the back. I can get him for you if you want," offered Vito.

"Thanks, I'd appreciate it."

Vito disappeared through the door to the back room and returned a minute later saying "Crusher will be out in a minute. He is putting beer in the big cooler."

"Thanks, Vito." Seaton stood at the end of the bar where Cuddles customarily sat, waiting. Five minutes later the door opened and a stern-faced Dennis Carson appeared.

"Hello, Crusher. I've missed you. I need to talk with you and ask a couple of questions. Do you have time for me?"

"Yeah, but not too long. I've been gone. Got a lot of work to catch up on."

"Thanks, Crusher. I won't take too long. Just a couple of questions. Can we sit at the table?"

"Sure. What do you want to know?" asked the big man as he sat.

"I'm still investigating the fire and death at Skip Williams' place. I haven't gotten very far, but I had a witness tell me that he thought you were out of the bar at the time of the fire. Is that true? Were you out of the bar?" Seaton tried to sound friendly.

"Nah, I was in the back stocking the beer cooler. I don't get out front much. Too many people out here." Crusher seemed relaxed. "I came out front when all the ruckus started. You know, the fire trucks and cops that came that night."

"I understand, but my witness says you left for a while and came back just before the excitement started." Seaton asked him again, "Are you sure you didn't leave for a while? My witness says you left in your old car."

"Your witness is full of crap. I told you I was here all night." Crusher was beginning to get edgy.

"Why would my witness say you weren't here? He seemed to know you were driving your car." Seaton was pressing the wrestler, irritating him.

"Your witness isn't very reliable. I was here all that night." Crusher was nervous, "Ask Cuddles, she'll tell you. She knows."

"OK, Crusher, I'll ask her again. By the way, where have you been for the past many weeks? I've missed you."

"I went to Kansas to visit my sister. She owns the family farm now. Had a nice visit, too." This answer came from a relaxed Crusher.

He was now telling the truth. It was plain to see he had previously been less than truthful. Seaton made a note to come back and dig at him again.

"Thanks Crusher, I think that's all for now. I may need to check with you again later. You can go back to work now." Seaton just wanted to keep the big wrestler off balance.

Chapter 20

Pamela Williams was not allowed to have contact with the outside world, but she was able to send word to Claudia Morris that she was doing well … although she was having a tough time resisting the urge for drugs. She had been a cocaine and methamphetamine addict for a very long time and it was a struggle for her to suddenly stop using the drugs. However, her determination to succeed was powerful and day by day she resisted the temptations. She was gaining weight and her color was beginning to resume the look of a live person instead of a corpse. The longer she was away from the drugs the more she was repulsed by how her appearance had deteriorated and the more determined she became to overcome her addiction.

The news of her struggle was welcomed by Cuddles. She had overcome her own addiction when she was injured and could no longer obtain the stuff on her own. She knew how hard it was to rid one's body and mind of the need for drugs. Cuddles was very pleased with her decision to help Pamela. Grant Cummings had given her each progress report as he received it. The lawyer had given the chances of success a zero, but even he had begun to have hope for this young woman.

Life at the Forelands Bar had returned to normal: Crusher was back and Vito now kept his hands out of the till, probably because of the size of the back-room-enforcer. Trooper Bob Seaton had not been in to harass them lately and Cuddles was grateful for that. She was seated in her usual place, working a crossword puzzle and wondering, what is an eight-letter word for shade tree, beginning with S?—when the phone rang. It was Buddy Phelps. "How is your winter going?" she asked the geologist.

"De Sylva and I are doing great. He bought another plane and has leased it to an oil company. He's a happy man. But the reason I called is to pass along some news. I don't want to do this on the phone and wanted to let you know I'll be down there next week. I'll probably only stay one day, but this is important." Phelps had never been an alarmist and Cuddles was taking him seriously.

"Let me know when you're arriving and I'll send Crusher to pick you up. See you next week." She hung up the phone wondering what that was all about. It was early evening when the door opened and a bearded man in Carhart attire entered. It was Chuck Hagel. He was shivering from the cold and had snow on his boots. Cuddles almost didn't recognize him without his Harley Davidson clothing.

"Get out of here if you came to make trouble," Cuddles ordered.

"Don't worry, Cuddles. I only came in to talk with you." There was no malice in his voice. He walked to the end of the bar where she sat.

"What do you want?" she asked.

"I don't know if you heard, but they've set a date for my brother's trial. He didn't do what they say, Cuddles. He told me. He gets mouthy, but he wouldn't hurt anyone. I know he makes that hard to believe, but I've known him all my life and … I know him." There was a note of sadness in his voice. "I just came in to ask if you'd remembered anything that might help him."

"How could I remember?" she said. "I wasn't even here when it happened."

"I know, but I thought maybe someone said something, you know, anything. He don't stand a chance without some help from somewhere."

"I'm sorry for you and your brother, Chuck, but I don't know anything. I guess I feel like the troopers. He tried to choke her just a few nights before and that sounds like he would kill someone to me. I can't help you. Sit down and I'll buy you a beer, but that's all I can do for you."

"No thanks, Cuddles, I can afford my own beer and it won't be in here. I think you know more than you told the troopers, but you want to get even with my brother." He turned to walk away, "It ain't right," he said as he walked away. He walked slowly to the door and out into the cold night.

Two mornings later Cuddles received a phone call from Phelps. He was in Anchorage and on his way to Kenai. She dispatched Crusher to pick up the mining engineer in her SUV. It was noon when the men returned to the bar.

Phelps was dressed in wool slacks, insulated dress shoes, L.L. Bean shirt and one of the finest insulated parka's she had ever seen. "You're looking pretty dapper today, Buddy," she said as a greeting.

"It's a lot colder in Fairbanks and up there I'm a business man. I have to look respectable." He seemed in a jovial mood. "Have you had lunch?" he asked.

"No, but I'll get something upstairs later. I have to watch my weight, you know." The two of them laughed at that. "You said you had something to say that you didn't want to do on the phone. Do you want to go up to the office for our business?"

"It might be best," replied Phelps.

He followed her up the stairs to the back room. "You should install one of those stair lift units. It would save you climbing the stairs all the time."

"I would, but this is the best exercise I get each day," she said, huffing and puffing and gasping for air.

In her office she dropped onto her chair with a heavy grunt. Phelps pulled another chair close and sat. He reached into an inside pocket of the unzipped parka for a large business size envelope. He said nothing while he pulled the papers from inside.

Finally he opened the papers and said, "Do you remember I took part of my payment in nuggets?"

"Sure, I remember."

"Well, I took them to a friend of mine who assays gold and other minerals. It took him a long time to get to them, but the assay was surprising, even to me. I had asked if he could determine the geographical origins of the nuggets. I was thinking he might be able to narrow our search down some."

"That was good thinking, Buddy. Did he find out where the mine is?" She was excited, expecting to learn the location.

"I did. Are you ready for this?"

"Don't keep me in suspense—tell me."

He pointed to the papers he had taken from his pocket. "This is the assay report on the gold, nugget by nugget. These nuggets came from all over the State of Alaska. Some were easy to identify—the ones from the old Valdez Mine, for instance. It probably didn't come from the Valdez Mine, but did come from the same valley on the Maclaren River. The assayer can check the foreign particles in the gold and, with some accuracy, determine where the nugget came from. He didn't identify all the nuggets but was able to get a location—not exact, but narrowed down—for most of the gold. It took him all this time to get it done."

"Are you going to tell me where they came from or teach me how to be a geologist so I can do it myself?" the anxious Cuddles demanded.

"I thought you'd be interested in how we determined the outcome." Explained Buddy Phelps, teasing her by withholding the information she was so desperate to hear.

"Just tell me."

Phelps was laughing now. "OK, Cuddles, OK, don't blow a gasket. Like I said they checked for general locations. The reason it took so long was that the gold didn't come from one location. They originated in locations all over the state. I checked the locations against the mining claims and they match. There are some nuggets that didn't come from any of the claim areas, but most did."

"What does all this mean," asked Cuddles, scratching her head with a pencil eraser.

"I don't know for sure, but my guess is that he never sold his gold. I think Otis hoarded it and kept it with him. Some miners are like that—they aren't interested in the gold as much as the search. Prospecting can become a disease, and once you catch it you can never get it out of your system. I think Otis was one of those." Buddy shrugged his shoulders in finality.

"What does all this mean then, Buddy. Does this mean there isn't any more gold out there to be found? Are we looking for something that doesn't exist?"

"Oh, I think there's gold out there. There's probably a lot of it, but it will take mining equipment to get it out. It looks like he panned the surface and took the big stuff, planning to come back and mine the rest sometime in the future. But, like I said before, prospecting is a disease. He was destined to keep looking, even after he found what he was after. If you want to go gold mining I think you'll be very rich. It takes permits, equipment, and a payroll. It takes a lot of money to develop a mining property. I don't know what you want to do with these claims, but if it were me, I'd contact some big mining company and sell them the rights. You have the proof of gold on the property and one or more of them will offer you good money for the claims." Buddy had not given her much detail, but she would understand it was not for her (hopefully).

She sat for a long while, thinking. "So you think my best bet is to sell the claims to some big mining company and let them do the work and make the money, is that right?"

"In my opinion, yes."

"Why would I want to do that?" she wanted to know.

"Because it will cost millions to develop each claim and take years to acquire all the permits. You aren't a miner, so you probably don't understand what this all means, but you'll be a rich woman if you sell. The mining companies will be even richer, but it will cost a lot of money to get it and a lot of time to make it work. There will be a lot of ulcers between now and the first load of smelted gold from any of the claims. You will have to make that decision. The claims belong to you." Buddy thought he had given her the best advice and most honest opinion he knew.

"I have to give this some thought, Buddy. I trust you and I know you're trying to look out for me, but it just goes against my nature to give away that much money." Her face was twisted into a thoughtful frown. "Have Crusher help you set up in the same room you had before. Spend the night and I'll think about it. I'll have him broil us a couple of steaks later. Drinks in the bar are on me. Let me think about it." She was again scratching her head with the pencil.

Buddy went to his room to wash up and leave the small overnight bag he had been carrying. He stuffed the assay papers in the side pocket of the bag before going downstairs to the bar. Cuddles remained upstairs but had called Crusher, presumably to instruct him about starting the barbeque.

In the bar Buddy officially met Vito. The two men chatted for a few minutes before Phelps ordered a beer. Vito brought the Alaska Amber and put it in front of Buddy.

"Have you known Cuddles for a long time?" asked the bartender.

"Yeah, a very long time; she's a good friend. I do a job for her now and again." He took a long drink of the cold liquid. "Aah! That tastes good." He took another smaller sip. "How long have you worked for her?"

"Her other bartender got murdered in December, and she need another one. I heard about it and asked for the job. She asked me to mix a couple of drinks and hired me. Funniest thing about the job interview was she told me to do what Crusher says, the big lummox in the back, and to keep my mouth shut." Vito was chuckling about that.

Phelps had known Cuddles for years and she was a strange individual. She had a big heart matched only by the mean streak she possessed. She was kindly and generous to her employees and vicious to her enemies. "She's a good gal, Vito. Treat her right and she'll treat you right. I've seen what she can do if you cross her: don't do it."

"I almost had a taste of that. I don't plan to test her again." He pointed at Phelps' empty beer bottle: "Another?"

"Yeah, one more, I have to get ready for dinner in a while." He was sitting at the far end of the bar when two bikers came in. Buddy recognized one of them as the starter of the bar fight right before Lil was killed.

Vito walked to the middle of the long bar. "OK, boys, that's far enough. If you're looking for anything other than a drink, just turn around and leave now."

"We didn't come to cause trouble," said Weasel Benton. He was a mousey little man with a scruffy beard and wearing the same leathers he had worn the night of the fight. "Skull and me just came in for a beer."

"As long as you keep it peaceful, have a seat." The two bikers sat at the bar.

Buddy was watching the proceeding when Crusher came into the bar and walked up to him. "What are you drinking with dinner, Mr. Phelps?" he asked quietly.

"I think scotch and water, Crusher, thanks."

"Cuddles wants to see you when you finish your beer." With that he turned and returned to the back room.

Buddy finished his beer and motioned to Vito. He tossed a five on the bar for the bartender and walked past the two men in black.

Back upstairs he met Cuddles again. "What's up, Cuddles?" he asked in a cheery voice.

"I've been thinking about what you said. I guess I would be stupid to pay for advice and then ignore it." She had made her decision.

"What are you going to do?" he asked.

"It depends. Will you represent me and sell the claims? I want the best price I can get, but I have no idea what that should be. I need someone to look out for my interests. Will you take the job? I'll pay you cash or a percentage, whichever you prefer."

"Wow, Cuddles, I didn't expect this." He thought for a moment considering his answer. "I have some contacts in the business. I have no Idea how much they will offer, but if you trust me to get you a good price I guess I should try."

"Thanks, Buddy. How does 30 percent sound to you?" she asked the engineer.

"That's far more than I would have expected," he replied. "I guess we're in business." The two shook hands. "I have one favor to ask, though."

"Name it and you got it," she replied.

"I would like to have copies of the claim certificates to show along with a few of the nuggets from the pouch. They are impressive and will make a good negotiating tool."

"Not a bad idea," said Cuddles. "I'll have them for you in the morning. What time is your flight?"

"At 10 with Era."

"I'll have them ready." She was smiling now. "Let's go eat."

Chapter 21

The following morning, bartender Vito entered the Forelands Bar through the rear door with his key. It was not uncommon for the lower level of the bar to be vacant when he arrived, but he had noticed Cuddles' Kia SUV was missing from its parking space. He went to the front and did some minor clean-up chores and turned on the lights. He needed his cash drawer for the till and decided to go to the office to find it. He climbed the stairs to the second floor and walked into the office. No one was there. He found his cash drawer on her desk—the usual place when she wasn't there to bring it to him.

The cash drawer was sitting on the desktop with a note detailing the cash amounts and denominations and amounts for the day. As he picked it up to check the figures he noticed something strange on the desk. It was a leather pouch tied with a leather thong. Curious, he set the cash drawer back on the desk and reached for the pouch. Untying the thong he peered inside to see the contents. What he saw amazed him. It was what appeared to be gold nuggets. He poured a few of the nuggets into his hand to admire them. They were heavy—they had to be gold. Old habits die hard and he lifted four of the nuggets from his palm and dropped them into his pants pocket. He was admiring the rest of the cache when the door opened and Crusher came rushing in. He recognized the pouch in the bartender's hand. "Close that back up and put it down," he ordered, his eyes narrowed and his face stern.

"Just looking, Crusher. I came in to get the cash drawer and was curious when I saw the pouch." His voice was nervous as he explained and tried to tie the pouch shut.

"Get out of the office, NOW," ordered the big wrestler.

"OK, OK, I'm going." He reached for the cash drawer, but was met by a huge hand and a mean thump to his kidney.

"I said NOW. Keep your hands off anything that doesn't belong to you. Get out."

"I have to have the cash drawer to open the bar," said Vito as he reached again for the drawer.

This time Crusher hit his forearm with a heavy blow. He grabbed the bartender by the right shoulder and spun him around. Vito held up a right arm to defend himself but was struck in the stomach by a hardened fist. Vito doubled over only to be struck on the side of the head. As he tried to straighten up he was again hit in the face. As he fell backward, something grabbed his right arm and jerked him upright again. His arm was twisted viciously around to his back, dislocating his shoulder. He began to fall, but was drug out of the office by his injured arm. Crusher dropped him in the hallway. As Vito attempted to stand the wrestler again seized his sore arm and, in a whipping motion, flung the weakened bartender down the stairs. He tumbled all the way to the bottom and lay there unconscious.

Crusher stood at the top of the stairs wondering if he had done the right thing. Just then Vito moved a little but did not try to get up. Crusher panicked. He went to the office and dialed the cell phone number for Cuddles. She answered on the third ring.

"Yeah, Crusher, what is it?" she answered.

"It's bad, Cuddles. I just threw Vito down the stairs and he's hurt bad. I caught him in the office and we got into a fight. He was looking at the pouch with the gold in it." Crusher was trying to explain without incriminating himself.

"Is Vito alive?" asked the boss.

"He's moaning and moving a little, but he ain't getting up. I think I hurt him bad."

"Call 911 and get him an ambulance. I'll be there in ten minutes."

Cuddles pulled into the back parking area as the EMS crew was entering the front door. The ambulance crew examined the victim and hooked him up to the electronic monitoring devices. Cuddles had to make her way around the crowd of medics in order to get up the stairs to her office. She had to clean up her desk before the cops came, as they were certain to do. She found the pouch and put the little bag in her safe, out of sight. She closed the door and left the office with the cash drawer in hand. She went to the bar to set up the cash register and await the arrival of the police.

Minutes later Trooper Jason Beeles came in the front door. He went past Cuddles to the back room where the medics were still working on Vito. He conferred with the fire captain in charge before returning to the bar to talk with Cuddles.

"Hello, Claudia, I'm Trooper Jason Beeles. I don't know if you remember me, but we met a few months ago."

"I remember," she said.

"Can you tell me what happened here this morning?" he asked in a businesslike tone.

"I wasn't here, I was in town. I took a man to the airport and went to the bank and my lawyer's office. I got here right behind the ambulance. Dennis Carson, who works for me, found the bartender, Vito, in my office. Dennis thought he was stealing something from the office and threw him out. He fell down the stairs, and that's all I know. You'll have to talk with Crusher: that's Dennis Carson."

"Where can I find him?" asked the trooper.

"I'll call him to come down. He's up in his room, waiting." With that she dialed the intercom number for Crusher's room and told him to come to the bar to see the trooper.

The medics finished stabilizing the victim and loaded him into the ambulance. Beeles finished his interview with Crusher and returned to his patrol car. His first order of business was to call Sergeant Bob Seaton.

Seaton answered his office phone. Beeles told him about the fight at the Forelands Bar and that the victim was being transported to Central Peninsula General Hospital with severe injuries. Seaton said he would meet the ambulance there and asked Beeles to meet him at the emergency room door.

While waiting for the doctors to examine Vito, Sgt. Seaton conferred with Beeles. "Are you going to arrest Crusher?" asked the sergeant.

"Not yet. There are some holes in the story he told me, but until I can talk with the bartender I don't have much evidence of wrongdoing. Their story, so far, is that Crusher found the bartender stealing something from the office. What he was stealing is a mystery at this point. The cash drawer was there and they indicated he was stealing money from there, but he needed the cash drawer to open for business. It just doesn't add up. I need to talk with Vito."

"We'll go talk with the doc and see when we can interview the victim." Seaton knew the emergency room doctors from his many visits like this one. The doctor in charge said it would be a couple of hours before Vito would be conscious and coherent.

"Let's get some lunch and come back," said Seaton. "The doctor told me he was going to admit Vito; he has a concussion and may need surgery on his shoulder."

When the troopers returned to the hospital, they found that Vito had been taken to the second floor to a private room, where a nurse was busy making him comfortable. He had been given some pain medications and was groggy, but awake.

"It looks as if you had a bad morning, Vito," commented Seaton.

"I think they fired me," mumbled Vito.

"Do you feel up to telling us what happened?" asked Beeles.

"Yeah, they gave me some drugs and I'm not hurting too bad." He looked terrible. His right eye was swollen shut, his arm was in a sling to immobilize it and there were cuts and bruises visible on his face.

"Crusher says he caught you stealing money from the cash drawer; is that true?" asked Beeles.

"No, I went to the office to get the cash drawer so I could open the bar. When I got it I saw a leather pouch on the desk. I was curious and opened it. It was full of gold nuggets. I was closing the bag when Crusher came in and started knocking me around." Vito was talking slowly.

"Wait a minute, Vito." The mention of the leather pouch was like a bolt of lightning to Seaton. "What did this leather pouch look like?"

"It was just tanned leather. It looked like someone had made it. It was about three inches across and about seven or eight inches tall. It was clear full of gold when I untied it."

"And Crusher caught you looking at the gold?" asked Seaton.

"He sure did. He started getting mad and ordering me out of the office. I tried to pick up the cash drawer and he hit me," said Vito.

"I went up to the office and looked around. I didn't see any leather pouch or any gold on the desk." Beeles had gone to the scene of the fight as part of his investigation.

"Crusher probably picked it up and put it in the safe," Vito surmised.

Seaton asked the next question: "Are you certain it was gold in the pouch?"

"My pants are in the closet over there. Get them and look in the right front pocket."

Beeles retrieved the black polyester slacks. Reaching into the right front pocket he came out with four small nuggets of varying sizes. Holding his open hand for the patient to see he asked, "Did these come from that leather pouch?"

"Yes. I did take something from the office, but it wasn't cash from the cash drawer. Crusher didn't know I had these or he would probably have finished me off and taken them back." Vito was beginning to get sleepy from the drugs.

Seaton was scowling and rubbing his chin. "Vito, I'm going to put a guard on your room. This goes much deeper than stealing from the cash drawer. I think you could be in danger if they figure out you have these nuggets."

Seaton motioned for Beeles to take a seat next to the bed and wait. He went to the hall and called his captain to provide a guard for the room.

An hour later Vito was asleep and the paid security guard was on duty. The troopers returned to their office for a strategy conference. The two men, along with the captain, sat in the office with the file containing information on the death of Larry "Skip" Williams.

"Explain to me exactly how you think Dennis Carson and Claudia Morris are responsible for the death of Larry Williams. Until now you've had suspicions, but no proof. Why are things different now?' asked the captain.

"Both the Nikiski fire marshal and I believed, from the beginning, this was a case of murder and arson," Seaton began. "There was no proof. The arson was proven by the chemical analysis of the residue at the scene, but no suspects could be named. It was the same with the murder, we knew Larry Williams had been murdered, but there was no way to prove who did it. Both the fire marshal and I searched the ashes of the burned mobile home for proof and for the remains of the plastic tool box containing the gold we knew Larry had. I documented its existence here in this office when Williams came to claim his property from Otis Fairfax's plane wreck." The sergeant pointed to notes in the file:

Williams picked up a plastic tool box with almost thirty pounds of gold inside.

It also contained several mining claim certificates.

"Until now, there has been no sign of the gold or the claim certificates. Crusher Carson caught Vito Hocker in the office of the Forelands Bar. Vito was holding one of the missing pouches containing gold nuggets. He described the pouch to me and it's the same one from the plastic tool box."

"What do you want to do now?" asked the captain.

"I want to run this by the district attorney. If he agrees with me, that we now have proof, we will ask the judge for an arrest warrant for Cuddles and Crusher for murder and arson." Seaton could hardly contain his excitement.

"Where are the nuggets you got from Hocker?" the captain asked.

"I bagged them and put them in the evidence locker," replied Seaton.

"OK, write it up and take it to the DA. If he agrees have him get the warrant. We'll have to move on this before they get rid of the gold." The captain understood the need for urgency. "Have Beeles help you with this. Keep him with you until it's finished."

"Thanks, Cap. We're on it."

Chapter 22

Seaton and Beeles had been cooling their heels at the court house for quite some time, waiting for the DA to review the evidence against Claudia Morris and Dennis Carson. It was finally decided: the warrant was allowed. The DA forwarded the information and a draft of the warrant to the Superior Court judge. The two troopers continued their wait. While at the courthouse, Seaton called Nikiski Fire Marshal Eustes Burns to give him an update and ask if he wanted to be present when the arrest was made. Burns thought about it a moment before answering.

"I have no compelling need to be there, unless you need some help with the arrest. Given the size of Cuddles' hired man, it could be a problem for you."

"I plan to take plenty of help, but I wanted to give you the option."

"Thanks anyway, Bob. I'll be around if you need me." Burns wasn't anxious to be in on the arrest action.

It was after five when the warrant was finally handed to the officers. Seaton called for two other officers to come to the Forelands Bar and back him up. Burns was right about one thing: Crusher Carson could be a serious problem if he chose to be.

The four patrol cars arrived at the bar together. Trooper Sergeant Bob Seaton had instructed one of the officers to park near the back entry to the building, covering the back door in case anyone decided to leave by that route. The remaining three troopers entered the front door. Luckily there were no customers in the bar at the time. One officer stood by the door while Beeles and Seaton walked to the end of the bar where Cuddles was perched on her stool.

Beeles spoke to Crusher who was tending bar tonight, "Come down here a minute, will you Crusher?"

"Sure, what do you need?" he asked as he approached.

Beeles stepped around the bar to meet the wrestler. Seaton stood behind Beeles facing Cuddles. He produced the warrants from an inside pocket of his jacket. "I have arrest warrants for both you, Claudia Morris, and you, Dennis Carson, on charges of murder and arson. Please step out from behind the bar, Mr. Carson," recited Seaton.

Cuddles was the first to react. "What kind of crap is this?" she asked.

"Please get up and turn around, Ms. Morris," ordered Seaton.

"You, too, Mr. Carson," ordered Beeles holding a pair of handcuffs in his left hand.

Crusher began to protest, but Cuddles stopped him. "Go along with it, Crusher. I'll call Cummings to come and get us out." He relaxed a little and turned his back to Beeles who snapped the handcuffs on the big man's wrists.

Seaton stood by as Claudia Morris struggled from the barstool to her feet facing the officer. He motioned for her to turn around and he snapped the handcuffs on her chubby wrists. "If you will tell me where the keys are located, I will have my officer lock the place up and turn out the lights for you."

She nodded toward the ring of keys sitting on the end of the bar where she had been seated. "Don't turn the heat down, just shut off the beer signs and lock the door."

"The warrant authorizes us to search the premises for evidence. I'll need for you to come with me upstairs and open the safe," Seaton asked politely.

"Not a chance, Bob. I don't have to do that." She was adamant in her refusal.

"I'm afraid you are mistaken, Ms. Morris. I do have the right, and if you refuse to open the safe I will be forced to have someone come out here with a cutting torch and open it. Save yourself a lot of expense and open the safe." Seaton knew she would comply, but not without an argument. "If you want legal advice in this matter I'll help you call your lawyer."

She was shaking her head, thinking. "Take these off me and I'll go open the safe. I want to know what you're looking for, though. Are you going to tell me?"

Seaton stepped behind Cuddles to unlock the handcuffs. "I'll be happy to. We have orders to look for two leather pouches containing a large amount of gold nuggets. We are also instructed to look for several mining claim certificates registered in the name of Otis Fairfax. Are these items in the safe?"

"I have two leather pouches of gold in the safe, but no mine claims," she answered.

"Where are the certificates?" he asked.

"Gee, I don't remember. Maybe I never had—what was it again—mining certificates?"

"OK, play it your way, Cuddles. Let's go open the safe and have a look." Seaton nudged her toward the back room door. He keyed his radio and ordered the man in the back to enter and meet him in the back room. When he came in out of the cold night, the three of them started the slow climb up to the second floor office and safe.

Finally in the office, Cuddles opened the safe and stepped back. Seaton saw the pouches in the safe but not the mining certificates. "We will have to inventory the contents of the safe, Cuddles. Have a seat while the trooper and I write it all down." She sat while Seaton called Beeles on his radio.

"You and the other officer take Mr. Carson to the Correctional Center and book him in on the charges using the warrant numbers. I'll be along as soon as we inventory the safe and lock up the bar."

"Roger that," replied Beeles.

It took almost an hour to inventory the contents of the safe which included a large sum of cash. There was jewelry, money, make-shift pawn tickets with different names, and a myriad of other items—some valuable and some not. "Are you willing to give me the combination to this safe, Cuddles? It will save us a lot of trouble and we will be able to lock it up. I am going to remove the pouches of gold, for which I will give you a receipt. You can lock it in the safe if you care to do so."

"You might as well have the combination. You know what's in there anyway. I want to call my lawyer before I go to town." She was complying regretfully, but she was complying.

She called Cummings and told him to meet her at the jail. She then gave the other officer instructions about closing the bar and turning off the lights. With that taken care of, the trio prepared to leave and the young trooper walked to his car around the back of the bar. Cuddles turned around to have Seaton put the handcuffs back on her wrists. The sergeant acknowledged, "I'm supposed to handcuff you before putting you in the car, but I think I can trust you to behave on the way to Wildwood." The backseat of the patrol car was uncomfortable at best and with the steel cage separating the front from the back there was little danger from her.

The booking process had been completed on Crusher and he was now sitting in a holding cell. Claudia Morris was being processed when Grant Cummings rang the bell out front. He was told to wait while fingerprints and photos were taken. Once done, Cuddles was admitted to the visiting area behind a glass barrier. Cummings had been here many times before, but never to see such a prominent client. He picked up the telephone receiver used to communicate with his client.

"What's going on?" he asked.

"The cops walked in and said they had warrants for me and Crusher. They put the cuffs on both of us. Said they had a warrant for murder and arson. Find out what's going on and get me and Crusher out of here. And I mean tonight! You hear me? Tonight!"

"If they're felony warrants, I won't be able to do that. They'll have to take you to court in the morning and have the judge set bail. I'll look at the warrants and see what I can do, but if those are the charges, you're going to be spending the night. Don't say anything to anyone. Do what they ask, but don't get mad and start talking."

"I don't like this, Grant. I want out of here." Cuddles didn't seem to understand she was no longer in charge of her own life.

"I don't think you will be out of here tonight," replied the lawyer.

Cuddles held up a fat hand and cupped the mouthpiece of the phone in her fist. "If you can't get us out tonight I want you to get my keys from the jailer," she whispered. "Go to the bar and find the phone book sitting on the bar. Inside there will be a number for Buddy Phelps. He has the claim certificates. Call him and tell him we have to dispose of them as quickly as possible. The troopers are looking for them. Get them sold—FAST."

"You'll have to give permission to take any property out of the jail," he said as he stood.

"Tell them I'll give you permission. Now get going!"

Cummings jumped through all the hoops to take Cuddles' property out of the jail while she was taken to an area where she was dressed in an orange jump suit. It was not at all flattering to her large frame.

When Grant Cummings arrived at the bar he found the door sealed with yellow police tapes. He ignored them and opened the front door. He found the book on the bar where she normally would be seated. He sat on the stool and dialed the Fairbanks number. It was answered on the sixth ring.

"Yeah, hello," croaked a sleepy voice.

"Is this Buddy Phelps?"

"Yeah, who's this?"

"I'm Grant Cummings. I'm Claudia Morris's attorney. She's been arrested along with Dennis Carson. Now listen carefully. She asked me to call you and tell you to sell the mining claim certificates as soon as possible. The troopers are looking for them. She said to get what you can as quickly as you can. She said you would know what to do."

"Yeah, I know what to do. It will have to wait until morning, though. Most business people are asleep this time of night." Phelps was beginning to wake up and grasp the situation. "What were they arrested for anyway?"

"Murder and arson, one count each. The troopers came to the bar and cuffed them up and took them to jail. They found the pouches of gold in the safe before they left, though. They mentioned the pouches specifically in the warrants. That tells me the gold is what ties her to the murder and arson cases. The mining claims were mentioned in the warrants also. That's why it's imperative you dispose of them quickly. And please, try to do this discreetly. I don't want to have to go to Fairbanks to get you out of jail."

"OK, I get the picture. Give me your number and I'll call you as soon as the job is done."

Cummings gave Phelps his number and hung up the phone. He stepped behind the bar and poured himself a very tall bourbon with a dash of water, locked the place up tight, and drove back to Kenai.

The following morning he learned court time for the two felons was at 10:15 am. He met his clients there and sat at the defendants' table with the two of them. "The judge will ask you for a plea on each charge. Plead not guilty to both charges. Tell Crusher to do the same. I'll be here, but the judge will want to hear it from you."

"OK, then can I get out of jail?" she asked.

"After you enter a plea, we'll ask the judge to set bail. The judge will ask the DA about that. After the DA is done the judge will ask us to justify bail. I think I can talk him into setting it low enough that we can arrange a bond. We'll see."

"Do what you have to do, just get us out of jail this morning. I have a business to run." Cuddles was ignoring the seriousness of the charges. "After all, I'm innocent until proven guilty, right?"

At that point the door behind the bench opened and the judge appeared wearing the black judicial robes of his office. Fifteen minutes later bond was set at $250,000 each and the judge exited the chamber through the same door he entered.

"Just sit tight. I'll call and arrange for the bond. I know the bail bondsman and should have you out of jail before noon."

The judicial services officer came and escorted Cuddles and Crusher from the courtroom.

Chapter 23

Several days later Cuddles was sitting at the end of the bar in the early afternoon, watching Crusher stock the beer coolers. Business had been slow at the Forelands Bar. She had not hired a new bartender, leaving Crusher to tend bar as well as do the cleanup and all the labor around the place. He never complained, just did what he was asked.

The front door opened and in walked two young women. One was heavy and dark skinned. The other was blond, well dressed, with long hair and erect stature. She walked directly to where the owner sat. Cuddles almost missed recognizing it was Pamela Williams!

"I don't believe it," a startled Cuddles said. "You don't look like the same person."

"I guess I'm not the same person," replied Pamela.

"What brings you out here?"

"I had to come and see you. I've been hearing terrible things about you and can't believe it," she began. "Everyone says you killed my brother. Is that true?"

"Of course not, Pamela, the troopers questioned me and Crusher, but we had nothing to do with his death. I didn't even know he had been murdered. I thought it was just an accident and fire. I don't even know why they think we had anything to do with it." Cuddles could lie as easily as she could breathe.

"Some of the residents at the Serenity House say they used to buy meth from Skip. I didn't want to believe he was making and selling the stuff. I heard you were selling his stuff here at the bar. How could you do such a thing and then turn around and help me to get off the stuff? I don't understand." There were tears in her eyes.

"Have a seat at the table, Pamela. Let's talk." Cuddles dismounted her stool and made it to the chair as the girl sat. "First of all, I want to say you look different. You look wonderful. I didn't know if you would make it, but it looks like you have. Believe me I know what you've gone through. It took me more than two years to do what you're doing in a couple months. I got hurt and couldn't go to a dealer to buy drugs. Nobody helped me. They just let me lie in that bed and suffer. I hoped you wouldn't have to go through what I did. The only relief I had was the drugs the doctors gave me. I finally realized what a waste it was and swore I would never use any of that stuff again. That was many years ago, and I never have. I have seen hundreds of people use every drug there is, but none of them ever got off them. Many of them died from using, others ruined their bodies and minds, all of them failed at life." There was sadness in her voice and in her eyes.

"What made you think I would get off the drugs?" asked Pamela.

"You'd reached the end of the road. Your next step was to die. When you have no hope you don't have many choices. I just gave you a better one than dying a lonely death. You saved yourself. I didn't have anything to do with that. All I did was show you a way out and you took it. Seeing you now, I'm glad I made the choice to help you, but you did the work. Congratulations."

"I will be in your debt forever, Ms. Morris, and I will never forget what you did for me, but I have to know if you are the one who had Skip killed—and why. He never had anything. He was a lot like me; he was struggling to stay alive. They say you had him killed because he owed you money. I can't believe he could owe you enough to make it worthwhile killing him." There were tears on her cheeks again now.

"I didn't give him enough cash to warrant killing him. I helped him for the same reason I helped you: he was a lost soul. He always paid me back, except this time—he never had the chance. Don't listen to the people who say I had anything to do with his death. You know how junkies like to make things sound bad; it makes it seem better to know there is someone worse than them." Cuddles hoped the girl believed this story.

"I don't know what to believe. I have to leave the Serenity House soon and I have no place to go. The lawyer says I own some of the property my brother had. I don't even know where it is. He says you'll help me, but I don't want to be a burden. I guess I can sell what he had and go back home, but to tell the truth, I doubt that's a good idea. I don't want to go back and get back into the same old friends and start doing drugs again." She sounded as if she were still lost.

"I've instructed Grant to give you any help you need. I will see he does." Cuddles was trying to explain the uncertain future they both had. "He'll see you have a place to live and help you find a job, if you want one. I need a bartender, but I don't think it would be good for you to work in this kind of place, at least for a while. We have a nice college here on the peninsula. If you want to go to school and learn a trade I'll see to it Grant helps with that, too. My life is a little complicated right now and I can't take time away from preparing for the trial. It's costing me a lot of my cash, too, but I'll be sure to have enough to help you when you need it. That means you'll have to go to work somewhere, but I want you to find something outside the world we are both too familiar with."

"You've been a real friend, Claudia. I wish you all the luck in the world with the trial. I still have a way to go with my rehab, but I'll make it, thanks to you." She stood to leave.

Cuddles struggled to her feet. "Good luck to you, Pamela."

Pamela walked around the table and hugged the short, round Cuddles. Wiping another tear, she turned to meet her escort at the door.

When she was gone, Crusher came from behind the bar to where Cuddles was standing. She seemed deep in thought. She was slightly startled as he approached. She smiled at the wrestler and moved back to her perch on the end stool. He went back behind the bar and stared at her.

"What's the matter, Crusher?" she asked.

"I was just thinking how many lives we changed when we did away with Skip." It was the first time Cuddles ever heard remorse in his voice.

"As it's turning out, it may have all been for nothing, too. I was hoping the troopers would take a lead from the arrest of Tom Hagel and pin Skip's death on him too. Now it looks like we may go down the same path as Hagel. I hope Grant can pull some rabbit out of the hat and take the heat off us."

"I have to tell you something, Cuddles." Crusher Carson spoke softly without making eye contact.

"What is it, Dennis?"

"It's about Lil."

"What about her? We had nothing to do with that." She dismissed it as an unnecessary distraction.

"That's what I have to tell you. I had to do away with Lil. She was telling Hagel that I wasn't here when the fire started at Skip's place. I thought if she told him that she might tell the troopers, too. I know I should have talked it over with you, but I thought the blame would fall on him. I guess I was wrong, I'm sorry."

"Are you telling me you killed Lil?" she almost shouted.

"Yes, I'm sorry. I know I let you down. I was just trying to help." He still had not made eye contact.

"Oh, Crusher, this is bad. I wish you had told me before." She sat quietly thinking, "That must be where they got the information about the gold claim certificates and the pouches in my safe. This is really bad, Crusher." She now had her head in her hands, rubbing her eyes. "I am going to have to go to the office and think about this for a while."

She was gathering her keys and papers from the end of the bar when the front door opened and two snow-covered bikers entered. It was Weasel Benton and Skull Bryant. "I hope you boys aren't looking for trouble," she greeted the two gang members.

"No, Ma'am," said Skull. "We just came in for a beer. Chuck Hagel is supposed to be here in a few minutes. He don't want any trouble either. We just want a quiet place to sit and talk."

"See that you stay quiet," she advised, as she exited the rear door, nodding to Crusher that it was okay.

The duo took a seat at a table, telling Crusher they wanted a couple of beers. Both men had their elbows on the table, talking quietly when Chuck Hagel arrived. "Bring one more," Hagel said to the bartender.

Crusher delivered the drinks and returned to his station at the bar. He was unable to hear what the men were saying but had the feeling they were plotting something. Hagel glanced at Crusher, annoyed.

"What are you looking at, man?" he asked in a harsh tone.

"Nothin', I'm just trying to figure out why you came in here. It don't seem right for you to be here when your brother is on his way to court this week. He killed our bartender, and now you want to come in and have a beer like nothing ever happened. It don't seem right to me." After his conversation with Cuddles he was not in a tolerant mood.

"If the Hunger Hut Bar was open we wouldn't have come in here. And if it weren't snowing we would have gone down the road to the Place Bar. Just shut up and bring another round," ordered Weasel Benton.

As Crusher approached the table with the new drinks Weasel stood to meet him. Crusher changed direction slightly to meet the man face-to-face, eye-to-eye. "Sit down or get out," Crusher said in a low tone. He was not taking anything from Weasel or the others.

"Sit down, Weasel," ordered Hagel, tugging at the sleeve of his jacket.

Weasel hesitated a moment, then sat. Crusher delivered the beer and returned to the bar. The men finished their drinks and Hagel was the first to stand.

"If my brother doesn't get off in court, I'm coming for you," bellowed Hagel.

"Come on ahead. I'll put you in the dumpster out back like Lil. And there will be room for your two friends." Crusher was not intimidated by the men in black leather.

"That sounds like you know who killed Lil—and it wasn't my brother!" Hagel was shouting now.

"That's it—get out of here. NOW!" ordered Crusher.

"Come on, guys. Let's go talk to the troopers about this." All three were now standing. Hagel led the march to the door.

When then men had gone, Crusher regretted his words and actions. He was angry with himself. He picked up a beer bottle from the table and flung it toward the back bar, breaking several bottles of whiskey and shattering some beer glasses. He was even angrier with himself now. He locked the front door and turned off the beer signs in the windows. It took him two hours to clean up the mess he had made. It would take a lot longer to correct the mistake he made in talking about Lil. Crusher was not a long range thinker but he knew he had created a problem he would have to deal with in the days to come.

Chapter 24

The three bikers drove directly from the Forelands Bar to the office of the troopers in Soldotna. The receptionist called Bob Seaton to the front to meet the men. It was easy to see they were agitated and angry.

Seaton greeted the men and asked what they needed. Chuck Hagel spoke for the group, "We just came from the Forelands Bar. We went in for a beer and Crusher was tending bar. He didn't like us being there and told us to drink up and get out. Weasel stood up to confront him, but I stopped it. Crusher got really mad. He said he would put me in the dumpster like Lil. He said there was room in there for Weasel and Skull, too." Hagel paused a moment to breathe, then continued, "He knows my brother didn't kill Lil. I think Crusher did it. He said he was the one who put her in the dumpster. He wouldn't do that unless he had killed her. You gotta do something, Trooper. My brother is going to trial next week and unless you know something I don't, they're going to send him away for life. You have to tell the DA and the judge what Crusher said."

"Slow down, Chuck. When did this take place?" asked Seaton.

"We just came from there. It just happened, maybe a half hour ago."

"Did you two hear Crusher make that statement?" he asked the other bikers.

"Oh yeah," said Weasel, "We heard it, alright." Skull was nodding in agreement.

Seaton pointed to a conference table in the office. "Sit over there. I'll get you witness forms. I want each of you to write down exactly what you heard and saw—in your own words—and I want you to sign the forms. Remember, this will be the same as sworn testimony. It will carry the same penalty if you lie on the forms. I don't want you to come back later and say you didn't mean it."

"Thanks, Trooper. We understand what you said and we are telling the truth." Hagel was again speaking for the group.

The sergeant opened a drawer on his desk and retrieved several witness forms. He handed one to each of the men along with some blank sheets of paper for any additional statements by each man. "Put your given name on the top of the sheet and you driver license number in the space marked ID number. I'll have an officer sit here while you write. I'll be in another office talking with the DA. Do you have any questions right now?"

"No," they said in unison.

A regular road trooper had just entered the building and Seaton commandeered him to sit in the office while the men wrote their statements. Meanwhile, he went into another office and called the district attorney office. The DA had just returned from court on another matter when Seaton called. It took only a short while to relay the story to the lawyer, who was astounded. He wanted to see the written statements from these new witnesses, and he wanted them signed and notarized. It was going to be embarrassing to go into court and tell the judge to release Tom Hagel, but it would be even more embarrassing to try to convict him when the state's only witness was now accused of committing the crime. Right or wrong, it would give the jury cause for reasonable doubt. It had to be done.

The three bikers completed their statements. Seaton read each one and confirmed the facts before having them notarized by the in-house notary public. He wanted no mistakes.

"OK," said the trooper sergeant. "Go home, and I mean home—not back to the bar. Go home. I'll call you when Tom is released. It may not be tonight, depending on what the judge says. Got it?"

"Yeah, we got it. Thanks for the help Sergeant Seaton. I didn't know it would happen this fast." The three men shook Seaton's hand and were led out of the office.

Seaton asked dispatch to locate Beeles and have him come to the office as soon as possible. He also asked the trooper who had sat with the witnesses to stay.

Once again he called the DA's office. "I sent copies of the statements by fax, did you receive them?"

"Yes, I got them. I called the Superior Court judge. He was still in his office. I'm going down now to show him the statements. If he accepts them, he'll sign a release for Tom Hagel right away."

"Will we need an arrest warrant for Dennis Carson or can we pick him up on probable cause?" asked Seaton.

"I'll have the judge sign a warrant, just to be on the safe side. He's out on bail right now for the other murder and arson case, but this new charge will nullify the bail." The DA was covering all the bases. "I should have the papers from the judge by the time you get here and you can go out to North Kenai and arrest Carson." He chuckled into the phone, "That friend of yours who owns the bar is going to be a little mad at you."

"I hope so," Seaton replied, chuckling along with the DA.

Seaton hung up the phone and called Beeles and the other trooper, Jordan Thompson, to his office to let them know the plan. After he spelled out the entire scenario and asked if they had any questions, the three men drove to the Kenai Court House in separate patrol cars. They met with the DA, who asked them to stop at the jail and deliver release paperwork for Tom Hagel. On the way to deliver the paperwork, Seaton called Chuck Hagel and told him the news; he said he could pick up his brother when he was released, which would be almost immediately. Chuck Hagel thanked Seaton over and over again.

On the way out to the Forelands Bar, Seaton learned there was another trooper in the Nikiski area and asked him to meet them at the bar. There was no need to jeopardize anyone for lack of manpower in the arrest of former pro wrestler—and now double-murder suspect—Crusher Carson. Trooper Thompson was told to cover the back door. The third trooper, Tim James, was stationed at the front door, covering Beeles and Seaton as they went in to confront Crusher.

Cuddles was seated in her regular spot and Beeles walked to that end of the bar. "Just sit still and don't speak until we're done," he said to her in a firm, low voice.

Seaton turned right to advance to where Crusher Carson was working, wiping the bar. As the sergeant moved toward Crusher he said, "I have a warrant for your arrest, Dennis Carson. Please step out from behind the bar."

"I'm out on bail, you can't arrest me," Crusher snarled, still in an angry mood at his self-made mess.

"Step out from behind the bar, Mr. Carson," the sergeant ordered again.

As Seaton walked closer, Crusher began to move to the end of the bar. He turned to look at Cuddles, who had not moved or said anything. "Call the lawyer and tell him what's going on. These cops can't arrest me, I'm out of jail on bail."

Beeles slipped around the end of the bar to look for weapons. As he passed Cuddles he whispered, "You can call the lawyer, if you care to do so." He continued to the other end of the bar, scanning the entire area for a weapon of any kind. At the other end he was met by Crusher, who seemed ever larger tonight. "Step out from behind the bar," he ordered the giant bartender. Crusher backed up a couple of steps, watching Beeles. As he stepped away from Beeles, Seaton gripped his right wrist from behind. Crusher's strength was incredible, but the sergeant held tight to his wrist.

Carson tried to turn around to face Seaton, but Beeles now had his left arm. Carson seemed to panic and pulled the two troopers out onto the open floor, all of them falling as they went. Carson was strong, but he could not shake the lawmen who held his wrists. The fight was only seconds old, but all the men were sweating profusely. This was making the wrestlers arms difficult to hold.

"Quit struggling, Crusher, you're only making things worse," shouted Seaton.

From the other end of the bar Cuddles now screamed, "Crusher, quit fighting! They will shoot you. Stop fighting, Crusher, stop fighting!"

At that point, Crusher Carson began to relax. Seaton and Beeles rolled the big man on his stomach and fastened the handcuffs. Trooper Tim James now went to the back room to open the door for Trooper Thompson. James had been unable to join the fight because of the confined area at the end of the bar where it started and then how quickly Seaton and Beeles subdued the prisoner. The two road troopers returned to the front of the bar as Beeles and Seaton lifted Carson to his feet.

"What's all this about?" Cuddles demanded. "Why are you here to arrest Dennis?"

The sweating sergeant reached inside his jacket to find the new warrant. "We have a warrant for the arrest of Dennis Carson for the death of Lil Danby." He turned to the two road troopers, "Load him up and take him to the jail."

"Don't say nothin', Crusher. I'm calling Grant," she shouted, as he was escorted through the door and to the back seat of a patrol car.

When he was out of the building she turned to Seaton: "What's this about another warrant? We're both legally out on bail."

"We have witnesses who heard Crusher admitting that he killed Lil and put her in the dumpster out back. With that kind of information we had to release Tom Hagel and arrest Carson. This was all cleared with the DA and the judge. Tell your lawyer he can get the particulars from the district attorney's office."

"This is harassment, plain and simple. You're just doing this to make my life miserable. I'm suing all of you." The officers turned to leave the bar as Cuddles dialed Grant Cummings.

Chuck Hagel was in the waiting room at the correctional facility when Beeles and Seaton arrived. They entered through the front door and met the biker who was awaiting the release of his brother, Tom.

"I saw them bring in Crusher. He's not happy back there," said Hagel, "Thanks for the help today. If there is ever anything I can do for you, just let me know." He paused a moment before continuing. "Me and my friends haven't always been model citizens, but I learned something out of all this."

"And what was that?" asked Seaton.

"You guys treated me and Tom fair all the way. I never expected that. In fact Weasel and Skull were really amazed at what you did. They talked about it all the way back to Nikiski. Thanks for everything, and if you need a friend in North Kenai, call me."

"We appreciate that, Chuck. Good luck to you and your brother. We have to go back and visit with Crusher, now. I hope you realize we acted on the information we had when we arrested Tom. It wasn't complete, and it turned out to be wrong, but it was the best information we had at the time and it's our job to protect the public. There was nothing personal about it, just doing our job." Seaton gave Hagel a complimentary short salute as he walked through the secure door to the booking area.

Chapter 25

The troopers had only been gone from the Forelands Bar about one minute when Cuddles dialed Grant Cummings. When he answered there were no conversational pleasantries, just orders: "We got big trouble. Get out here—now!" With that she hung up and walked behind the bar to pour herself a tall glass of vodka.

Fifteen minutes later Cummings came into the bar looking like he had just been roused from bed. "What's so important you want me to rush out here? I have a life of my own, you know."

"You won't have, if things keep going the way they are. The troopers just came out here and arrested Crusher. They say he told someone he killed Lil and put her in the dumpster. We have to do something, or he may just wreck everything. If he was dumb enough to tell someone he killed Lil, he may be dumb enough to admit he killed Skip Williams. We have to prevent him from talking." Cuddles was beginning to show signs the vodka was working on her.

"And just how do you propose do that?" asked the irritated counselor.

"That's why I pay you—to figure that out!" she spat.

"The only way to stop him from talking is to kill him, and I can't do that while he's in jail. The problem is I don't think the judge will allow bail on this second murder charge. I think there may be another way, though."

"Yeah, and what would that be?" She was back on her stool, after three tries to mount it.

"He may start talking to the troopers to save his own skin. It won't work, but he could try," Cummings was trying to explain it without making Cuddles more belligerent than she already was. "You and I both know he's going away for this. The trick is going to be to save you from the same fate." He studied her to see if she understood any of what he was saying.

Her large glass was nearly empty and she was visibly tipsy, but she understood. She looked at him with a pair of red eyes and said, "You want me to throw Crusher under the bus!"

"It's the only way to save yourself. If you want to get out of this without going to prison for the rest of your life, you'll have to sacrifice him. He's loyal enough to you that he'll take it and think he's doing you a favor, which of course he would be." Cummings tried to assess her mood, but the booze was clouding her feelings. "It's either him or the two of you. Make up your mind."

Cuddles was unsteady on her stool. "I'm going to close up and go to bed. I want you to go to the jail and see Crusher. Convince him he has to take all the blame for killing Skip. Convince him it's to save me from prison. You're right … he'll do it for me. Tell him we won't let him down and we'll help him any way we can, but he has to take the fall for the both of us." Her head was beginning to clear slightly. "I have to call Phelps. I need him here right now."

"You do what you have to do, and I'll do what I have to do. This is going to cost you, Claudia. It's going to cost you a lot." Leaving her with this threat, he picked up his briefcase off the bar and walked out. It was snowing hard.

Cuddles was near tears. She had been the best of friends with Crusher for many years and it hurt her to think she was about to betray him like this. Choking back the emotion, she locked the front door and turned off the beer sign hanging in the windows. She turned the overhead lights off and made her way upstairs to her apartment. She took a shower and put on a flannel nightgown. The vodka was wearing off and her head was clearing as she sat at her desk. She dialed the Fairbanks number for Buddy Phelps.

"I hope I didn't waken you, Buddy," she said in greeting.

"Not at all, I was just sitting here looking at the papers for the deal on the mining claims. I sold them, but the price wasn't as good as I hoped because you said to get rid of them right away. How are you doing, anyway?"

"Not so good, Buddy. The troopers arrested Crusher and me for killing Skip Williams. We got out on bail and then the troopers came back and arrested Crusher again, this time for killing Lil Danby—my bartender. All that happened just today!" She was nearly in tears. "I am going to need some help with the bar, Buddy. Can you come down and help me? I'll pay you for the time."

Phelps paused a few seconds before answering. "Sure, Cuddles, I'll come down there in the morning. I need to bring the paperwork on the claims for you to look at. I'll call you when I get to Anchorage to let you know what time I'll get to Kenai. See you tomorrow. And don't worry, we'll work all this out. See you tomorrow."

"Oh, thank you, Buddy, thank you." There was relief in her voice. She turned off the lights and fell into bed.

Grant Cummings entered the jail and asked to see his client, Dennis Carson. The two men were locked in the attorney visiting room to discuss legal matters. An hour later Cummings left the jail and Crusher was locked in a holding cell for the night.

Amazingly, Cuddles had no sign of a hangover the following morning. She was in good spirits knowing Buddy would be there today. She had just finished breakfast when the phone rang. It was Cummings.

"Arraignment will be at 10 this morning. We will enter a not guilty plea and ask for bail. I doubt the judge will give it to us, though. Are you coming to the hearing?"

"No, I have to meet Buddy at the airport. I don't know the time, but I think it will be fairly early. He likes to get stuff done. Call me when the hearing is over and tell me what happened. Tell Crusher I'll do whatever I can for him."

"I'll do that. He told me to tell you he was sorry for all the trouble he caused."

"Did you broach the subject of him taking all the blame?" asked the bar owner.

"Yes, I did. He said he would think about it," said Cummings. "He loves you, Cuddles. I think he'll go along with the idea."

"I want you to get the deeds to Skip's properties transferred to his sister. Do it right away. Stay in touch with Crusher. I don't want him to him getting lonely and feeling sorry for himself. If he asks for anything, get it for him." Cuddles seemed compassionate, but it didn't last long. "Keep nudging him about taking the full responsibility for the killing. He did the Lil killing and he's sure to be convicted for that one. Convince him the second one won't add to his life sentence."

"You're such a softie, Cuddles. I'll tell him. He's considering it."

There was a beep on the phone line. "I have to go; Buddy is calling," said Cuddles.

She hung up and answered the second call. "Hello, Buddy. I was on the phone with Grant Cummings. What time will you get here?"

"I'm in Anchorage and about to get on the plane to Kenai. I'm supposed to arrive at 9:45. Will you be there to pick me up?"

"I'll be in the SUV at the curb when you arrive. See you then." She felt good that something was going her way.

In court the proceedings went quickly and pretty much as Cummings had predicted. Dennis Carson entered a not guilty plea to the charge of murder in the first degree. The charges had been read and the defense attorney, Cummings had asked for bail, reminding the judge that since the defendant had already posted a large sum in another case, it was unlikely he would try to leave the area. The DA countered with a statement that he thought it would make it doubly likely the accused would flee. After only a moment of consideration, the judge ordered bail: the new amount was set at one million dollars, cash only. With that he banged his gavel and left the courtroom. Crusher was returned to the correctional facility to await trial, for which the date had already been set.

Cuddles sat in her white KIA in front of the Kenai Municipal Airport waiting for Buddy Phelps. At 9:55 he came out of the building, towing a medium-size suitcase on wheels. He recognized the SUV and walked directly to it. He opened the back door, and tossed the suitcase inside. Opening the front passenger door he poked his head inside and said, "Hi."

"Get in, Buddy," she greeted the mining engineer. "Are you hungry? Want some breakfast?"

"No, let's go to the bar and do some business. You'll have to explain to me what you want me to do for you while I'm here."

"Good enough." She slipped the SUV into gear and drove out of the airport lot. "How was the trip?"

"It was OK, but you know the flight from Fairbanks—it seems longer than it is. By the way, you said Crusher was to go to court this morning. How did he make out?"

"Cumming hasn't called me yet. They're in court right now, but I expect to get a call soon. As they pulled into the Forelands parking lot, her phone rang. It was Cummings. "How did it go?" she answered.

"Almost word for word as I predicted. He set bail at one million, cash only. Crusher is resigned to staying in jail," Cummings reported.

"Get the other items on the list completed. I may have some more work for you soon. Buddy and I are going to figure out what to do now."

In her office, the two sat at her desk. She had a small spiral notebook open to make notes. Buddy had a manila folder containing his notes made on yellow legal pads. He sorted them while she prepared her notes with dates and times.

"OK, Buddy, let's get down to business. You said you sold the claims and got a decent price. What did you get for them?" Now she was all business with no sentiment.

"Try to follow me. This is all smoke and mirrors except for the bottom line." He began to explain the process of selling the certificates. "I contacted several mining companies. Three of them are big, world-class mining companies. All the small companies offered low bids, hoping to steal the claims from some bankrupt miner. The three large companies were into the bidding with gusto. I had shown them each of the assay reports connecting the assayed gold with each of the claims. Because each claim had already produced measurable gold, the three remaining bidders got serious. The high bidder was Apex Gold LTD of Toronto. They're partnered with a South African company. Apex topped the other two bidders with a bid of US$145,000. They had some provisos, though: they wanted to have the claims signed off by the legal owner."

Cuddles eyebrows went up, "How did you get around that one?"

Phelps was grinning; he had done this before. "Otis Fairfax was the registered owner, but only as the president of Sunset Mining Company. I showed Otis as dead and that the board of directors of Sunset Mining had appointed me the new president. Stockholders voted at a meeting in Fairbanks. The stockholders are De Sylva, you, and myself." He looked her in the eye, smiled, and said, "Thanks for your vote of confidence."

"You're welcome," she replied.

"Apex was satisfied and wrote a check payable to Sunset Mining Company. I opened an account in that name at the Fairbanks branch of First National Bank of Alaska. Once all the papers were signed and the check deposited, I had the bank open an account for me here in Kenai, under the name of Phelps Mining Engineers. I transferred the money to that account and tomorrow I will get certified checks in the names and amounts you designate. I assume you will stick to the 30 percent you offered me to do the deal."

"I always honor my deals, Buddy." She was scratching away at her notebook. "Here's what I want you to do: get one check for $40,000 payable to me, Claudia Morris. Get one check for $40,000 payable to Pamela Williams. You keep $40,000. Send $15,000 to De Sylva and $10,000, by check, to Grant Cummings. I'll deliver the two for Pamela and Grant. You did a great job, Buddy. This whole mess is getting out of hand." She knew she had chosen the right man to take care of this bit of business. She hoped Grant would do as well with Crusher.

Chapter 26

"Crusher is really despondent," Cummings reported to Cuddles. Her legal counsel had come to the bar to report in person, as opposed to calling her. There were other things they needed to discuss, one of which was money: Who was paying for Crusher's defense? How much could he expect to get for doing the paperwork transferring the ownership of the Williams and Fairfax properties to Pamela Williams? He had invested a great deal of time and effort into this and had not seen one thin dime for any of it. And then there was the issue of the mining claims. Where was his share of the sale of those?

"It's your job to keep him happy. I told you that. You have to convince him to take the fall for both killings. It won't do any good to send me to jail along with him," Cuddles said, thinking only of her own future. "He has to absolve me of any complicity in the Williams case. I can't afford to be connected to it in any way. He has to see that."

"All I can do is try," said the lawyer. "I think he's in love with you and I think he'll go along, but you're going to have to sweet talk him a little."

"There's no evidence to connect me with either of the killings. The troopers can say anything they want, but they haven't any proof. I was here in the bar that night. Everyone saw me here. The reason he killed Lil was that she said he wasn't here during the time of the murder and fire. That alone should get me out of the equation." Cuddles was trying to think like a lawyer.

"The DA is going to have to make those points, Claudia. I can't do it if I'm representing Dennis in his defense," explained Cummings. "There is one way to get around it, though."

"Good, what way is that?" she asked.

"If we can talk Dennis into making a deal with the DA by offering to change his plea on both charges and taking you out of the Williams case. The

DA might just go for it in order to clear two murders and one arson case from his case load. The troopers will scream their heads off, but I think the district attorney will tell them to shut up. I think he'll make the case that this is in the best interest of the State of Alaska. There's a statute to cover that."

"How do we get Dennis to go along with the plan?"

"He will have to convince the DA he did it on his own to steal the gold. I think it's pretty thin, but if Crusher tells it right it'll work."

"Make it work, Grant. I have too much riding on it not to take the chance." She was still thinking. "There is one more thing to consider. The troopers found the gold in my safe. How do we explain that?"

"Dennis will have to tell them he asked you to keep it for him." Cummings had a word of warning for her: "I have to remind you not to call him on the jail phone or, if he calls you, don't discuss it with him. All the conversations are recorded and it would be dangerous."

"OK, Grant. Let's go this route. I'll have some cash for you tomorrow. We sold the mining claims and the money will arrive at the bank tomorrow. I'll get a certified check to you when it arrives."

"Speaking of the mining claims, they've never surfaced in the investigation. I'm hoping they fell through the cracks and no one is looking for them. Those certificates are a hazardous loose end and could come back to haunt us."

"They've been sold to a foreign company and transferred in the name of a dummy company. I think the sale is safe from detection. Buddy handled it and has some experience in that area." Cuddles almost smiled, knowing she had beaten Grant to the punch on this item.

Cummings left the bar, stepping out into 10-degree-below-zero weather. Pulling his collar up around his ears he was engrossed in the problems he must solve. He made one decision on the spot: he needed long underwear beneath his overalls and flannel shirt.

Cuddles got up from the table where she and Grant had been planning and made her way back to her barstool. She wanted to talk with Buddy Phelps, so she called up to his room. He came down and leaned on his elbows on the other side of the bar.

"Life is becoming very complicated, Buddy. I have a lot of things I have to take care of and I need you to help me do them. I want you to hire a bartender. I'm going to need you outside the bar sometimes, and if you're tending the bar it's impossible for you to get away." She opened her spiral notebook to a page in the back. "Here's a list of people who have applied for the job. I've interviewed a few of the names. Don't call the ones with red checkmarks unless you run out of names. Just call them and have them come down here for an interview. You set the times. If you find one you like, let me know who it is. If I approve, you can hire."

"I can do that," said Buddy. "What do you have in mind for me? Nothing criminal, I hope?"

"I make a good living here, Buddy. I'd like to take you on as sort of a partner—not a co-owner, but in for a percentage of the gross. It takes 30 percent to run the place: wages, heat, lights, insurance, and upkeep. I'll split the other 70 percent down the middle with you. I want you to run the bar. With Crusher in jail I have to know there's someone I can count on to do the things I'm unable to do. Do you understand what I'm proposing?" Cuddles wanted a clear understanding of what she was proposing.

"Oh, I think I understand, Cuddles. And there's one thing I want you to understand: there are certain lines I will not cross. You know I'm not above bending the rules a little, but I'm not going to butt heads with the law. I'll work for you and do my best to keep you safe, but I'm not Crusher." Buddy hoped she understood what he meant.

"I think we understand each other. If there's something you don't want to do, just say so and we'll find someone else to do it. With all the legal intrusions in my life right now, I won't be coloring outside the lines much. Welcome aboard, Buddy. I'm glad to have you." Cuddles relaxed a little. She had been honest with her new partner. She needed him, badly. She was beginning to trust Cummings less and less. He was becoming too familiar with her private business. She felt if Grant knew too much he might use it to blackmail her every time he needed more money. With Buddy on board she could sidestep Cummings on most sensitive issues. This was a good move on her part, she thought.

Late in the afternoon applicants began to enter and interview with Buddy Phelps. She watched the first two interviews and was satisfied he was doing it the way she wanted. By early evening Buddy had made his choice. She was a thin, nearly six-foot tall, brunette; soft-spoken, but not a push-over, and attractive. Buddy had watched her mix several drinks. He instructed her in bar cleanliness, ID-checking, and the consequences of dishonesty. Her name was Carol. In spite of the bitter cold several customers wandered in and she greeted each one with a friendly smile. Buddy was satisfied she would work out well.

Phelps took a seat next to Cuddles and watched the new bartender at work. "What's next on the list of things to do, Boss?"

"We'll talk about it in the morning. They're several personal legal issues I want you to handle for me. We can start with them tomorrow. I like the way you handled things today, Buddy. Thanks."

He was about to answer her when the Hagel brothers came in. Tom was arguing with his big brother Chuck. "Calm down or take it outside," said the new bartender.

Immediately the two men turned to look at the new voice. Chuck Hagel presented a huge smile and greeted her: "Howdy-do, and who are you?"

"I'm the new bartender, and if you expect to get served you'll have to keep me happy. My name is Carol; what's yours?"

"Well Hellooo, Carol. I'm Chuck Hagel and this is my brother Tom. We come here a lot so I expect we'll be seeing a lot of you."

"You're seeing all you will ever see of me, Chuck. I just tend bar," she smiled and tamed the biker.

Tom Hagel wasn't impressed. "I hate uppity women," he snarled.

"Calm down, Tom. We just met the lady. We don't want her to get the wrong impression," brother Chuck said.

"The last time I had a conversation with the bartender in here they put me in jail."

"Boys, I'll be happy to fix you a drink, but if you want a fight you'll have to go somewhere else." She was pleasant, but stern.

Chuck Hagel took his brother by the arm and led him to a table. "Come on Tom. She doesn't even know us. Calm down."

The two other customers at the far end of the bar had begun to make motions to leave. Carol saw their intent and went to the end of the bar. "It'll be OK, boys. Have another one, on me." They relaxed and took the beers.

Carol walked from behind the bar to take the order from the Hagel brothers. When she arrived at the table Chuck Hagel said, "You're a big ol' girl, ain't you?"

"My new boss said she wanted someone big enough to kick a biker's butt," she said, smiling. "What'll it be?"

They ordered and Carol returned to the bar. She delivered the drinks and took their money, including a large tip. Both Cuddles and Phelps were satisfied she was going to work out well.

"I'm going up to the office. I have some things to take care of tonight. Stick around and make sure she doesn't get into trouble on her first shift." She slipped off her stool and made her way to the back.

The rest of the evening was uneventful and Buddy helped Carol clean up the bar and re-stock the beer coolers for morning. The cash drawer showed a good night in spite of the shortage of customers. Her tip jar, too, was full. It looked like this new bartender was a winner.

The following morning Buddy found Cuddles in her office. She was busy tallying the receipts and making out a bank deposit slip. With all the figures in place she looked up and said, "Good morning, Buddy. Have a seat."

"Good morning to you, Boss. Did you sleep well?" he asked in a friendly tone.

"The best I've slept in months, thanks to you and the new bartender."

"Glad you approve."

"I have some things I want you to do for me today. Between you and me, I am beginning to lose confidence in Grant Cummings. He knows way too much about my business and I think he may try to take advantage of me with it. I can't trust him anymore." She began by picking up a sheet of paper and handing it to him. "This is the name of another lawyer in town. I want you to contact him. See if he will come out here and see me. I want him to draw up a will for me. He may say something about the arrest and about Crusher, but assure him this has nothing to do with those issues."

Buddy took the paper and read it.

"I also want you to go to the bank for me. I have a deposit to make in the business account. Get an account name change sheet. I want to put you on the account so you can sign checks and pay the bills."

"Are you certain you want to do that?" asked Buddy, astonished at the request.

"Oh, yes, I'm certain. Crusher was loyal but could never be allowed to think for himself. I believe you are trustworthy, loyal, and have great intelligence. This is going to be a good partnership for the both of us."

Chapter 27

The following day brought an unusual change to the weather. The temperature had risen from yesterday's sub-zero temp to a high of 42 degrees, making the roads extremely hazardous. In spite of the conditions, John Quimby, youngest of the associates at a prominent local law firm, entered the Forelands Bar. Unzipping his light jacket and surveying his surroundings, he asked if Claudia Morris was in.

Buddy Phelps said she was in and was expecting him. Phelps led the young man to the office of his boss and partner. He returned to the bar and left the two alone.

"How do you do? I'm John Quimby. I understand you requested a meeting." He introduced himself in a professional way.

"Have a seat, John." She pointed to an empty chair near the desk. "I'm Claudia Morris. I own this place. I asked for you because I've known your father for many years, though it has been a long time since I've seen him."

Pat Quimby had begun his career as a truck driver. He was ambitious and energetic. He started dealing in used trucks during the early days of the pipeline, when every aspiring young trucker wanted to own a new rig but found that making the payments required more than they had or wanted to give. He bought up used trucks and resold them to other operators. He managed to acquire several trucks of his own and several route permits for operational rights. Later he sold the permits to well-financed companies and expanded his trucking business with leases. His sales volume increased and he opened a diesel shop, reputed to be the best in Alaska.

In those days, the elder Quimby knew Cuddles professionally. When she was brutally injured by another one of her clients, he offered to help her. He picked up the medical bills during the time before she was paid off by the abusive client's father. Cuddles never forgot his kindness. When she learned that his son was now a local lawyer, she knew she wanted him to represent her in her personal affairs.

"He's well, living in Arizona with my mother."

"He is one of the finest men I have ever met. I owe him a great deal. You should be very proud of him." Cuddles wanted the young man to know about his father's good deeds but did not want to go into detail about the nature of their association.

"I'll tell him you send your regards," said the younger Quimby. "How may I be of service to you, Ms. Morris?" he asked politely.

"You must have heard I was arrested recently for a crime I didn't commit. I had an employee who involved me in some terrible things without my knowing about them. Those charges are not what I want you to represent me in. I have several personal business items to deal with, and I want you to help me with those." She explained the general situation.

He took a large yellow legal pad from his briefcase and placed it on the edge of the desk. "I cannot and will not represent you in any criminal proceedings. I will do my best for you with business and personal issues. Where would you like me to start?"

"I admire your forthrightness, John. You remind me of your father. He, too, was an honest man." There was a short pause. "Now, to business. There will be several items, the first of which is the matter of a partnership agreement between me and the man you met downstairs, Buddy Phelps."

"Is Buddy his legal name or a nickname?" asked the lawyer.

"It's his legal name. I'll get his date of birth for you before you go." She went on to explain the agreement she had made with Buddy. When she had finished with the partnership matters she went on to lay out a last will and testament. "I'm not planning to check out soon, but you can see I'm not exactly the picture of health and I want to have my affairs in order if something happens to me."

"Fair enough," he said, turning to a new page on his legal pad. "Let's start with the required items: name, age, date and place of birth."

These items were simple, but the terms of her will were complicated and she read them from the notes in her notebook. "In the event of my death, I want my estate to pay all my debts—there shouldn't be any, but be sure they're paid. Next I want my new partner to get half the real and personal property." Quimby was writing as quickly as he could. "The other half of my property is to go to Pamela Williams. I'll have to get her date of birth and such; I don't know what they are right now."

"Are either of these heirs related to you in any way?" he asked.

"No, I have no relatives that I know about. These are just good friends to whom I owe a great deal for helping me during my lifetime."

"Do you own this property outright or is there a lien on the property?"

"I own it all. The deed is in my safe along with a couple of others: I own a rental house in Anchorage and a business location in Nikiski, as well as two undeveloped lots on the Kenai River. I own them all outright, free and clear. All the deeds are in the safe." She wanted this will to be accurate and unbreakable. "I have two bank accounts in Kenai—I'll give you the account numbers—and one in Anchorage. That one is in a savings and loan; I'll give you that number, too."

Item by item the young lawyer listed the legal requirements and the personal preferences required by the client. The list was long and began to fill many pages of the legal pad.

This same day Sergeant Bob Seaton sat at his desk reviewing the files on the murder and arson case, as well as the Lil Danby murder. The district attorney had advised the trooper that a trial date had been set and he wanted Seaton to have his facts straight. During his review he noted that the Vito Hocker case was referred to as a cross-reference. For some reason it triggered a thought Seaton could not get out of his mind. It had to do with the bags of gold nuggets. It was strange that these bags kept showing up in different investigations. They disappeared at the time of the fire and murder of their second owner, Larry "Skip" Williams. Vito Hocker was in possession of four of the nuggets when he was attacked and beaten by Dennis Carson. The bags were found in the search of Claudia Morris' safe. One other missing item from the tool box in the plane crash—the original investigation in this chain of events—was the mining claim certificates. What had happened to them? They had vanished. Seaton had photo copies of the claim certificates in the crash investigation file, but the originals were nowhere to be found. The more he studied all the files the more he wanted to know about the claims. He was leaning back in his desk chair, thinking about it when suddenly he had a thought: "The nuggets—where did they come from? Did they originate at the claims on the certificates?"

Seaton looked in his private contacts file for the number of a man he knew well—a state geologist living right here in Soldotna; he would have the answer to that question. Bob dialed the number and got his voice mail. Hanging up he stood and walked to the coffee pot, more for the exercise than the coffee. His phone was jingling when he returned to his desk.

"Sergeant Seaton," he answered.

"Hi, Bob, Dick Reger here. I have a message you called."

"Yes, Dick, I called to see if you were in town today."

"As a matter of fact I am—and heading to the post office right now. What do you need?"

"I have a geology question for you. Can you come by the office?"

"Sure. Will twenty minutes be soon enough?" asked Reger.

"Perfect, Dick. See you in a few minutes." Reger being in town was a stroke of luck for the trooper. He might have been out in the field and not returned for weeks.

Seaton was studying the files on his desk when the receptionist notified him he had a guest at the front desk. Bob went out to escort Reger to his office.

Once there Dick asked the trooper, "What you got?"

"I have a case going to trial and I would like to tie some evidence together for presentation. It has to do with some gold, both nuggets and fine gold. What I need to find out is if it can be determined where the gold came from. I have some claim certificates and I want to know if it can be determined whether the gold came from these claims. The claims are located in various areas of the state. I was thinking that there may be a way to tell, geologically, if the nuggets actually came from these claims."

"Not from a geological view; what you need is an assay. Gold nuggets are not pure gold. They have impurities in them. An assayer can test the impurities and sometimes tell where they came from. The makeup of these particles is slightly different coming from, say, central Alaska versus nuggets from Nome or Eagle or Hope. The assayer probably can't tell you which mine in each of those areas the gold came from but he could tell, with reasonable certainty, in which area they originated."

"This case will be going to trial soon, so I need to find out about this as soon as possible. Can you recommend an assayer to do the job? The gold we'll be testing is evidence in several felony crimes, so handling them will be touchy," Seaton tried to explain some of the issues.

"I know a fella in Fairbanks. He's state certified and has a PhD in the field. I use him on a regular basis. I can call him and see if he can do the job," Reger volunteered.

"It would be wonderful if you could do that for me. Do you have his number with you?" asked Seaton.

"I sure do," Reger replied, reaching into his shirt pocket for his cell phone. He scanned through his contacts and came up with a number. "His name is Roger Comstock. His office is in Fairbanks. Give me a minute and I'll introduce him to you."

Seaton was elated; this was better than he had hoped. Reger reached the Assayer and talked with him a few minutes before putting Seaton on the line. Bob explained the problem and told Comstock he could fax copies of the mining claims to him. Comstock said he would put it all at the top of his list of priorities. He needed samples of the nuggets to test; Seaton wrote the address in his notebook. Other details were noted before Seaton thanked him and hung up.

"I really owe you, Dick," the sergeant commented. "How about lunch?"

"I'll take it. This will be the best paying job I ever had!" Both men laughed and Seaton notified the dispatch he was going to be out of the office a while.

Two days later, in mid-afternoon, he received a call from Comstock. "You won't believe this, Sergeant. I did an assay a few weeks ago for a mining engineer here in Fairbanks. He said he needed it to verify the origination of some gold nuggets he had. They perfectly matched the claim certificates he had. The mining claims you sent me are identical to the ones he had. And there are matches between the nuggets you sent and these claims. When the tests and the certificates all matched, I looked it up. I'll send you copies of both tests and copies of his mining certificates. What's going on down there on the peninsula?"

"What? You can't be serious. Who's the engineer you did the test for?"

"A local guy I do work for sometimes. His name is Buddy Phelps."

"Phelps, Phelps, somehow the name rings a bell. I'll have to look him up. Anyway, thanks. Send me a bill and get the evidence back here as soon as you can. I really appreciate what you did." Seaton was having trouble placing the name Phelps.

Chapter 28

The name Phelps finally came to him. He went to the file and pulled up the Lil Danby case. Buddy Phelps was one of the two bystanders in the bar helping break up the fight the night Lil was choked by Tom Hagel. He knew he had to drive to the Forelands Bar to ask Cuddles about the man. It seemed this case was taking another twist toward the bizarre.

He decided it was time to ask Cuddles again about the mining claims. She had pointedly omitted them from any statements she had made about this entire affair. He called Officer Beeles and asked him to meet him at the Forelands Bar. He volunteered a short version of the talk he had with the assayer in Fairbanks. Beeles seemed excited.

Less than an hour later the two entered the bar. A new bartender was wiping the tables. "Can I help you gentlemen?" she asked pleasantly.

"We would like to see Claudia Morris, if she is available," said Beeles.

"She hasn't come down yet, but the manager is in. Can he help you?"

"I don't think so, Ma'am. When do you expect Claudia to be available?" asked Beeles.

"She usually ..." she was cut off by the back door opening and a tall man carrying two cases of beer entered. "Here's Mr. Phelps, perhaps he can help you," she continued.

"Well, he certainly can," agreed Seaton, who kept a poker face.

Phelps set the beer cases on the floor behind the bar. He stood and stretched his back.

"What can I do for the troopers today?" he asked.

"Mr. Phelps, I'm Sergeant Seaton and this is Officer Beeles. I don't know if you remember us, but we met the night Tom Hagel attacked Lil Danby during a fight."

"I remember. You two saved my neck that night. Thanks."

"Mr. Phelps, we would like to talk with you for a few minutes, if you have the time." Seaton was trying to be cordial and friendly.

"Sure, let's go to that table over there," he said, pointing to a table past the end of the bar.

The three men shook hands and sat. Seaton took his notebook from his jacket pocket and put it on the table. "Mr. Phelps, do you know an assayer by the name of Comstock in Fairbanks?"

"Sure, and call me Buddy. I've used him on many occasions to do assays for different mining company projects I have worked on. Why do you ask?"

"It's sort of complicated. I asked the state geologist for some advice about a case I was working on. He personally couldn't give me what I needed and recommended Mr. Comstock. I wanted to find out if it was possible to determine where some gold nuggets I had in my evidence locker originated. I also had some copies of mining claim certificates and asked him to match them if possible," Seaton explained.

"Yes," said Phelps, "I have him do that sort of work for me quite often. He's very good at it. Was he able to help you?"

"As a matter of fact, that's why we're here, Buddy. Your name came up in our conversation. He told us you had the exact same job done recently, matching gold nuggets to the same mining certificates we gave him." Seaton was looking directly into the engineer's eyes. "It's a coincidence I just couldn't ignore."

"You must be talking about the nuggets and claim certificates I brokered a sale for from a local mining company to a Canadian outfit, Apex Mining LTD. I needed the assays to prove the gold came from the claims they were buying."

"Who hired you to do the brokering?" asked Beeles.

"I had some stock in Sunset Mining Company, who owned the claims. The owner and president of the company died and the board voted me the new president. I represented the company in the deal. I own a lot of mining stocks I've acquired in doing work for different mining companies. The exploration companies never have any money and I take a portion of my pay in mining stocks. It's a common practice." Phelps seemed matter-of-fact about the dealings.

"I mean who, exactly, hired you—not the name of the company, but the name of the person," Beeles inquired again.

"It was a board decision; the directors of the company met and asked me to broker the sale."

Seaton was now asking, "Mr. Phelps, it seems you are avoiding the question. What are the names of the members of the board of directors of the Sunset Mining Company?"

Phelps was hesitating, thinking: the names of board members are a matter of public record, so he could not stop the troopers from learning the names. "The voting members are Gene De Sylva, Claudia Morris, and myself."

"How did you come to possess the actual mining claim certificates?" asked Seaton.

Phelps was becoming uncomfortable, "Claudia Morris had them in her possession and gave them to me to arrange a sale."

"When did she give you the actual certificates?" Seaton persisted.

"Gosh, I don't remember for sure. It must have been a couple of months ago." Phelps was nervous.

"Are you aware these claim certificates were the property of a man who died?" Seaton asked.

"Yes, Otis Fairfax—former president of Sunset Mining—was killed in an airplane crash."

"He was the original owner… but when he died he left his property to a man named Larry Williams. Mr. Williams was subsequently murdered and his home set afire, apparently to cover the crime. Dennis Carson, who once worked for Claudia Morris, is about to go on trial for killing him. Now, perhaps you can see why we are so interested in how you came to be in possession of the certificates." Seaton was trying to shake the story Phelps was telling.

"I can see you need to find out where they came from, but I was only working at the request of the board of directors. I'm a hired hand in this deal." Phelps was trying to keep the story from crumbling.

"I guess we'll have to stick around and talk to one of those board members." Seaton turned to Beeles: "Jason, ask the bartender to go get Claudia and have her come down here for a chat."

The bartender came back in a couple of minutes and said Claudia would be down soon. It was more than twenty minutes before she actually showed. She was wearing a yellow dress with red flowers and fresh makeup. She was smiling, but it was difficult to tell if the smile was genuine. Seaton guessed it was not.

The first to speak to her was Phelps, "Good morning, Claudia."

"Good morning to you, Buddy," she answered before turning to the two troopers. "What do you two want?" she growled.

"I'm sorry if we disturbed your morning, Claudia, but some things have come up and we need to talk with you about them." Seaton tried to be nice, but it wasn't easy. "We have learned some information that we need to confirm. We learned you had been in possession of some mining claim certificates once owned by Otis Fairfax. After the crash, I had them in my evidence locker. I gave them to his heir, Larry Williams. Williams was killed and his house set afire. The certificates went missing. Now I learn the certificates have been sold by a company of which you are a board member. That seemed strange to me and I came out here to find how it all came about. Tell me, Claudia, how did you come to be the sole owner of the mining claims?"

"Well, wise guy, we ain't got no bank out here in North Kenai and sometimes customers will ask to borrow money. Sometimes I ask them for collateral and sometimes not, depending on the amount. Larry Williams came in looking for a loan, a substantial loan, and I told him I had to have some kind of security. He put up the mining claims as security for the loan. It's as simple as that. When Skip died, I asked Buddy to find a buyer for the mining claim certificates in order to recover some of the money I loaned Williams. There ain't nothin' magic or sinister going on here." Claudia pitched a good story.

"So, you had them, with the pouches of gold, all along?" asked the sergeant.

"Yep," answered Cuddles.

"Why didn't you tell us about this when we were here investigating Skip William's death?"

"Well I didn't have them on me at that exact moment," she said, with a satisfied look. "Now, if you want to know anything else, I'm going to call my lawyer to come out and give me advice. You got any more questions?"

Seaton finished writing the notes he was making in his little book before answering. "No, Cuddles, I think that does it for now, but we will probably have to ask you some more questions later. Thank you for cooperating with us." He picked up his notebook and motioned for Beeles to follow him to the door.

They sat in Seaton's car to debrief. Bob asked, "Well, Jason, what did you think of them and what they told us? Do you think there's any chance they're telling the truth?"

"It looks to me as if they concocted a pretty good story and it may convince a jury, but I don't believe it," answered the junior investigator. "What's our next move?"

"How do you feel about running this story past Crusher? We're going to be passing the jail anyway. Maybe we can make him mad enough to say something we can use."

"What's the worst that can happen? He might tell us to go away." Jason Beeles was grinning as he said it.

Correctional officers brought the wrestler to the attorney visiting room where the troopers waited. "I'm not supposed to talk to you guys," he said.

"That's OK, Crusher. We just found out a couple of things and wanted to confirm them with you. Sorry we bothered you." Seaton stood to leave.

"Don't go just yet, trooper. What is it you want to know?" Crusher thought he might learn something he could use.

"Not much, Crusher. We went out to the bar and talked with Cuddles and your replacement, Buddy Phelps. They have a new bartender. A big tall gal; she seems to be doing a good job."

"What do you mean, 'my replacement'?" Crusher asked.

"Phelps is doing your job while you're in here. Cuddles likes him."

"He can't do the things I did for her," Crusher bragged.

"What kind of things?" asked Seaton.

"You know, things she didn't want anyone to know about."

"You mean like stealing the tool box from Skip?" Seaton suggested.

"Yeah, stuff like that." He knew as soon as he said it he was in trouble.

"So," Seaton followed up, "she did send you out to Skip William's trailer to get the little plastic box with the gold in it?"

"I ain't supposed to say," Crusher was pulling back.

"It might help your case if you tell us the truth. It sure can't hurt you any." Seaton hoped the wrestler would crack.

"Don't tell her I said so, but she sent me to see Skip that night. There wasn't any other way to get the box except to choke him out. When I did I could tell he wasn't breathing anymore, so I set the fire to make it look like an accident. I guess it didn't work very well. She wants me to take all the blame, but it was her idea." Now the cat was out of the bag and Cuddles was implicated.

"Thanks for telling us, Crusher. I'll tell the DA you helped us and maybe he'll go a little easier on you." Both troopers stood to leave.

"Don't tell Cuddles, though. She'll get really mad if you do."

"OK, Crusher. We won't." The troopers left the jail and drove to the courthouse to see the DA.

Chapter 29

Seaton and Beeles stopped at the office of the district attorney as they came through Kenai. The clerk notified the DA and escorted the two men to the office. His office was a mess: files on the desk, files on the credenza behind him, and files stacked on the floor. Seaton had seen it before, but Beeles was appalled at the disarray. He stole a glance at Seaton with a smirk on his face. Seaton concentrated hard to ignore the look.

"What do you fellas want?" asked David Zane, the current DA. "I'm busy."

Seaton did the talking: "We just had an interesting conversation with Dennis Carson. We stopped at the jail to ask him about some information we gained in an interview with Buddy Phelps, who now works for Claudia Morris. We've always believed Claudia had Carson go to Williams' place and rob him of the gold he had just inherited. We just learned, from an assayer in Fairbanks, that Buddy Phelps had an assay done on the same gold, establishing it came from the same claims we were checking. Phelps said he brokered a sale of the claims, claiming he was president of the company whose name was on the certificates. Those certificates came from Larry Williams, along with the pouches of gold we took from the safe of Claudia Morris. In our conversation with Dennis Carson, he admitted he was sent by Claudia Morris to take the box containing the gold and the mining claim certificates. He admits he killed Williams, but by accident, and set the fire to cover the death."

"You just created a month's work for me! I think this is the third time you have been here to change the basic case. Carson denied Morris sent him to the Williams trailer that night and accepted full responsibility for the death. Now you say he denies *that* and instead says he *was* sent by Ms. Morris to rob Williams." Zane was shaking his head in disbelief. "Bob, you have a real talent for wrecking my cases. Last time, I had a case against Tom Hagel and then you came back to say Carson did it and asked me to release Hagel. This time, we're eliminating Morris as a suspect in the murder/arson case, and you waltz in and say she's the one who ordered it! Can you explain to me how I can convince a jury beyond a reasonable doubt that Carson—alone—is guilty, when you keep creating doubt?"

Seaton held up a hand, "Hold on, David, I never believed Hagel killed Lil Danby. I told you so when we arrested him. I never believed Dennis Carson robbed and killed Larry Williams on his own; I have always maintained Claudia was the brains behind it all. You are the one who wanted to eliminate doubtful suspects because there wasn't enough evidence. Well, now there is enough evidence. Proving it in court is your job. I'm just doing mine." Angry and frustrated, Bob Seaton stood and motioned for Jason Beeles to follow. "Call me when you decide what you are going to do. I've given you the evidence; you do with it what you think best." The two troopers stormed out of the office without saying goodbye.

"I've never seen you angry before, Sarge; I like it!" Beeles was keyed up and laughing now. "How 'bout I buy you a cup of coffee and you can cool off before you shoot someone."

"Let's go to the office to have it. I don't think I should be seen in public right now."

The captain was waiting when they arrived. He wasn't happy. "What did you say to the DA, Bob? He called and wants your head."

"Not much, I just told him to get off his can and do his job."

"You're kidding, right?"

"Not really. I brought some new evidence to him and he didn't want to hear it. The guy is a nut. He's so far behind in his work load he can't see the truth when it comes right through the door. I just got tired of dealing with his incompetence."

"I can see this isn't going anywhere. Stay away from the DA for now. I'll try to get it ironed out." The captain returned to his office and the two troopers proceeded to the coffee pot.

Back in his office, Seaton looked at Beeles and commented, "That went well, don't you think?"

"I guess this is why some cops drink a lot. Calm down, Sarge. Everyone's angry right now. You can't win. Let it settle and then make the point. If you keep this up, you'll be working for me—and I don't want to supervise *you*!" Beeles was grinning but giving sound advice.

"Yeah, it would be a dirty trick for *me* to have to do what *you* say." Bob took a long drink of his coffee and a deep breath to clear his mind. "I think I'd better quit for the day and go to the gym … get some of this out of my system. Thanks for standing by me, Jason. I appreciate it," he said, sticking out his hand to shake the hand of a friend.

Beeles was in the office early the following morning and met Seaton when he arrived. "I'll wait for you in your office while you get a cup of coffee," he told the sergeant.

Minutes later the two men were in the office with the door closed. "Things were a little tense after you left yesterday, Sarge. The captain called me to his office and asked me to explain what happened. I told the truth and he listened. When I finished he called the colonel and discussed it with him. He did explain to the boss that what you said was the truth and that the DA's office has often been slow to nonresponsive in the past few months. I don't know what the colonel said, but the cap said he would wait for a call back. I don't know what they plan to do, Bob, but I wanted you to know this has been sent to the head shed with your name on it."

"Thanks, Jason, I appreciate the heads up. I feel a little better today, but I still think I was right. I probably shouldn't have unloaded on the DA like that, but I think he had it coming."

Just then his desk phone rang. It was the captain requesting an audience. Seaton excused himself and walked down the hall to his captain's office. "Come in and close the door," ordered the captain.

Seaton closed the door and the captain motioned for him to have a seat. "I just got off the phone with the colonel. He spent last night and this morning with the attorney general. You succeeded in stirring up a hornet's nest. I'm going to have to put a letter of reprimand in your file. If you stay out of trouble for a period of time, it will be removed and forgotten. That's the way it goes when you cause my boss to call his boss."

"I'm sorry Cap, but I just couldn't take it any longer. It got the best of me and I let him have it with both barrels."

"Off the record, this has been brewing for a long time. You just lit the fuse on a situation that's been in the making. The colonel called the attorney general and discussed it with him. The AG is sending a DA from Juneau to take over the Kenai office until it all gets sorted out. And, off the record, I'm surprised you lasted as long as you did, but I can't allow unprofessional outbursts to go unpunished, even though I thank you for the result."

"Am I still on the case, Cap?"

"You're still on the case, as is Beeles—who, by the way, is being promoted to corporal, as of today. You can deliver this good news if you want. I want you to review the entire case and write a summary for the new DA. Claudia Morris is still out on bail and her charges are still pending; they have never yet been dismissed. We'll use your summary to attempt to get an arrest warrant for Buddy Phelps on a felony charge of receiving and selling stolen property. That warrant will have to come from the new DA."

"Who are they sending us, do you know yet?" he asked his captain.

"I'm not sure, but the word I got from headquarters is that it's a lady from the Juneau DA's office. She's supposed to be a real fire-eater by the name of Nancy Collins. The AG has sent her other places in the state to shape up an office. I hear she's really good." The captain's phone rang. "Go back to work now," he said, picking up the call.

Back in his office, Seaton called Beeles in. The two men talked about the outcome of the meeting and the senior officer gave him a full account, minus one important item.

Beeles exhaled, "Whew! Things turned out pretty well, then. I thought for a while I was going to have to find a new partner," he smiled and winked.

"Well, there was one other thing I forgot to tell you," Seaton said, dragging out the news.

"Oh oh, here it comes. What did they do, fire me instead of you?" asked the junior partner.

"No, but only because they didn't think of it," Seaton held back, building the suspense. "The captain asked me to tell you something, so don't be mad at me."

"What now?" asked Beeles.

"As of today ... you are officially my partner: you have been promoted to corporal as of this morning." Seaton smiled broadly, with a twinkle in own eye now.

Beeles could not believe his ears. He had wanted to become an investigator and now it had happened. "Tell me, Sarge, what does an investigator corporal really have to do?"

"Everything I say, Partner, everything I say," Seaton laughed and shook the new corporal's hand.

"OK, then, where do we start?"

"We have to review and summarize the case for the new DA. That will take all day and maybe part of tomorrow, but at least we can expect some action on it."

While researching and writing the summary it became apparent this was no simple, straight-forward case. There were many side factors and victims. The two men began to make an outline and diagram the path of the gold, tying the victims and the suspects to the story, with the lust for gold as the motive for all the individuals involved. Otis Fairfax was obsessed with the gold, it ruled his very existence. Larry Williams became obsessed with the gold, dreaming it would change his life. Instead, it ended his life. Claudia Morris lusted for the gold for the sake of riches. Buddy Phelps lusted for the gold for the same reason. The only one who wasn't interested in the gold was Dennis Carson: he committed his crimes first on orders from his employer and then to protect both himself and Claudia. He had no personal interest in the gold; his interest was only to please his boss.

As it stood now, everyone who touched the gold was a loser. Otis was dead from the plane crash. Larry Williams had been murdered. Claudia had been arrested, though was out on bail. Phelps was about to be arrested for the sale of the mining claims. Lil Danby was killed because she knew about the likelihood of Carson being the thief and arsonist who killed Williams. Even Bob Seaton had come close to losing his job, succumbing to the frustrations caused by the gold. Privately he wondered what would eventually become of the cursed pouches of bright yellow misery—$1.75 million in misery, to be exact.

The two troopers worked late that night writing the summary for the new DA. Both men were exhausted by the time they finished. "There's gotta' be a restaurant open this late," hoped Beeles.

"Froso's is open for another hour and they have great Italian food. Come on, I'll buy dinner to celebrate your new stripes." Seaton stood to stretch his aching muscles. He had hated coming to work this morning not knowing how it would turn out. He was now satisfied and grateful with the turn of events. It had been a good day, after all.

Chapter 30

Nancy Collins was in her mid-30s, a slight red tint in her hair. She dressed in a beige business suit and carried herself with a no-nonsense look. Neither Beeles nor Seaton had met the lady before and didn't know what to expect.

"Come in, gentlemen," she said when they arrived; "I've been expecting you. I understand you are investigating a rather complicated set of cases. Sit down and give me the Reader's Digest version."

Proper introductions were made before Seaton made the presentation of evidence to the new district attorney. At the end she asked, "How would you like to see me proceed?"

"I think it would pay off to go out to the jail and let Dennis Carson know that you think Claudia Morris is throwing him to the wolves. I think he loves her, and if we can convince him that she is using his feelings for her to get him to take all the blame, he might try to get even. He's not a quick thinker, and I'm not sure he understands fully how dire his situation really is." Seaton didn't know if Ms. Collins would consider getting her hands dirty.

She sat quietly a moment before answering. "It sounds like a good plan. The case against her is pretty weak. If we can get him to officially incriminate her, it would make things a lot easier. I don't know how much bargaining leverage I have, though. He's up for two murders and one arson charge. I can't offer him anything that will even get him out of jail before he dies."

"Try this," Seaton offered, "—convince him that she has a new *beau*. Tell him that you know she's hired Phelps to take his place, and I mean to take *his place*. Dennis might get mad enough to want some revenge. Like I said, he isn't a quick thinker, but he's emotional and impulsive."

"It might work, but don't bet the farm on it. I guess we won't lose anything by trying. Give me the file and the summary you wrote. I'll review it this morning and try to get to the jail to meet with Carson by this afternoon."

"Thank you, Ms. Collins. I think it will be a pleasure working with you," said Bob Seaton.

"Stay here a minute; I'll have my clerk go to the judge's office and see if the warrant for Buddy Phelps has been signed. You might as well take him out of the picture as soon as possible. I don't know how long he'll stay out of it, though. The judge will probably grant him bail. If he does, we're right back where we started." She checked her files, "By the way, who is this goofy lawyer Claudia Morris has? He looks like some homeless guy. I understand he represents Dennis Carson also."

Both Seaton and Beeles chuckled, "You have him pegged. But, don't underestimate him. I've seen him pull some big rabbits out some small hats. He uses that country-boy look to his advantage. Be careful with him."

"I'll take that advice, Bob." Her intercom buzzed and she answered, "Bring it in." Looking at the troopers she said, "Your warrant is coming up now."

Seaton turned to his new partner, "I guess we had better go to work." He thanked Nancy Collins again and went to the outer office to pick up the warrant for the arrest of Phelps.

The two troopers had decided to take both their cars out to the Forelands Bar. They arrived and entered the bar together, with Seaton in the lead. Both troopers said good morning to Cuddles, who was seated on her perch.

"What do you two want now?" she snapped.

"We'd like to have a word with Buddy Phelps, if he is available."

"I don't know if he wants to talk to you." She turned on her stool and called toward the open back door, "Buddy, get out here. The troopers want to talk with you."

As they waited, Seaton asked Cuddles, "Who's the new bartender?"

"Her name is Carol. Leave her alone, she's a good one. I have trouble keeping help when you come around. Where is Vito? I haven't seen him since you took him to the hospital. He hasn't even come back to get his check."

"The last I heard he was in therapy for his shoulder. I think he's living in Soldotna," Beeles answered, not wanting to offer too much specific information.

At that moment Buddy Phelps appeared at the back door of the bar. Dressed in jeans, a flannel shirt, and wearing a white apron, he looked like he was working. "Yeah, what is it? I'm kinda busy right now."

Seaton stepped up next to Phelps. "I have a warrant for your arrest for dealing in stolen property. Please put your hands behind your back."

"You what?" said Phelps, stepping back a step.

"We are placing you under arrest. Stand still and put your hands behind your back." Seaton had the handcuffs ready.

Phelps began to protest, but Cuddles interrupted. "Go with them, Buddy. I'll call Grant and have him meet you. I'll have you bailed out before these two can finish their report." Buddy relaxed and put his hands behind him. They led him to Beeles' car and placed him in the backseat. The two cars had not yet left the parking lot when Cuddles dialed Grant Cummings.

Beeles drove into the admitting port at the jail, but Seaton parked outside the gate and walked into the area behind the other patrol car. Beeles opened the rear door of the car as Seaton approached. The two troopers helped Phelps out of the car and into the secure area of the jail where the booking would take place. Seaton walked to the entry door of the booking cage and noticed Nancy Collins in the attorney visiting room across the hall. He entered the booking area to speak with the duty sergeant and pass the warrant numbers to him for the booking.

"Is that Dennis Carson in the attorney room with the DA?" Seaton asked Sergeant Bell.

Bell was tall and lean. His job was to manage the prisoners and staff of the pre-trial facility. He managed 150 prisoners with eight officers. It was a high-stress job, but he did it well and with a sense of humor. "Yeah, Carson should be grateful for a visitor with her looks. It makes me want to be tossed into jail," he smiled playfully.

"Be careful, Bell. She's a lawyer," Seaton smiled back with a wink. By the way, Carson and this new prisoner know each other. They both worked at the Forelands Bar."

"I'll put them in the same dorm and they can discuss old times," said Bell.

"It should be all right; they aren't close friends, as far as I know." Seaton signed the booking remand slip and left the office. Beeles was waiting and the two exited together.

Nancy Collins introduced herself to Carson. She explained to him that Seaton had recommended she stop by to see him. "I understand you have some further statements to make, Mr. Carson. Trooper Sergeant Seaton explained a little bit about it to me because I'm new here. I have read your case file. Before you say anything to me, I must advise you that what you say can be used against you in court. My advice to you is to have your lawyer present while we talk."

"I don't want him here. I want to talk to you." Carson was speaking in an angry tone. "The trooper told me I was going down for two murders and one arson charge. I know I'm going away for a very long time. If I give you some information and cop a plea, will it make a difference in the length of my sentence?"

The new DA was shocked. "Mr. Carson, once again I advise you to have your lawyer present."

"I don't want him here. Cuddles hired him and now she wants me to take the blame for it all, while she and her new hand stay out of jail. I ain't doin' it. She has the same lawyer and he'll sell me out to protect her, 'cause she's payin' him." He was still very angry. "Have you got a tape recorder?"

"Of course," she replied.

"Well, get it out, and I'll say all this on the tape."

She opened her briefcase to get out the micro-recorder. She turned it on and spoke into it, identifying herself and Dennis Carson, adding the date and time as well as the location of the interview. Then she placed the recorder on the metal table and faced Carson. "Mr. Carson, have you been advised to have your attorney present during this interview?"

"Yeah, and I don't want him here."

"Would you like to have another lawyer present to advise you?"

"No, I know what I'm doing. Now get on with it," he said.

"Mr. Carson, you are charged with murder in the death of Larry Williams. You have pled not guilty to the charge. Do you now want to go before the judge and change that plea?"

"No, I didn't kill him intentionally." He paused and said, "Let me start from the beginning. Cuddles, that's Claudia Morris, is my boss. She knew Skip—that's Larry Williams—had the gold. She wanted me to go to Larry's place and take it. I was told there were two leather pouches in a plastic tool box. I went to Skip's place and asked him to show me the gold. He got it out and showed it to me. It sure was purty. There just wasn't no way to take the pouches away from him, so I asked him to get me a soda. When he turned around, I reached an arm around his neck and choked him out. I knew I was doin' wrong and must have been scared, 'cause I squeezed him too tight and too long. It killed him. I didn't mean to do it, but he was dead—I could tell. Skip cooked meth and his lab was out the back door. I got some of his chemicals and spread them around the kitchen floor and in the lab. I picked up the little plastic tool box and dropped a match in the chemicals on my way to the door. I took the box to the bar and went in the back door and upstairs and gave the box to Cuddles. She told me I did a good job, and I went back to work. Now she wants me to take all the blame while she keeps the gold and runs around with her new boyfriend. Cummings, her lawyer, wants me to just say I did it and let her go free. But Ms. Collins, I did what she said and got the gold. I didn't mean to kill ol' Skip. I liked him. He was always nice to me." Carson paused and seemed to be finished.

"Mr. Carson, I'm impressed with your story. We'll have to go over it to clarify several points, but right now I believe your story. If it all checks out,

I will try to get the charge reduced to murder 2, which means you did not intentionally kill Mr. Williams. It will hinge on the fact that you went to Williams' house on orders from your boss, Claudia Morris, with the intent to steal, not kill." This statement by the DA seemed to make Crusher relax somewhat. "Now, let's go back to the start and see if we can iron out some of the points."

Meanwhile out front, the jailers had searched, fingerprinted, photographed, and dressed Phelps in the official jail uniform: an orange jump suit. Two officers escorted him to the pre-trial dorm and assigned him a room. They gave him blankets and necessary toilet items. Once done, they locked the dorm door, allowing him to get into a commons area outside his cell. There were several other inmates in orange jump suits sitting around watching television. He introduced himself and sat, waiting for his lawyer to come to the jail.

An hour later Crusher was returned to the dorm. He was surprised to see Phelps. "What are you doing here?" he asked the new prisoner.

"Time, same as you," answered Phelps wryly.

"Stay away from me while you're here," said Carson, moving to another table.

Chapter 31

Bob Seaton was in his office working on the reports for his arrest warrant service and subsequent incarceration of Buddy Phelps. The report was nearly finished when the phone rang. It was Nancy Collins. She sounded excited.

"I have some good news for you, Sergeant."

"I could use some good news right now," he replied.

"Your friend Dennis Carson fell for the bait you had already suggested to him. He's willing to testify to the fact that Cuddles Morris gave the order to steal the gold from Larry Williams. He was extremely irritated when I added that she denied giving the order and said it was all his idea. I advised him to consult his attorney before making a statement, but he was more interested in making a deal with me than getting legal advice. I have his entire statement on tape. He claims she ordered him to go to the Williams residence and steal the plastic tool box with the gold in it. Carson said he went there and was looking at the gold with Williams when he choked the victim out from behind. He claims he did not intend to kill Williams but in the excitement crushed his throat. He admits setting the place on fire to cover the crime."

"It will be his word against hers in court, Nancy. Will it stand up when the jury hears it?"

"I think it will. Carson has nothing to lose. He knows he's going away for a long time. Even with the first charge of murder one being reduced to second degree, plus arson, he'll probably never see the street again. He'll get life on the other murder charge for killing Lil Danby," she assessed the jury probabilities and a judge's decision. "Dennis is going to spend the rest of his life behind bars."

"What do you think Cuddles will get out of this?" asked the trooper.

"It will be a separate trial and a new jury, but I think I can put her away for life, also. This one will be a little tougher because she'll go down screaming her innocence, but you found the gold in her safe. She claimed ownership of the claim certificates and was the one who stood to gain the most from this plan. I think Phelps will back us up on who possessed the claims when he sold them to that Canadian company. I think he'll testify for us to reduce his own sentence." Nancy Collins was sounding pleased.

"You did a great job, Nancy. I hope it all holds up when it gets to the jury. Thanks for all your help. By the way, I'll have a report on the Phelps arrest by the end of the day and get it to you in the morning." Seaton was glad that he and the new DA were working so well together.

The investigator was home and getting settled in for the night when his telephone rang. There had been an altercation at the pre-trial facility and a prisoner was injured. That prisoner was Buddy Phelps. Seaton put his uniform back on and drove to the jail. An ambulance was parked inside the secure entrance to the jail. The trooper parked in the lot, walked to the front door, and rang the bell for entry. Inside he was met by the shift supervisor who explained what had happened.

"No one told us that Carson and Phelps were enemies. Dayshift put Phelps in the same pre-trial dorm as Carson. There was a confrontation this afternoon, but nothing really happened. Tonight, about an hour ago, there was a fight in the commons area of the dorm. Carson and Phelps were having it out. The other inmates all went to their cells. Carson beat the holy crap out of Phelps before the control room heard anything. We locked the entire dorm down and called an ambulance for Phelps. It took five officers to get Carson into the segregation dorm and locked down. He was one mad monkey. I've seen a lot of mean prisoners in my time, but he's the prize winner."

"How bad is Phelps hurt?" asked Sergeant Seaton.

"He's going to need some stitches. The medics are taking him to the hospital. Our transport officer is going to escort the prisoner. The medic said he didn't think anything was broken, but he was bruised and cut up pretty bad. They're taking him out to the ambulance right now. Do you want to talk to Phelps before he goes to the hospital?"

"No, I'll see Carson first. I'll stop at the hospital on the way back to the office."

"Good enough, Sarge. Come on back and I'll escort you back to the seg cells." Shift Supervisor Sarah Britton was a large woman, both in height and width. She was extremely competent and took no sass from anyone, inmate or staff. She led the way into the secure area of the jail.

Britton opened the outer door to the segregation unit and locked it again behind them. She ordered Carson to step to the back of his cell.

Before unlocking the door she asked the prisoner, "Carson, are you calmed down enough to talk with the trooper like a man or do we have to do this through the door?"

A weak and calm voice on the inside answered, "I'm OK. I'll talk with the trooper."

She glanced at Seaton, "Don't take any chances, Sarge; he's big and he's mean. If there's trouble I'll pull the door closed; it opens inward." She unlocked the cell door and opened it slowly. Carson was seated on his bunk, a swollen eye beginning to close.

"Are you OK, Crusher?" he asked.

"Yeah, that puny guy couldn't hurt me much without a weapon." Carson must have a different definition for "hurt me much" than most folks do.

"Do you want to tell me what happened here tonight?" asked Seaton.

"We were both in the same dorm. After I saw the DA today, he was in my dorm. I told him to stay away from me, but he kept coming to my table and saying things. I finally couldn't take it anymore and took him down. I didn't want to kill him, just mess him up a little. He just wouldn't shut up."

"What did he say to you, Crusher?"

"He knows I really like Cuddles and he kept saying things about what she used to do for a living and how she was now his girl and how she was going to be glad when I go to prison for her." Crusher had his head bent to hide the tears forming in his swollen eyes. "She isn't really bad, Trooper Bob, she just had a tough life."

"Are you sure you don't need a doctor? They have a medic here in the jail. I'll stand by while he comes in if you want to get medical help." Seaton thought the injuries were worse than Crusher was letting on.

"I'm OK. I just want to go to sleep. I'll be OK in the morning. Thanks for coming to see me, though. I ain't mad at nobody here, just Phelps. I'm OK."

"Get some rest, Crusher. I'll be back to see you tomorrow, but don't give the guards any problems tonight, you hear me?"

"I won't, Trooper Bob." He nodded and lay down on the bunk.

Seaton and Britton backed out of the cell and locked the door. On the way back to the supervisor's office she said, "You sure have a calming way with him, Sarge."

"I've known Crusher for a long time. We get along all right. Send me a copy of the incident report when you finish it, will you Sarah?"

"Sure, I'll put it in the trooper pouch in the morning."

She let him out of the institution and waved goodbye. He pulled his collar up against the cold and walked to his patrol car. It was late and Seaton decided to return home and finish the report in the morning, but first he had to stop at the hospital and interview Buddy Phelps—if he was conscious.

Phelps had been treated and taken to a room where a guard had been posted. The doctors had put more than forty stitches on his face and head. He had also suffered a concussion. Seaton found the room on the second floor.

He said hello to the guard, a man Seaton had met on several similar occasions. The guard remained outside the door when the trooper entered. Seaton found Phelps awake but in obvious pain.

"Thanks for getting me a nice room at the jail," Phelps mumbled through swollen lips.

"Hey, I'm not a tour guide, just a hard-working trooper trying to make ends meet." Seaton could see the damage to his head and face but wondered about the damage to the rest of his body. "Are you up to talking with me right now? Or would you rather I come back in the morning?"

"They have me doped up, but I'm OK. I can't sleep anyway." Phelps was a mess. "What do you want to know?"

"I came to hear your side of the story. Why did Crusher attack you?" Seaton had his pen and notebook in his hands.

"I guess I said something he didn't like."

"Exactly what did you say that set him off?"

"He wasn't in the dorm when they put me in there. Later he came back and got mad right away when he saw me. I really don't know what got him so riled up."

"He said you made some comments about Cuddles," Seaton prompted, to get more specifics.

"I might have mentioned her—but nothing that should have made him go ballistic like he did."

"Do you want to tell me what kind of arrangement you and Claudia have?" asked the trooper.

"Not much of an arrangement. She had asked me to sell some mining claims for her, which I did. I came down here from Fairbanks to give her the paperwork on the sale. Crusher had been arrested and her new bartender was in the hospital. She asked me to fill in and hire a new bartender. Claudia and I go back a long way. She calls me once in a while to do a job for her. I owe her and she pays me well. It's a good arrangement for both of us." The talking must have pulled at his stitches because he reached up to feel them.

"It's really none of my business, but do you and Cuddles have a personal relationship on the side?"

Phelps tried to smile, "No, I like my girls a little slimmer, but Carson thinks we have. That's why he went off on me in the jail."

"If what you say checks out, I'll have to file assault charges against Crusher. I don't think he really cares, given that he's already charged in two murders. Do you think she'll be in his corner when he goes to trial?" Seaton didn't expect an answer.

"I think she wants to stay far away from him. She wants him to take it like a man and accept all the blame." It was an unexpected statement from Phelps.

"Did she tell you she had anything to do with the death of Williams?" he asked.

"She never said, but she asked me about the gold when she first got it, right after the fire. I have to think she told Crusher to go over there and take the gold, no matter what it took." It must be the drugs causing him to talk, thought Seaton.

"I know you're hurting tonight; I'll come back tomorrow with a statement form and we'll make it out then. Get some rest. I'll see you tomorrow." Seaton stood. Phelps nodded and closed his eyes.

In the hall he said good night to the guard and drove home. It had been a long and eventful day. He needed the rest. He checked his watch and decided it was too late to be calling Beeles. He would fill him in on tonight's events when they came to the office in the morning.

Chapter 32

Seaton was in the office working on the report from the night before when Beeles came into the station. He gave Beeles a rundown on the fight at the jail and the interview with Phelps. Seaton wanted to finish the report and drive to the hospital for a statement from Phelps. When he had the witness statement in hand, he wanted to visit the DA and try to convince her they had enough corroborating information to arrest Claudia Morris. Beeles helped enter part of the information into the computer and between them it was finished in less than an hour. They rode together to the hospital to have Phelps make his statement.

A different guard was stationed outside the hospital room this morning. Seaton had never seen this one before and introduced himself and Beeles. Inside the room Phelps was just finishing his breakfast. His face was even more swollen this morning and the bruising much darker.

"Good morning, Buddy. Are you feeling any better this morning?" asked Sergeant Seaton.

"Yes, a little. Sore as the devil, but I feel better. I was kinda out of it last night when you were here, but I remember it all this morning. I suppose you want me to make out a statement form."

"Actually, if you prefer, Beeles here can write it up if you want. When we finish you can read it to make sure it's correct and sign it. Do you want to have Jason write it for you?"

"Yeah, I think it would be best. My head hurts really bad if I move around much; thanks." Phelps adjusted his pillow to a more comfortable position then nodded he was ready to start.

Corporal Beeles sat on a chair next to the bed, using a clipboard for a writing table. Seaton asked questions and Phelps narrated his answers. The process took more than an hour. Phelps needed to rest often. When they finished, Beeles handed the multiple sheets of text to the patient/prisoner. Phelps read it and agreed to sign.

The troopers were preparing to exit the room when the doctor came in to examine the patient. They waited until the doctor was finished and asked him about releasing Phelps to return to jail. The doctor said he would like to keep him one more day because of the concussion but thought he could go back to jail tomorrow morning. The troopers thanked the man in the white coat and left the hospital.

Their next stop was the courthouse to meet with Nancy Collins. She had just come from the courtroom on another case when they caught up with her.

"I got word there was a fight at the jail last night after I left, involving Dennis Carson and the prisoner you brought in, Mr. Phelps." It was more of an inquiry than a statement.

"That's right. Old Crusher beat the heck out of Phelps. He's in the hospital. The doctor said he will release him back to jail tomorrow. He has a concussion and a lot of stitches and bruises. I talked to both of them and, as long as they stay separated, it should be OK for Phelps to return to the jail." Seaton handed her the report they had just finished, along with a copy of the witness statement by Phelps.

She scanned through the sheets, nodding now and again. "How are the jail people going to want to deal with this? Are they going to handle it in-house or do a criminal complaint for assault?"

"We haven't been to the jail yet. We'll be going there next. I'll call you and let you know." Seaton and Beeles stood in the office.

"Is there something else, Sergeant?" she asked.

"I hope so," said Seaton, going on to explain it to the DA: "In the course of investigating the assault, both parties mentioned the gold. Crusher confirmed Claudia sent him to steal the gold. And, while talking with Phelps, he confirmed she was in possession of the gold the night of the murder and fire at the Williams place. I think all this confirms she sent Crusher to get the pouches, making her an accessory before the fact and a party to the murder. She's already charged with the crime, and is out on bail, but she thinks Crusher is going to take the fall for her and she won't have to go to trial. I want to nudge her a little. I want her to know I'm going after her for Skip Williams' death. It might shake her enough to make her do something stupid."

"Are you saying you want me to give you permission to harass a suspect?" she asked with a tongue in cheek tone.

"Of course not. I would never do that, nor would I harass a suspect, however I might use some small misleading statements to influence her actions." Seaton knew the legal games and played them well.

"If you do, I don't want to know about them." She played the legal games well, also.

Sarah Britton was the shift supervisor on duty again today. Beeles and Seaton entered through the front door where Britton met them. She led the two men to her office.

"How is Carson today?" asked Seaton.

"He's OK. He's not a problem, but I wouldn't want to have to deal with him if he was. He's a big man. We already know he's a mean one."

"I have a question for you, Sarah. The DA asked if you were going to handle this in-house with a disciplinary hearing or send it to the DA for criminal prosecution?"

"Both these men are only here temporarily, both pending trial. If you want to add to the already pending charges we can give it to the DA, but it will save time and money if we handle it with a disciplinary hearing. Your choice, Sarge." Britton had seen it all before and knew an assault charge on top of the felonies they were now facing wouldn't even be noticed.

Seaton thought a moment. "I don't think additional charges will make a difference. How about we let you handle it? Have the disciplinary committee keep Carson in segregation until his trial. That way these two will be separated and there shouldn't be any further problem with them."

"Sounds good to me. I'll call the chairman of the committee and let him know how you want to play it." She made a note on the desk pad.

"Thanks Sarah, we have other issues to deal with, if you'll let us out." She escorted them to the front door and let them out into the cold, snowy day.

In the car Seaton turned to Beeles, with a grin: "Why don't we go pay a visit to our favorite bar owner?"

"Now that sounds like a fun thing to do!" said the enthusiastic Corporal Beeles.

The two men motored to North Kenai and the Forelands Bar. It was snowing hard now. They stomped the snow off as they entered the bar, which was empty except for the bartender.

"Nice day out there, isn't it?" Carol joked as they entered.

"If you're a polar bear," replied Seaton, unzipping his coat. "Is Cuddles in?"

"No, she said she was going to Kenai to see her lawyer about something."

"Did she say what it was?" asked Beeles.

"No, but she and the lawyer have been doing some stuff for a woman in Kenai. I think she was the sister of the guy killed the night of the fire back behind here."

"Skip Williams?" Seaton was astounded. "I didn't know he had a sister."

"I'm new here, but I don't think anyone knew. I know she was in rehab for some time and is out now. Cuddles has been helping her out. From what

I've heard when the lawyer was here, Cuddles is signing the property the brother owned over to the sister. I heard her tell another lawyer she wanted to leave half this place to the sister if she dies. I thought that was a wonderful thing to do." The new bartender had not been privy to the entire story, but she was right about it being a nice thing to do. This was totally out of character for Cuddles.

"The lawyer—was that Grant Cummings?" asked Beeles.

"No, it was someone named Quimby. I think he's a new one. When he was here they didn't seem to really know each other."

"Thanks Carol, we'll catch up with her later," said Seaton, nudging Beeles toward the door.

Outside, Seaton commented to Beeles, "The new bartender is pretty chatty. I don't think Cuddles will take kindly to her bartender telling us of her business. It could get her fired. We did learn some things, though. We need to find this sister of Skip Williams. Carol said she's been in rehab. Let's go to Serenity House and ask a few questions. We might get lucky."

"Let's hope so. And I agree about Carol; it wouldn't do to have a good ear like her fired from her job," said Beeles.

Back in Kenai the troopers stopped at the office of Serenity House. They have an excellent record with drug and alcohol users, and Seaton knew the director well. The two went inside to confer with her.

An ex-user herself, Teena Watts was, by far, the most knowledgeable person to ever hold the post. It wasn't easy to fool this savvy director. "What can I do for you boys?" she asked when she came to the front desk.

"Hello, Teena, I would like you to meet my new partner, Corporal Jason Beeles."

"Pleased to meet you, Beeles. What brings you to this place?"

"We understand there's been a resident here by the name of Williams. Are you allowed to tell us where we can find her?" asked Beeles.

"No, I can't, but I'll contact her and ask her to get in touch with you."

Seaton handed her a card. "Have her call me at this number, will you please, Teena? It's important. Tell her she's not in any trouble. We just want to see her about her brother. We would have contacted her earlier, but we didn't know about her until today."

An hour later, Seaton's cell phone rang. It was Pamela Williams. "Teena Watts said you wanted to talk to me about my brother. He's dead, you know."

"Yes, we know, and we're sorry for your loss. Please, can we meet you somewhere and talk?" Seaton asked pleasantly.

"Yes, I'd like that. Where would you like to meet?"

"Can you come to the trooper office?" asked Seaton.

"Yes, if I can come now. I have a job and have to work later this afternoon."

"That will be fine. We're in Kenai right now, but I'll head to the office and meet you there. Ask for me, Sergeant Seaton, when you get to the front desk." He hung up and said to Beeles, "Let's go to the office, partner. We have to meet her there. He put the car in gear and made his way toward Soldotna.

"I hope she's friendly," commented Beeles from the passenger seat.

When Pamela Williams arrived at trooper headquarters, she was met at the front desk by Beeles who showed her to the office of the Sergeant.

"How do you do," she said as she entered. "I'm Pamela Williams."

"I'm Corporal Jason Beeles and this is Sergeant Investigator Seaton. The sergeant was acquainted with your brother."

"How do you do, Sergeant. I'll get right to the point: I have some questions of my own. I want to know what happened to my brother. No one will tell me exactly how he died. I know he died in a house fire, but that's all anyone will tell me. Can you tell me any more than that?"

"Please sit down, Ms. Williams." She was a thin, good-looking woman but showed the ravages of long-term drug use. She sat, folding her hands in her lap. "I'm sorry to be the one to tell you this, but your brother was murdered. We have the suspected killer in jail awaiting trial. I'm sorry I can't give you much more information than that at this time because an investigation is still on-going. Please accept my sympathy. I knew Skip and he was doing his best to turn his life around when he met his end."

There were tears in her eyes. "I suspected something like that. I came up here to get Skip to help me, but when I got here he was dead. I didn't know what to do, but Claudia Morris from the Forelands Bar said Skip was a friend of hers and offered to help me out. She has been so wonderful. She got me into rehab and she is giving me the other property Skip owned so I'll have a place to live. She is so very kind."

"Did she tell you how Skip came to own the second piece of property?" asked Seaton.

"No, she just said she got it from the court because of the money Skip owed her. She said she didn't know he had a relative either. Like I said, she's been wonderful to me."

"What I'm about to tell you is confidential information. You must not tell anyone, especially Claudia Morris. Do you understand?"

"Of course, but what is this all about?" She sat wide-eyed, wondering what she was about to hear.

"The original owner of the property your brother inherited was a man by the name of Otis Fairfax. He died in an airplane crash. He had no relatives and was friends with Skip. He left a handwritten will, giving all his possessions to your brother," Seaton explained.

"That was so nice," she exclaimed. "The trailer is in very good condition and is very clean. I was impressed with the neatness. It isn't much on the outside, but inside it's really nice."

"The part you must not tell anyone is this: Skip inherited some other items also. Among them were a number of mining claim certificates. They're involved in the other investigation I told you about." Seaton looked her in the eye for acknowledgement. She nodded and pulled her body to the edge of her seat. "The other thing he inherited from old Otis was two small leather pouches filled with gold, a rather large amount of gold. I seized it and have it here in our evidence locker. Once the criminal proceedings are complete, the court will probably give the pouches to you."

"Good gracious, Sergeant, no one told me about this. How much gold is there?" She was excited.

"We've had it weighed by a jeweler and have an estimate. Based on the price of gold at the time we had it appraised, it was near $1.75 million. You will be a very rich woman, Pamela."

"What?" Her eyes flew open wide. "I don't believe it! I never expected ... Oh, Sergeant I don't know what to say." There were tears in her eyes.

"I want to caution you again about saying anything about this. There are some dangerous people out there who would do anything for this gold. Be very careful," advised Seaton. "I'll be available if you feel threatened or have questions. Don't hesitate to contact me."

"Thank you both for being so kind and caring. I'll stay in touch with you." She shook the hands of both men and Beeles escorted her to the front door again.

Chapter 33

Claudia Morris was on her throne when a well-dressed man entered her establishment. He wore a wool felt hat, custom-tailored overcoat, and scarf. Upon entering the bar he took off his hat and unbuttoned the overcoat to reveal a three-piece suit. He walked directly to the bar and asked the bartender if Claudia Morris was in.

"At the end of the bar," she said, pointing toward Cuddles.

"Thank you," he said politely, before walking to where cuddles was seated.

As he approached, Cuddles eyed him suspiciously and asked, "What do you want?"

"Are you Miss Claudia Morris?" he inquired.

"Yeah, what do you want?" she asked again.

The stranger reached inside his suit coat and produced a thick bunch of paper with her name on the cover sheet. "I am Serge Winter. I represent the court and am presenting you with this summons. You are to appear in a civil action at the Kenai Court on the listed date and time. This action is brought by one Vito Hocker for damages. If you have any questions or cannot appear, you must notify the clerk of the court. Do you understand what I just told you?"

"Vito! Why is he suing me?" she asked.

"You will have to ask the court that question. I just serve the papers and you have been legally served. Thank you." With that he turned and walked out the door.

The big woman read the papers. Vito was suing her for personal damages, medical expenses, and loss of work, as well as the cost of retraining for another occupation since his injuries precluded him from returning to his bartending profession.

She was shaking as she dialed Grant Cummings. "Grant, get out here. I was just served some papers saying Vito is suing me. Get out here now."

He grumbled and growled but said he would come as soon as he finished with his current task. He failed to mention she had awakened him from a pleasant nap. An hour later he appeared at the Forelands Bar.

Cuddles landed off the stool with a thud and motioned for the lawyer to follow her to the office. Once there she handed him the summons. He read the several pages without looking at her. Once done he handed the papers back to her.

"OK, so Vito is suing you for his injuries. That shouldn't surprise you. He was working at the time and another employee attacked him. Why are you calling me?"

"Listen to me, you fat hillbilly, I pay you a lot of money to keep me out of court. So do what I pay you to do!"

"Don't get nasty with me, Cuddles. I know where all the skeletons are buried around here. I know what Vito did in your office and why Crusher beat him up. My advice is to just pay Vito. You don't want all this coming out in court. Remember, you don't have Crusher to change Vito's mind. In fact, he may become a witness for Vito. Since I represented Crusher in another matter, the court may not let me represent you in this case. Get another lawyer."

"Why, you pompous windbag! Get out of my office and my bar. For that matter, get out of my life! I don't need you. I want all the records of our business delivered to me by tonight. If it isn't, I may bail Crusher out of jail and send him to get it."

The lawyer turned to look at his one-time friend. "Is that a threat, Cuddles? I'm holding the aces here. So back off and shut up. You can't fire me and you know it. Call me when you calm down." Without another word he walked out of the office, down the steps, and out of the bar.

Cuddles sat at her desk for a long while, thinking, cursing, plotting, and crying. She was running out of options as well as money. With Crusher out of the picture she had no one to do her dirty work. Buddy was in jail. She was out on bail. The troopers had taken the bags of gold from her safe. Cummings was refusing to help her. She was running out of people she could use. She stood up and pushed the door closed to cry in private.

Once she had composed her emotions and taken a shower, she was sitting in her office wearing a chenille bathrobe and drinking a cup of hot tea when the phone rang. "Hello, this is Claudia," she answered.

"Hello, Claudia, this is Pamela. I'm at work and can't talk long, but the troopers called me today to come to the office. They said they had no idea Skip had a sister and therefore had not contacted me. They told me Skip was murdered. Why didn't someone tell me?"

"We just wanted to spare you any heartache, dear," Cuddles explained weakly.

"You should have known I would find out sooner or later. Is that why you have been helping me?"

"Partly, but not entirely. The truth is, I saw myself in you. I was once just like you: on drugs, falling deeper and deeper into a pit I couldn't dig myself out of. I got hurt and couldn't do anything for myself. That's when Crusher came to my aid. I fought my way back into life. I took the settlement I got from my injury and bought this place. I've been sitting here at the bar getting fatter each year, feeling sorry for myself every day. I wanted to keep you from the same fate. I wanted you to be able to get back into life as it really is—good and bad. I hope you don't hate me for that."

"I don't hate you, Claudia, I'm just confused. Everyone says you are a hard woman, but you have been sweet and kind to me. I thank you for that. You are the best friend I have ever had, but I still don't understand why I wasn't told about my brother."

"Forgive me, Pamela, I should have told you. My life has become very complicated in recent months. I made a bad decision and I'm sorry."

"I don't blame you, Claudia. I have to get back to work now, but I'll call you tomorrow and perhaps we can talk."

"I'd like that. Good night, Pamela." Cuddles was crying again as she hung up the phone. No good deed ever goes unpunished, she remembered someone once saying.

The following morning a prison transport officer came to the hospital and picked up Buddy Phelps for the ride back to Wildwood. He was searched and dressed in a clean prison jumpsuit and returned to his original cell. Phelps was sore and aching but glad to be out of the hospital. The booking officer had told him Crusher was isolated and would not bother him again.

A few hours later, Grant Cummings came to visit with him. In the attorney visiting room, Cummings he explained he no longer represented Carson and would handle the case for Phelps. The jail supervisor had informed the lawyer there would be no criminal charges against either of the combatants, but a disciplinary hearing would be held to determine what was to be done with the two fighting prisoners.

"What about the original charges, dealing in stolen property?" Phelps asked.

Cummings leaned back in his chair and tucked one hand under the strap of his overalls. "I've been thinking about that," he said. "The DA doesn't want you. They want Cuddles. They already have Crusher. I think we can make a deal with her."

"What kind of a deal?" asked Buddy. "How much time will I have to do?"

"Are you willing to give up the money you got from the sale of the mining claims?" the lawyer inquired.

"I think it's already gone. I'll never make a profit from this deal."

"I agree. Now, here's what I was thinking: we agree to forfeit the proceeds of the sale in return for a reduced sentence. I'm hoping to get it down to time served. The DA has a full calendar and I think she'll go for the deal. That would get you out right away. How do you feel about it?" Cummings asked.

"It sounds good to me. Is Cuddles picking up the tab for your fee?" asked Buddy.

"I'll see that she does," said Cummings, not letting on he had a fight with her.

"OK, take it to the district attorney and get me out of here."

Within days a deal had been made. The terms offered by Cummings had been accepted by the state. Phelps would forfeit all proceeds from the sale of the mining claims and in return he would be released with time served. Cuddles said he could come back to the bar and work for her, if he cared to. He had to do something for the rest of the winter and it was warmer in the Forelands Bar than in Fairbanks. Two days later he was released from jail. His life could now go on, with a few changes. First off was the fact he now had a felony on his record. He was not happy about that, but it was better than serving a long sentence. The second bad change was all his cuts and bruises, along with the several stitches on his head and face. He was in no shape to travel or do heavy labor, but working for Cuddles did not include either. She picked him up when he was released and drove him to the Forelands.

There was little conversation during the drive. Arriving at the bar, she told him to occupy the room he had earlier, to rest up, and they would discuss what was to happen next. In his room he showered and put on a clean set of clothing. That act alone made him feel better. He stretched out on the bed and fell asleep, the first restful sleep he had experienced in many days.

When he awoke, he washed his face and started down to the bar, but the smell of steak cooking stopped him. He followed the aroma to its source and found his boss busy in her apartment kitchen.

"Come in, Buddy. I thought you'd be hungry when you came around. I broiled a couple of rib steaks, and there's a baked potato and salad. Do you want a drink with your dinner?"

"Not tonight, thanks. I am hungry, though. Do you have any coffee?"

"In the electric pot next to the stove. Help yourself." She was busy setting the table. Buddy thought she sounded particularly cheerful tonight.

At dinner she asked about Crusher and how he was doing. He asked about what his duties were to be now. She said they would discuss it later. After dinner she cleared the table and poured two glasses of a good Merlot. Finally she sat.

"I have been thinking all day on what I want you to do. I think I'm going to take a little vacation and I'd like you to run the place for me while I'm gone. Do you think you are up to it? Physically, I mean. You still look pretty beat up."

This wasn't the answer he was expecting. "You sort of caught me by surprise, Cuddles. What brought this on?"

"Things have not gone well for me recently. I've had so much to worry about, I can't take it any longer. I need to get away for a while. The lawyers are hounding me, the troopers are hounding me, and I have always had Crusher to insulate me from problems. Now he's gone and things are coming at me faster than I care to admit. I've been thinking I should go somewhere warm and sunny for a few weeks. You know—California, Arizona, or Florida. Just get away for a while." She had a strange far-away look in her eyes. "Do you think you can handle this place while I'm gone?"

"I'm sure there are some things you'll have to fill me in on, but I think I can manage. That new bartender is darn good and I can count on her to help me. Yeah, I can do it, Cuddles. When do you plan to leave?" asked Phelps.

"Within a couple of days, I think. We can begin to talk about the bank accounts and billing tomorrow. I'll make a list of the quirks in the building you need to know." There was sadness in her face. "Thank you, Buddy. This takes a big load off me. Thank you."

Chapter 34

Cuddles was in an unusually good mood the following day. She came down to open the bar wearing a large, long, bright yellow dress. She was humming a tune while she worked. She opened the front door to see the weather. The sun was shining, making it seem warmer than the zero on the thermometer. She closed the door and prepared the drawer for the cash register. The lights were turned on, the cash drawer in place, and the bar ready for business when Buddy Phelps came into the room.

"Nice day outside," Buddy commented.

"Yes it is," she replied. "Have you had breakfast? I want to get started on what you'll have to do each day."

"I'll have breakfast later if you're ready to give me my marching orders now," offered Buddy.

"I've started a list for you. You already know most of it. It's just the daily routine—how to pay the vendors and who to call if the heat or refrigeration breaks down. When I leave, you can drive me to the airport and keep the Kia to use while I'm gone."

"OK, I can do all that easily, but here are some things I don't know—personal things, like your bank account numbers for making deposits and where to contact you if there is a problem." Buddy was uncomfortable with some of the responsibilities.

"I'll get you the account numbers, but run this place like you owned it. You're the boss while I'm gone. If you make a mistake, it's OK. I make them all the time. I chose you because I think you're a good businessman. You'll run this place as well as me. I don't expect you to run it like I do but like you think it should be run. Try not to lose too much money, because I'm running low right now." She snickered at him with the last comment.

"I'll try to keep you solvent, Cuddles. Now, where can I contact you if the need arises?" he asked, ready to write down the numbers.

"You can't, Buddy. I don't know where I'll be or how long I'll be gone. I'll try to call you a couple of times a week to check in."

"What if there's an emergency of some kind?"

"That is one reason I don't want to be found. *You* handle them."

"OK, boss, if that's the way you want it. Don't you think the troopers or the court or your lawyer will be asking where you went or how long you'll be gone?"

"I expect they will. Don't even tell them I'm gone, especially Grant Cummings. The troopers will be looking for me, undoubtedly, but they can worry on their own. If you don't know you can't tell them, right?"

"Will you be accessing your bank account from wherever you are? I'll have to know how much money I have to work with for stock and any repairs and wages. And what about our tax payments? These folks will want their share." Buddy was, indeed, a good businessman.

"All the tax numbers are on my desk. I'll stop by the bank with you and put you on the accounts before I leave. Any other questions?"

"I can't think of any right now, but I probably will as soon as you're gone." Buddy Phelps was realizing the enormous responsibility with which he had just been entrusted.

"Good, I'm going to my office and try to book a flight to somewhere warm and pleasant." She plopped off her stool, humming again, and disappeared out the rear door.

Phelps continued with his morning duties, stocking the coolers behind the bar, taking out the trash, and filling the coolers in the back of the bar. Carol came in at her usual time and began her morning routine, wiping down the bar and tables, sweeping the large floor, and wiping glassware. Buddy spent his time reviewing his list of responsibilities, trying to think of any unanswered questions. His list was complete and he could think of nothing that Cuddles had not covered in her briefing.

It was noon when Phelps climbed the stairs to his room and Cuddles' office. He was going into his own room when she poked her head out of the office door.

"Got a minute, Buddy?" she called.

"Sure." What now? he wondered.

"My flight out of Kenai is at 10:30 tonight. I'll pack this afternoon. I'm catching the redeye out of Anchorage. C'mon, Buddy, we'll go into town to the bank and I'll buy your lunch." She seemed almost giddy in her mood.

"You seem pretty chipper today, Boss," commented Phelps, smiling. "I feel like you're about to play some dirty trick on me."

"I am, Buddy," she smiled broadly and winked. "I'm leaving you in charge and I'm getting away from it all for a while. I want to thank you for giving me the opportunity. Now, go tell Carol we're going to town."

Buddy was driving the SUV when he asked one last time, "Are you sure you want to do this, Cuddles?"

"I'm more than sure; I'm desperate. I need this time off more than you can imagine. My health is going downhill, fast. I have to get away. I know people are going to think I'm running away, but it's not true, Buddy. Please don't tell anyone where I'm going or what I'm doing. I'll be back when I can, but I don't even have a return date. I'm counting on you." She normally spoke without looking at the other person, but today she stared directly at Buddy Phelps, with sadness in her eyes.

Their first stop was the bank, where Buddy signed a signature card and the forms to add his name to the account. While he was filling out the papers she was at another window withdrawing a large amount of cash. With their business finished at the bank, the next stop was Louie's Restaurant where the same small, slim waitress with the long braid down her back came to their table to wait on them. She was pleasant and obviously remembered Buddy with, "I see you're back in town."

Cuddles didn't drink often, especially outside her own establishment, but today she ordered a bottle of Pinot Noir. She noted the inquisitive look on the face of her new partner. "It's five o'clock somewhere," she commented, raising her glass and taking a large gulp. "What you are about to do for me is a monumental task. You're married to the business. I know how hard it's going to be, Buddy, and I promise I'll make it worth the trouble."

"You pay me enough, Cuddles. You just go and get your life straight. I'll be here if you need me. If you get worried, just call." Buddy tried to be reassuring, but he didn't think it came across that way.

The two had their late lunch and returned to the bar. Cuddles went to her room to rest and pack for her evening flight. Buddy checked in with Carol at the bar.

"It looks like you'll be working for me for a while, Carol. I hope that doesn't pose a problem for you."

"Nah, I like you, and from what I've seen you're easy to work for." The comment came from a very experienced and self-assured person. "Is there anything you want me to change to suit you?"

"No, you do a great job and I'm happy to have you here. Between us we should be able to keep the joint running until she returns. And before you ask, I don't know how long she'll be gone or where she's going. She didn't tell me."

There was a blast of cold air when the front door opened. Two big men in work clothes entered. Carol recognized the occasional customers. "Come on in, boys. It's warm in here," Carol greeted them when they closed the front door.

Phelps decided to study the bookkeeping and try to make his figures look as good as those of the boss lady. Both Phelps and Cuddles spent a quiet evening upstairs above the bar. It was getting late when she called to him.

"OK, Buddy, I guess it's time to go. Any last minute questions?" she asked the new manager.

"They probably won't arise until you're out of sight," he smiled at his boss. "Have a great time, Cuddles, wherever you go."

The two rode quietly during the trip down to Kenai and the airport. She seemed relaxed; perhaps it was the bottle of wine at lunch, thought Phelps. At the terminal he carried her luggage to the check-in and waited with her until her flight was called. He put an arm around her shoulders and hugged her, "See you later, Boss." She nodded and shuffled to the plane, struggling with the stairs on the boarding ramp. Phelps stood at the window watching until the plane was in the air, wondering if he was up to the job. He had just turned to leave the terminal when his cell phone jingled.

"We got trouble, Buddy," Carol notified him. "Those two construction guys are getting pretty rowdy. The Hagel brothers and two of their friends are here and there's going to be a fight. I asked them to leave, but nobody is going."

"Stay behind the bar and be safe. I'll call the troopers. You did your job when you asked them to leave. I'm on my way." Buddy dialed 911 and reported the disturbance. The roads were icy and he pushed the speed as much as he dared, arriving at the Forelands Bar in ten minutes. Two trooper cars pulled into the front parking area as he drove to the back of the bar. He ran inside and found Carol standing behind the bar with a whiskey bottle in her hand, held by the neck.

The six patrons were leaving her alone but taunting each other. The Hagel bunch, led by Tom, was threatening the construction duo. One table had been broken and chairs overturned. Broken glass covered the floor behind the damaged table.

"Break it up," shouted Phelps, as the troopers entered the front door.

The appearance of the uniforms distracted the combatants and the two groups began to separate. "Everybody, calm down and sit down!" shouted one of the troopers. The men all obeyed and the hostilities seemed to calm. One of the troopers went to the bar and asked Carol if she was alright.

The troopers each took a group of men to interview. The first trooper sat with the two construction workers, while the second stood near the four bikers.

The first trooper recognized one of the construction men: "Didn't you just get out of jail for a bar fight in Kenai?" he asked the larger of the two.

"Yeah, we did ten days for disorderly. That's why we came out here to have a drink."

"Who started the brawl tonight?" asked the trooper.

The answer came from the same man as before. "They did. We didn't have any problem until those bikers came in."

"What was the argument about?" the trooper asked.

"I don't know. They came in and started to insult us and we stood our ground. It just escalated from there."

"Stay here and stay in your seats. I'll be right back." The trooper stood and walked to the bar where Carol was standing, Buddy now alongside her.

"You guys got here in a hurry," Buddy commented.

"We were both out north when the call came. Which of you was tending bar when the fight started?"

"I was," answered Carol.

"The big guy says they were peaceful until the bikers came in, is that true?"

"Pretty much; they had been drinking all afternoon and I was about to shut them off when Hagel and his bunch came in. Those two said some nasty things to the Hagels and it went downhill from there. Funny thing, though, these two kept it up. They wouldn't quit. The Hagel bunch tried to ignore them, but they just kept it up. The table got broken when Chuck Hagel jumped up to face the two over there. There weren't any punches thrown, but I tried to get the two construction guys to leave. But they just kept it up."

"We'll take these two off your hands. Have they paid their tab?" asked the trooper.

"Not yet," answered Carol.

The trooper stepped over to where the other trooper was talking with the leather-clad bunch. "What did they say took place?" he asked.

"These guys say the other two started it. Tom Hagel says he got word someone was coming to the bar to trash it, someone who just got out. Dennis Carson asked them to do the job for him—according to Tom Hagel."

"I don't know about the motive, but the bartender says the Hagels tried to avoid a confrontation and the other two persisted. Did you get ID from all of these men?" asked the first trooper.

"Yes, I got it," said the second.

"OK, let's take the other two in for disorderly and defrauding an innkeeper. They're going to be a handful if they decide to resist," said the first trooper.

"Don't worry about it, Trooper. My brother and the others will back you up if they start anything," Chuck Hagel spoke for the first time.

The two troopers approached the construction workers and ordered them to put their hands behind them to be handcuffed. At first they stiffened to resist but saw the bikers willing to back the troopers and complied. They were led out to the patrol cars and driven to jail.

Chuck Hagel spoke to Carol when the troopers had gone. "We came down here to stop those guys. Sorry about the mess; we'll help clean it up. Tell Cuddles we got word there was going to be trouble and we came to stop it. Crusher hired those guys to mess up the place. He wanted you taken down, too," he said to Buddy Phelps.

Buddy was truly grateful for their help. "We'll take care of the mess, Chuck. Sit over there and Carol will bring you a round on the house."

The bikers moved to another table and Carol brought them a fresh round of drinks. Buddy went to the back room for a broom and a mop and returned to clean up the damage.

Finally the bar emptied and Carol and Buddy were alone. "Not bad for a first day, eh, Carol?" the new manager smiled and shook his head.

"I hope it isn't going to be like this every day working for you," she smiled and wiped the bar.

"How do you feel about coming upstairs for a drink and some dinner? I'll help you lock up."

Carol liked the offer, but refused. "I'd better not tonight, but thanks anyway. Some other time, maybe?"

Chapter 35

District Attorney Nancy Collins was at her desk, up to her eyebrows in cases when her phone rang. It was Sergeant Bob Seaton. She had been expecting the call, since there had been two more arrests at the Forelands Bar.

"Hello, Bob," she answered, "What are you boys doing over there? Are you trying to see how much I can take?"

"Something like that," was his cheerful answer.

"What do you need this morning, Bob? I'm really busy. You folks keep arresting North Roaders."

"As a matter of fact, I'm calling about that very thing. Last night we arrested two guys for fighting at the Forelands Bar. The word we get is that the fight was paid for by Crusher Carson."

"Wait a minute. I thought Carson was in segregation at the jail. How could he do that?"

"Jailhouse telegraph. We got the information third-hand by the same route. Nothing can be confirmed, but I believe it." Seaton was leading up to something.

"What does this have to do with me?" asked the DA.

"I called to see if we can get the two fighters something more than misdemeanor disorderly charges? Is it possible to boost the charges to a felony, somehow?" he asked.

"How much damage was done to the bar?" she asked.

"According to the arresting officers there wasn't much damage. The Hagel brothers and friends stopped it."

"I'm sorry, Bob, but I don't see any way we can do anything except disorderly and defrauding an innkeeper," she judged. "We can't go around making up charges, you know that."

"I know, but there's more to it, even though I have no real proof." Seaton was apologetic and frustrated.

"Carson goes to trial in a couple of weeks. He's going away for the rest of his life. I think that will end the threats to the Forelands Bar. But, if you can find a witness to back felony charges against the two combatants, I'll file on them," she explained her limitations.

"OK, Nancy, it was just a thought. Thanks; I'll let you get back to work."

The next several weeks were quiet for Seaton and Beeles. They were thankful because it gave them time to review and rewrite all the reports before the trial dates.

Carson had been seeing his public defender, Alan Lewis, on a regular basis. When the trial date arrived in late February Carson was in court dressed in a new suit. A jury had been selected and seated, but the public defender asked the judge for a private hearing. Once the jury was led away, he asked the judge if it was appropriate for his client to enter a change of plea in accordance with the agreement reached with the district attorney. The judge agreed and the hearing was short. The judge asked the DA if she wished to change the plea agreement from what the public defender had stated. She said it was acceptable as is. The judge ordered a sentence in accordance with the agreement: Dennis Carson was sentenced to serve two consecutive life sentences without parole. There was to be no appeal.

Crusher Carson stared at his huge fists resting on the defendant's table during the entire hearing. His jaw muscles bulged with the tension, but he never uttered a word. The jury was dismissed and Carson taken back to Wildwood. Prior to leaving the courthouse, he conferred with his public defender one last time, asking him to come to the jail; there were some papers he wanted the lawyer to file for him before being transferred to another prison. The State of Alaska would decide where he would serve his time. In all likelihood it would be at the maximum security prison, Spring Creek Correctional Facility, in Seward, Alaska.

Seaton sat in the rear of the courtroom with Fire Marshal Eustes Burns during the hearing. When it was over and Carson was led from the courtroom, Seaton turned to Burns and asked, "Well, Burns, How do you feel now?"

"Relieved … I think justice was done. The best part was, I didn't have to testify. I liked that part." Burns was wearing a satisfied grin on his face. "This is one case I am happy to close."

"I know how you feel. It's been fun working with you, Burns. If we ever have another case like this I hope we can work it together again. Thanks for everything." Seaton shook the hand of the fire marshal as they left the courthouse.

It was after lunch when Alan Lewis entered the jail to see Crusher Carson. He waited in the attorney visiting room while Carson was brought up. Crusher was quiet and subdued as he came to the meeting.

"Sorry I couldn't get you a better deal, Dennis. The state was dead set on a long sentence. I want you to know if there is ever anything I can do for you, please ask."

"There is something I want you to do for me before they ship me out of here." He retrieved several sheets of notebook paper from his pocket. "I've written down some investment company numbers on here. I have two investment accounts started by my old manager when I was wrestling. He knew I'd have a short career and wanted me taken care of when I was done. This one," he pointed to a number on the first sheet, "is the largest. I've never taken anything out of it, just rolled the interest over and re-invested it. The second," he pointed to an account number on the second sheet, "is a smaller account I use occasionally, if I need some cash. The third is a regular First National Bank of Alaska savings account. The number is here. I want you to have the name on these accounts changed to the name on this page," he pointed out the name and address of his sister, Darlene Carson, in Kansas. "She doesn't know about all these goings-on. She has the family farm now. I want her to have all my assets. I'll never get out to use them, and she should retire from the farm. Maybe this will help her."

Lewis looked at the sheets in amazement. "There's a lot of money in these accounts, Dennis. How did you get a public defender when you have this much in liquid assets?"

"The lawyer I had before is a crook and had a conflict of interest with another person in the case. He told the court he couldn't represent me in my case. I think the judge thought I was broke and appointed you. It didn't matter to me, so I took the deal."

"I'm surprised you have this much money, Mr. Carson—" he said as he scanned and estimated the totals, "$265,000 in the first account, $92,000 in the second, and $41,000 in the savings account. Are you sure you want to sign all this cash over to your sister?" Lewis was impressed with the amounts and Crusher's willingness to give it away.

"I'm never going to get out of jail. I'll never use it. I want to give it to her so her life can be a little easier," Crusher spoke in a sad tone.

"All right, Mr. Carson. I'll have it typed up today and be here tomorrow for you to sign the papers. The facility here has a notary public on staff. She'll stamp the papers for us." He put the notes in his small briefcase. "Is there anything else I can do for you?" Lewis asked.

"Nope, that's all. Thank you for helping me." Carson stood at the door where the guard could see him, ready to leave.

Late the following morning Lewis brought a bundle of papers to the jail for signing. He explained each sheet to Carson before asking the guard to bring the notary to the visiting room. The officer with the notary stamp sat at the table, watching as Carson signed each sheet. When they were done, Lewis gave a copy to Carson and left the jail. Carson was returned to his segregation cell, resigned to the fact that this was to be his way of life for as long as he lived.

A month later, the weather beginning to look like spring was coming. Buddy Phelps was seated at the end of the bar in Cuddles' spot, watching Carol and a customer at the other end, when the phone rang.

"Forelands Bar, how can I help you?" answered Buddy.

"I guess the place is still open, then," said a pleasant voice on the other end.

Phelps was surprised at the caller: "Cuddles, is it really you?"

"Of course it's me! Who were you expecting anyway?"

"I've been wondering where you were. How are you?"

"Better than ever, Buddy. I've been thinking about coming home. Has anyone been around looking for me?"

"The troopers have been in a couple of times and I told them you weren't here right now and they left. When are you coming?" he asked the boss.

"I think, if the coast is clear and no one is anxious to see me, I'll be headed that direction in a couple of days. Are there any problems you know about?"

"No, things are quiet. The weather is warming up and the ice in the parking lot is beginning to melt. It looks like breakup is on the way."

"How's the bar doing?" she asked.

"We've managed to put a few bucks in the bank for you. I hung a 72-inch flat screen TV on the end wall in time for the Super Bowl game. Customers liked it so much, I left it there. With hockey and basketball season on we're getting quite a crowd in the evenings. It seems to be good for business, especially on fight night." Phelps caught himself talking about business and knew this was not a good time. "It will be good to have you home, Boss. Call me when you have an arrival time."

"I will, Buddy. I just wanted to be sure it was safe for me to come back. Have you seen Grant? I need to know when my court date is scheduled." Now Cuddles was the one talking business.

"Nope, he hasn't been around."

"I'll get caught up on the gossip when I get there. I'll call you tomorrow with my schedule. It's good to talk to you Buddy."

"Good to hear from you, too, Cuddles. And it will be good to have you here again." They hung up and Phelps sat on his stool, wondering what was bringing her home now. He wondered why she had not contacted him, even to ask about the business, for all these weeks. It made him wonder how she had managed to stay away for this amount of time without anyone asking to see her face-to-face. Even the trooper sergeant had been absent. Things would surely change when she came back.

After Carson's trial, the court awarded the property in the evidence locker to Pamela Williams. Seaton had not seen her since that day they had met in his office, but he was able to locate her and make arrangements to meet and hand over the property. The following day Pamela visited trooper headquarters once again and was led to the office of Sergeant Bob Seaton to acquire her new wealth, just like her brother had done months before.

"Nice to see you again, Trooper Seaton, it's been a while." Beeles was out on another matter and missed this meeting.

"Nice to see you again, Ms. Williams. How have you been?" he asked the lady.

"I'm doing well. In fact, I'm doing better every day. I want to thank you for your kindness. I know my brother was a pain for you sometimes." Something was different about her. It took a few minutes for Seaton to figure it out … it was her teeth! She now had perfect teeth: straight, white teeth.

"You *look* wonderful, too. I hear you're working in the Serenity office now," Seaton smiled with genuine satisfaction at the turn in this woman's life.

"Yes, they've been good to me. Which brings me to another question, Sergeant. I keep hearing from people who come to the rehab center that Claudia Morris had something to do with the death of my brother. Is that true? Did she have that man, Carson, kill my brother?"

"I really can't comment on an open case, Pamela."

"She's been so nice to me since I came here. She's given me so much and taken care of me. I can't believe she would do such a thing. I have to know what happened."

"I understand, but I can't tell you anything at this time. Come on now, Ms. Williams, we have some pleasant business to conduct. You are about to receive a large amount of gold. If you like, I will escort you to a bank where it can be locked in a vault until you decide what you want to do with it. It is such a large amount you may not be able to find a local buyer who can handle the cost. Someone at the bank may be able to help you with the sale. I'm not qualified to advise you about this. But, I will make sure you get it to the bank and locked up safely."

She agreed to allow the escort and signed all the papers releasing the gold to her. Seaton followed her to the Soldotna branch of the First National Bank of Alaska. Inside, he stood by as she opened an account and conferred with one of the bank executives about her options. Once the pouches were weighed and listed they were placed in a safety deposit box. Seaton felt a huge relief when the gold was locked away.

Chapter 36

Buddy was waiting at the Kenai Airport Terminal when Cuddles' plane arrived. He waited inside, knowing it would take her a while to come from the plane to the terminal. He watched through the window for her to deplane but never spotted her getting off the aircraft. He was still watching the plane when a voice from behind him asked, "Are you waiting for someone?"

He recognized the voice and turned to face Cuddles. He was shocked. He had not recognized her when she walked from the airplane. "Good Lord, Cuddles, what happened to you?"

She laughed, "I wondered if you would know me when I arrived. How do I look?"

"I'm stunned. What did you do?" She was 100 pounds thinner and wearing a smile. She looked wonderful.

"I had to leave here to get some surgery. I was dying and felt horrible. That's when I decided to hire you to run the place and give me the chance to do this. I still have to lose another 75 pounds, but I feel better already." She was smiling, showing her personal pride.

"How did you do this in such a short time?" he asked, still amazed at the sight of her.

"When I left here I went to a clinic in San Diego. They evaluated me and put me at the top of the list for surgery. I had a gastric bypass. They removed most of my stomach. I lost half this weight before I left the hospital. The doctors said I'd be dead in six months without the surgery. I can't eat what I once did, but I feel so much better now. I can walk, I can breathe. I can smile now. I can't believe it myself—how much better I feel."

"Well, let me get your bags and we'll leave here." She had two large suitcases, which she pointed out as they came around the carrousel. Luckily they were both on rollers, making the trip to the car easier. She didn't want to stop for lunch … just wanted to get home to the bar.

The sun had a little heat in it today and water was forming at the edge of the once-again black pavement. Winter was on the way out, though not without a fight. There would probably be more snowstorms and cold, but the accumulation would be less than the melt from now on.

"Take my bags upstairs for me, will you, Buddy?" He made two trips up the stairs to get the bags to her room. She stopped to enter the bar and say hello to Carol. Cuddles was surprised to see the differences in the place. The tables were arranged differently and the huge television covered the north wall. It was turned on to Fox News with no sound, but closed captioning was displayed on the screen. Carol was squatted down, working behind the bar and had assumed it was Buddy coming in the rear door. When she stood she saw Cuddles, not recognizing her for an instant.

"Well, look at you!" Carol said, I almost didn't recognize you. You don't look like the same person who left here a couple months ago. Welcome home."

"Thanks Carol, it's good to be home at last. How have you been?" inquired Claudia.

"I've been great. We haven't had any trouble here since the first day you left. Business is picking up and with spring and summer coming there will be the fishermen starting to get their beach sites ready." Carol was showing good business sense and working hard to improve the old place. "How do you like the new décor?" she asked.

"I like it. I can see now I should have had that television installed a long time ago. How come the tables are moved so far down toward the front door?" Cuddles asked her bartender.

"Sometimes, when there isn't a game on, we turn on the Sirius Radio channel and some of the customers have taken up dancing. There are more ladies coming in with their guys nowadays."

"It looks like you and Buddy have done a great job while I was gone. I'll try not to interfere with success. I'm going up to my room and rest a while. You two did great, thanks." It was not the same old Cuddles who walked upstairs. This one had a little spring in her step and a smile on her face.

Buddy came back to the bar a few minutes later carrying two cases of cold beer for the cooler. It was his habit to sweep the place out each morning before any customers came in to track snow on the floor. When he finished he sat on the stool at the end of the bar. "I guess I will have to find another place to sit in the mornings," he commented, laughing.

"I'll bet it doesn't take long for the locals to hear she's back in town," said Carol, chuckling for her own amusement.

"I'll bet business increases when the word gets out she's back and looking like a real person," Buddy wagered.

Shift changes at the Tesoro Refinery always meant business for the Forelands Bar. This evening was no exception. The first two customers in were old timers who knew Cuddles. The tall one saw her first. He turned to the shorter, heavier one, "Hey Ed, look who's here tonight!"

When Ed spotted the bar owner he let out a squeal that was heard for miles. "Cuddles, you old darlin'! Where have you been? We've been pining away without you here. Have you been sick? You look awfully skinny."

His partner was clearly happy to see her as well. "We've missed you, darlin', come over here and give us a kiss!" He puckered up and made a wild kissing sound, "Mmmm …wa!"

She laughed aloud, "You devils didn't even miss me, did you?"

"We asked about you every day, didn't we, Carol?" bluffed Ed.

"Buy these two liars a drink, Carol," Cuddles ordered. "Have you two been true to me while I was gone?"

Ed looked sideways at his partner and back at Cuddles, "Never gave another girl a glance, did we, Donnie?"

"I knew there was a reason I came home," she smiled as the front door opened again and Chuck Hagel walked in.

Hagel stopped dead in his tracks when he saw her. Immediately, he reached into his shirt pocket for his cell phone and dialed his brother: "Get down here, Cuddles is back." He walked up to where she was seated and gave her a huge hug. "Missed you," he said quietly.

"I missed you too, Chuck. The first round is on me." She was surprised and pleased at the reception she was receiving.

Hagel walked down the bar to converse with the two Tesoro hands. Tom Hagel and two friends entered five minutes later. The trio screamed, "Welcome home," when they entered.

Cuddles motioned for Carol to set up the bar once more, "Don't get used to drinking for free, boys. From now on you'll have to pay for my attention." They all laughed and raised their full glasses in salute to the returned Cuddles.

Tom Hagel walked down the bar to speak with her. "We really did miss you, Cuddles," he said as he put his arm around her shoulders and gave a gentle squeeze. "I suppose you heard about Crusher's trial?"

"Actually, I haven't had time to talk to Buddy about that. What happened?"

"They gave him two consecutive life sentences, one for Skip and one for Lil. It's hard for me to believe he did those killings, but he finally admitted to them. They sent him to Spring Creek prison in Seward. I just wanted you to know I don't hold any hard feeling toward you over any of this. You couldn't have known. Are we still friends?" asked Tom Hagel.

"Sure we are, Tom. I never meant to harm you or your brother. Let's let bygones be bygones. Let's be friends," she said earnestly.

Tom Hagel joined his brother and the others at the other end of the bar. Someone yelled, "Turn on the Texas Honky Tonk channel. Let's have some music around here!" Carol clicked on the satellite radio and the entire bar joined in singing "The Yellow Rose of Texas."

Cuddles smiled at Buddy when he entered the rear door. "I like what you've done with the bar. It's a friendly place now. Good job, Buddy."

"Glad you like it. I guess everyone is glad to see you back home again," he smiled, noting the happy tone of the crowd.

"I'm glad to be here, too. Tom Hagel just told me Crusher was given two life sentences, is that true?"

"Yes, it is. Grant called a while back and said to tell you that the charges against you had been dismissed because they exceeded the 120-day rule, whatever all that means. And he said he got his bail money back. You're off the hook."

"I'm happy to hear that. I still have some legal things to clear up before I can get back to business. You've done a bang-up job of running this place and I want you to keep on running it. I'll come down and sit here and pretend to be the boss, but I want you to take care of things. I haven't healed up entirely and can't take the responsibility for a while. Is that all right with you?"

"You pay me well, Cuddles. I'm happy if you're happy."

She stepped off her stool, much more easily now than before, and exited through the rear door. She was exhausted from the long day. Tomorrow she would have to contact Grant Cummings and learn the details of the legal proceedings.

Buddy took her place on the stool at the end of the bar. He checked the time and decided to call his old friend, Gene De Sylva.

"De Sylva," a brisk voice answered.

"You sound grumpy, Gene, what's the matter? Your date stand you up?"

"Hey, Buddy. Good to hear from you. I've been wondering whatever happened to you. Someone told me you were thrown in jail. What did you do, molest some farmer's daughter?" Gene was laughing aloud.

"Ha ha. I'll tell you about it when you get down here, Gene. What are you doing these days?"

"Not much. The bush strips are too soft to land on, and the ice is too weak for skis, too thick for floats."

"If you aren't busy, why don't you come down for a few days? I'll buy the beer."

"You could be sorry you said that, Buddy," Gene warned.

"Will you fly your plane or come by commercial?"

"Is the snow off the Rediske strip?"

"Mostly, it's been plowed all winter and should be in good shape," Buddy reported.

"OK, I'll call you when I get in. It'll probably be two days. Anything you want from Fairbanks?"

"Just bring your smiling face. See you in a couple of days." Phelps felt good about his old friend coming to visit. The two always had a good time when they were together.

Phelps was still sitting at the end of the bar when the front door opened and the local patrol trooper came in. He looked around, assessing the crowd, and made his way to where Phelps was seated.

"How's your night, Buddy?" he asked.

"Pretty quiet so far, how about the rest of the north road?"

"Your competition in Nikiski doesn't have a customer in the place. I see you have them all here." This trooper was always friendly. "I'm disappointed you haven't had a good bar fight here for months. I may forget how to use my pepper spray if this keeps up." The trooper winked and turned to leave. "See you next time," he waved as he walked to the door.

Buddy liked the troopers making bar checks. Their presence kept the rowdy behavior to a minimum. He was about to begin planning for De Sylva's visit when Carol came over and said she was about out of Bud Light. Oh well, back to work, he thought.

Buddy had finished stocking the bar cooler when the biker crowd stood to leave. The Hagel brothers walked to his end of the bar. "We're glad Cuddles is back. We missed her," said Chuck.

"Me too, Chuck, me too," Buddy nodded.

As the biker bunch left, the construction pair stood to go. "See you next time," said the big one, as they went out the door.

Carol waited until they were gone: "It was a good night, Buddy, but I'm glad they've all left. I can start to clean up now." She looked into his eyes. "You've made this a decent place to work. Thanks."

She was right. It had turned into a nice place to make a living.

Chapter 37

Darlene Carson and the hired hand had finished breakfast and were planning their day when, through the window, she saw a very large, very black Lincoln sedan stop in front of the house. Two men dressed in dark suits stepped from the vehicle. To Darlene they looked like government men or lawyers; neither sort were welcome on the Carson ranch. They stepped up on the porch and knocked. Darlene walked to the living room to answer the door.

"Hello, what can I do for you?" she asked.

The older and taller of the two spoke first. "We are looking for a lady by the name of Darlene Carson. Have we come to the right place?"

"Yes, that's me. How can I help you?"

"I'm Winston Marshall and this fellow is Seth Goodman. We are with the firm of Madison and Marshal of Topeka. If you will allow us to come inside we have some things to discuss with you."

Lawyers. She had guessed right. "What for?" Is someone suing me?"

"Oh, nothing like that," replied the lawyer kindly.

"OK, come on in." She held the door as the men marched into the living room. "Have a seat," she said, pointing to the sofa after closing the door.

After sitting, the younger lawyer opened a briefcase on his lap and withdrew a thick, large manila envelope, from which he pulled a stack of legal papers. He handed them to Marshall, who continued to speak. "Perhaps we should be alone for this conversation," he said, indicating the hired man at the kitchen doorway.

Darlene turned in her seat to look at the hired man, "It will be OK, go out to the shed and finish the tractor repair. I'll be along soon."

The hired man never spoke, only nodded, and turned to walk out the back door.

Once he was gone the lawyer continued. "Ms. Carson, I know of no easy way to tell you this, but your brother, Dennis, was convicted on two counts of murder and one count of arson. He has been sentenced to two consecutive life sentences and will never get out of prison."

Darlene gasped. "He was just here a few months ago. It was the first time I had seen him in years. We had such a wonderful time and he never said anything about any of this." She was sobbing now and pulled a Kleenex from a box on the end table.

The lawyers gave her a moment to regain her composure before continuing. "After his conviction, your brother requested his lawyer draw up papers giving you all his assets. There is a letter from him included in this packet of papers. We will let you read it after we leave you alone. We are here to help you take possession of his assets."

"It couldn't amount to much … he worked in a bar," she said, wiping her cheeks again.

"On the contrary, Ms. Carson, he has a great deal of money in savings and investments to give you. There are two investment accounts, and a bank account, which will become yours when you sign the final papers. We would like you to know that our firm, Madison and Marshal would be proud to represent you with your investment accounts, if you choose to continue them."

"Just how much is in these accounts?" she asked.

"The two investment accounts are approximately $265,000 and $92,000. The bank account is $41,000. These figures are approximate, due to the interest they are accumulating."

Darlene was without words. She stood and paced the living room floor. Finally she returned to the couch and sat. "Are you saying I'm getting $400,000 from my brother?"

"Yes, that's about what it comes to. I know this comes as a surprise, but when you decide what you want to do with these accounts, please feel free to contact me." Marshal was not going to allow someone else to manage an account like this, if he could help it.

"OK, what do I need to do?" she asked.

The younger lawyer spoke for the first time. "It would be easier if we reviewed the forms at the kitchen table." Once at the table he began to explain each sheet, and at the end of each group of paper he asked her to sign the form, which he notarized. There were a lot of pages and a lot of signatures before she finished. "The bank account is now in your name and you are free to add to or withdraw funds from that account. I would advise you to consult with Mr. Marshal before changing any of the terms of the other two investment accounts. They are very good investments and well managed. Each is drawing excellent interest in today's market, which is being reinvested in the accounts.

It was thoughtful of your brother to pass these accounts on to you before he left for prison." Seth Goodman was smooth and professional. "Are there any other questions to be answered, Ms. Carson?"

"I'm sure there will be, but I can't think of any right now."

Both men stood and Goodman closed his briefcase. Marshal handed her his card and a sealed envelope, "Feel free to contact me at any time. I will be happy to assist you in any way possible. Please, read the letter from your brother privately, as I'm sure he intended. We will leave you now. Remember we will be there to assist you at any time."

"Thank you both. I'm sorry I was so abrupt when you came. I seldom have good meetings with lawyers. You have been kind and gracious; thank you. I will be calling." She showed them to the door and watched them enter their big black Lincoln. She stood in the doorway until they were out the front gate. Once the lawyers were out of sight she returned to the kitchen table and opened the letter Dennis had sent her. She was trembling as she opened the envelope.

In the letter he apologized to his sister and wished her well. He confessed to her that he had, indeed, killed Skip Williams in order to get the gold pouches from him. Claudia was so obsessed with finding the source of the gold she wanted it at any cost. Lil Danby knew Dennis was not in the bar when Skip was murdered and had said so. In order to cover his tracks he killed Lil and placed her body in a dumpster behind the bar. "Don't feel sorry for me, Darlene, I did these things willingly. I am now paying for my mistakes. I will never be out of prison and I want you to have a more comfortable life. Please take these accounts and use the assets for anything that will make your life easier. I'm sorry I can't be there to help you." The words were kind and out of character for Dennis. Darlene knew he was sincere. He explained his manager had saved the winnings from his wrestling matches in these accounts in order to provide a future for him when he could no longer fight. He did not know about them until much later in his life. He had never needed the money; consequently, the accounts had grown.

Darlene was crying with sadness and joy simultaneously. She read the letter again, this time trying to feel what Dennis had been going through when he wrote it. When she finished, she sat at the table for several minutes. She had made up her mind, the money was hers and she would use it as Dennis suggested—to make own her life easier. She stood and put on her coat before stepping to the back door. She opened it and to the hired man, "Lester, lock up and come in here. We're going to town."

<<<.>>>

De Sylva called to notify Buddy of his arrival at Rediske Airpark. He had finished tying down the airplane and was ordering fuel when Phelps drove up to the tie-down spot. De Sylva had opted not to cover the wings. There would be frost at night, but he knew the peninsula weather would melt it all during the daylight hours.

Phelps rolled down his driver side window, "Hey, Gene, good to see you!"

"Good to see you, too, Buddy!" He gathered his belongings and loaded them in the SUV.

"Want some lunch before we go to the bar?" Phelps offered.

"Yeah, how about that place in Kenai? It's been a long day," said Gene as he stretched his legs.

"Hey--what happened to your face? I've seen men in aircraft accidents who looked better than you."

"It's a long story, Gene. I was arrested for dealing in stolen property and tossed in jail ..."

"What stolen property?" interrupted De Sylva?

"Those mining claims we were searching for—well, it turns out they were stolen from a man who was murdered. I didn't know about all that, and I made a deal for Cuddles to sell the claims to a big mining company. It turns out old Claudia wasn't always completely truthful with us. I've learned she wasn't satisfied with the $1.75 million dollars in gold nuggets she already had; she wanted more. That's why she sent us to find the source—pure greed."

They were pulling into the parking lot of Louie's Restaurant. Inside they were met by the little waitress who had tended them before. She looked tired but was pleasant and efficient, walking quickly with her long braid flipping from side to side. De Sylva and Phelps chose a booth. The waitress brought two cups of coffee and took their order.

"So, back to your face –?"

"You remember Crusher Carson?"

"Sure, the big wrestler who worked for Cuddles."

"Yeah, that's him. The troopers arrested him for murder—two different counts—and I got thrown in a jail dorm with him. He started giving me guff about Cuddles and the bar and, you know me, I couldn't keep my mouth shut. He beat the hell out of me, gave me a concussion, and sent me to the hospital for stitches. I'm almost healed up now."

"What happened to Crusher?" asked Gene.

"They just sentenced him to two life terms plus some other time for arson. He'll never get out of prison. Too bad. I kind of liked him. He was quiet and worked hard. He looked out for Cuddles every minute. She was safe with him around. I think she wants me to take over for him, but it's not my kind of work." Buddy laughed, "Want a job?"

De Sylva nearly choked on his coffee, "No thank you! It's not my kind of work either."

The two men passed the time during the rest of the meal and the drive back to North Kenai with small talk of old friends and Gene's business.

When they arrived at the Forelands Bar, Buddy told him to put his belongings in the same room he had shared with him the last trip here. De Sylva rested most of the day while Buddy tended the business of the bar, taking deliveries and making orders. He was sitting on the end stool when Carol came over and asked, "Who's your friend? He's cute."

"Watch out for Gene, he's a lover," Buddy teased.

"Hey, I'm just being friendly to the customers. You know what I mean. ... What does he do?" she persisted with her questions.

"He's a pilot and he owns an aircraft leasing company in Fairbanks. He's a good guy and I have trusted him with my life on a number of occasions. You could do a lot worse, Carol."

"Hey! I'm not shopping for a husband, I'm just curious, OK?" she said indignantly as she moved to the other end of the bar.

Cuddles entered through the rear door, wearing a light coat and tall breakup boots. "I'm going into town to finish up some legal work. I'll be back in a couple of hours. I'll be on my cell phone," she said, as she went back through the door she had just entered.

The front door opened and four oil field hands dressed in Carhart overalls entered. Two of them had been here before. Neither Carol nor Buddy recognized the other two. "What'll it be boys?" asked Carol.

"Bud Lite all around," answered the big man. They sat at a table close to the door.

The bartender delivered the beers and returned to the bar. They were a quiet bunch today.

Minutes later De Sylva came through the back door.

"What can I get you?" asked Carol.

"Coffee," replied Gene, sitting on a stool next to Buddy. "What are we doing?" he asked his old friend.

Carol approached with a steaming mug of black coffee. "Watch out for her, Gene. She's prowling for a spouse. I think she has you in mind. She combed her hair when she saw you come in." Buddy kept up the teasing.

"Buddy Phelps, you're rotten!" she declared and flounced to the other end of the bar. Both men laughed.

"Is there anything going on today?" asked De Sylva. "Anything I can do to help out?"

"No, we're just here to keep the peace, although Carol does a pretty good job of that on her own. She really is a good one, Gene. She won't have anything to do with me. That says something about her good character."

Two hours later Cuddles came back to the bar. She looked tired. "I'm going up to my room for a while," she said without any explanation and disappeared back through the door.

Gene held up his empty coffee cup for Carol to see.

It will be another boring evening, thought Buddy, as he turned the newspaper to the crossword puzzle.

Chapter 38

The reception desk at Serenity House had been a busy place today. It seemed every client who needed to check in and take a drug test had done it today. Pamela Williams sat at her desk finishing the filing and checking names off her list. She had a large stack of files on her desk to be placed back in the locked cabinets. She was tired, but she was happy not to be one of those coming in to be checked. This woman with a new lease on life was standing at her desk drinking bottled water when the phone rang.

"Serenity House," she answered.

The voice on the other end said, "Hello, this is Grant Cummings. I am trying to contact one of your employees, a Pamela Williams."

"This is Pamela," she replied.

"Oh, hello, Pamela. You sound very professional, and I didn't recognize you. One of my clients has transferred some items to your name. I wondered, could you stop by my office to sign some papers and accept title to these items?"

"I suppose so." They made arrangements to meet when she finished work later in the day.

It was after five when she left the Serenity office and started Skip's old truck. It ran well and got her where she needed to go, but it looked terrible. She vowed to buy a new one soon; she could afford it now. Pamela was surprised by the look of Cummings' "office," as she had been the first time she was there. She parked in front and walked to the porch, tapping lightly on the door. It seemed an eternity before the unsightly, bearded man wearing overalls, opened the door.

"Good to see you again, Pamela. Won't you please come inside?"

She hesitated a moment before entering, but decided to hold restrain her judgments and enter the house. He led her to the kitchen table, where legal papers were stacked in the center.

"Have a seat, Ms. Williams. Let me explain. I was hired by Claudia Morris to transfer ownership of some mining claims and an airplane she held as collateral on a loan she made to your brother, Larry. Unfortunately he was killed and his house burned. I represented the man accused of killing your brother, as well as Claudia Morris for a period of time. She was charged with conspiracy in the case. I ended up in a conflict of interest because she pled not guilty and the other party eventually changed his plea to guilty. At this point I could no longer represent both parties. The other party, Dennis Carson, was an employee of Claudia's. She was paying me to represent the both of them, therefore I had to drop the other client. I know this is complicated, but do you follow me so far?" he asked.

"Yes, I follow you." She took notice of the connections Cummings made, tying Cuddles to Crusher. She had not been told this prior.

"The property is now yours, including the lot where his trailer burned and the one where you are living now, as well as some mining claims and an airplane. The mining claims and plane belonged to an old prospector who was killed in an airplane crash. He left them to Skip in a hand-written will. The old man's name was Otis Fairfax. He was a nice old guy, completely obsessed with gold mining. The claims were sold during the time she owned them and prior to the time we knew you existed. Therefore, I will ask you to accept ownership of the sale price. Here is the check paid by the mining company for the full amount of the sale." She looked at the check. It was a very large amount. "If you agree to accept this check as payment for the mining claims, and I would advise you to do so, please sign this line on the last page. It explains the terms of the sale and transfers this payment to you. Will you accept the terms?"

She scanned through the pages, not understanding most of what she read, but finding the transfer wording and the amount to be as Cummings had represented. "Yes, I'll sign," she said, asking for a pen. Once done, he handed her the check. "I would like a copy of these papers, Mr. Cummings."

"Certainly, I'll make you copies of all the papers as soon as we finish." He set the first set of papers aside, picking up the second. "These are the titles to both of the real properties your brother owned. The names have been changed to acknowledge you as the new owner." Again he pointed out where she was to sign, and again she scanned the papers signing them on the last page. Cummings put this document with the other.

"The last one is registration of a Piper PA-11 owned by Otis Fairfax. It was willed to Larry and has now been registered in your name. The aircraft is located at Rediske Airpark in North Kenai. It is yours to keep or sell as you wish." He handed her the registration certificate and a document to sign, stating she had received it. Again she perused the document and signed on the last page, placing the registration form on top of the check from the mining companies.

"Mr. Cummings, I thank you for helping in this matter. But I have a question."

"I'll answer it if I can."

"You said Claudia was implicated in the death of my brother. Whatever happened to those charges? Were they dismissed?"

"Unfortunately no, she is still out on bail on those charges. The other trial was never held because the suspect, Dennis Carson, pled guilty. No disposition has been rendered in Claudia's case. I expect the district attorney will soon review this case and dismiss the charges. It should have been done long ago because the trial date has exceeded 120 days, the maximum under Alaska statutes. If she dismisses, it can be re-filed ... but I don't think she will do that because Dennis admitted his part in the death."

"Are you telling me Claudia was charged in the murder of my brother but never went to court?"

"Well, yes, I guess you could say that."

"Please make those copies for me, Mr. Cummings." Her tone was as cold as an Alaskan glacier.

"Of course, Ms. Williams, it will only take a few moments."

Pamela climbed into her old truck and began to drive north. She drove slowly, mulling the revelation about Cuddles being implicated in the death of her brother. Could Cuddles really have paid Dennis Carson to murder her brother? Could the district attorney really dismiss the charges against her? Is her guilt the reason she is being so kind and helpful? Cuddles seemed so compassionate; could she really be this cunning and hateful? There were only questions with no answers. The further she drove, the angrier she became. She drove directly home where she stashed all her papers in a small, two-drawer filing cabinet. The longer she thought about Claudia the more it disturbed her. Everyone had said Claudia's treatment of Pamela was totally out of character. She sat in her kitchen searching for answers, but found none. She only became more confused and more upset.

An hour later she climbed into her truck and drove the mile to the Forelands Bar. Phelps and De Sylva were sitting at a table in front of the huge television set with the sound muted, eating a large pizza. Cuddles sat at the end of the bar. Her dinner consisted of two hard boiled eggs. Pamela entered the bar wearing a long insulated coat and carrying a large cloth purse, hung from her right shoulder. Claudia watched her walk in and greeted her in a friendly voice.

"Hello, Pamela, good to see you." She turned to the nearby table, "Boys, this is Pamela Williams, sister of Skip Williams."

"Pleased to meet you," said Phelps.

"Me, too, Ms. Williams," spoke Gene De Sylva. "I'd like to talk to you about that Piper that you own now."

Pamela ignored the two men, focusing on Claudia. Her expression was cold and harsh. "I want to know why you didn't tell me you were charged in the murder of my brother!" Her words to Claudia came in a loud and rapid sequence, like the fire of a machine gun.

Cuddles was taken aback, "Who told you that?"

"It doesn't matter who told me. What matters is whether or not it's true. Is it?" She stood with her legs apart, staring at Cuddles.

De Sylva was still standing and moved around the table toward Pamela. "Calm down, Ms. Williams, please."

"Go back and sit down. This has nothing to do with you." She reached her right hand into the large purse and produced an old, worn-looking Colt 1911A.45 caliber automatic pistol. In her small hands it looked gigantic. "Tell me the truth, Claudia. Did you have anything to do with the death of my brother?"

"Hey, Pamela, that's not the way to go about this," De Sylva spoke very calmly. Again he attempted to step around the table.

"If you don't want to get shot, get back." She swung the pistol in the direction of De Sylva, snapping the safety off as she turned. It was plain to see she was familiar with the gun. De Sylva moved back.

"Pamela, honey, why are you angry with me after all I've tried to do for you?" soothed Cuddles. There were tears in the bar owner's eyes.

Carol was halfway down the bar. She caught Phelps' eye, motioning toward the phone under the far end of the bar. Phelps gave a small nod and Carol inched her way to the far end of the bar.

Phelps and De Sylva were both standing now. Phelps took the lead: "Pamela, nothing can be solved this way. Please put the gun down and sit down with us. We can talk about it in a calm manner." While he was confronting Pamela, Carol was dialing 911, cupping the mouthpiece with her hand in an attempt to be silent.

When the operator answered she whispered, "Gun, Forelands Bar, come now," and hung up.

The two men were inching their way around the table toward Pamela. "Back off," she shouted, "I came to find out about my brother. I'll shoot you if you try to stop me." She turned back to Cuddles, who was now terrified and crying in fear. "Answer my question, Claudia. Did you have anything to do with my brother's death?"

"Of course not, Pamela," she sobbed. "I don't know how you could have come up with an idea like that."

"Cummings said you were arrested along with Carson and that he pled guilty to protect you. I wondered all along how you came to be in possession of so much of Skip's property. And now I know that you had all of Skip's gold. I was so blinded by your helping me I couldn't see that you were the one who ordered him killed. It was all for greed. It was all for the lust for gold. The troopers told me everyone who touched this gold was either dead or in jail. Well, I own it now and I'm willing to go to jail to find out if you killed Skip. I've thought about it a lot and there simply is no other answer."

The siren of the first patrol car was approaching and could be heard in the bar. The second was minutes behind and another behind that one.

"Pamela, the cops are coming. Give me the gun and get out of here before they get here," Phelps was advising her. "They're going to arrest you when they come. Give me the gun and get going."

"I don't think so." She pointed the gun at Cuddles, "Just tell me, Claudia, tell me you killed Skip."

"All right, all right, I paid Crusher to go to Skip's place that night and get the gold. But the killing was his idea, not mine." The siren was closer now, "Now get out of here. You heard what you came to hear."

There were tears in Pamela's eyes now. "Yes, Claudia, it's what I expected to hear." Pamela looked Cuddles in the eyes with her own hard glare. "Explain it to Skip when you get there." Pamela pulled the trigger and instantly a bullet struck Claudia at the top of her breastplate, shattering the bone and destroying her windpipe and arteries. Cuddles flew off her barstool to the floor in a bloody heap.

Pamela lowered her arm and placed the Colt on the table with the pizza. She backed into a chair at a table behind her and sat. De Sylva picked up the 45 and carried it to Carol, who stashed it behind the bar. The smell of cordite was still in the air when the first trooper entered, gun drawn.

"It's over," Phelps informed the trooper. "Pamela here just shot my boss, Claudia Morris. I think Bob Seaton is going to want to know about this."

The trooper took a pair of handcuffs from his belt and snapped them on the wrists behind the back of Pamela Williams. He walked to where the body lay before speaking into his radio. "Dispatch, we will need a supervisor. Our victim is 10-99. Please advise Sergeant Seaton."

The second trooper arrived and the gathering of information began. When the third trooper arrived, they transported Pamela to the pre-trial facility for booking.

Chapter 39

Bob Seaton and Jason Beeles arrived minutes after the call was made. Both had been off-duty when the call came and both responded in civilian clothing but with duty belts and weapons strapped on, ready for business.

The first trooper on the scene met the investigators at the door and gave a brief report of, what had happened. Seaton thanked him and said he would take the investigation from here. Beeles was taking ID information from all the witnesses. He was checking Carol's identification when Seaton approached the table where the three were seated.

"I asked the trooper to call you, Sergeant. After all that has gone on in this bar over the past few months, I thought you would want to see how it ended," Phelps was explaining.

"Where were you when all this began?" Seaton asked Phelps.

"De Sylva and I were sitting here at this table eating a pizza when Pamela came in. Carol was behind the bar and Cuddles was sitting on her regular stool. There weren't any other customers in here at the time she arrived."

"Was she carrying the gun when she came into the bar?" asked Seaton.

"No, it was in her big purse and we didn't see it until later. She came in and walked over to where Cuddles was sitting and confronted her about paying Crusher to kill Skip Williams. Cuddles denied it at first, but Pamela started saying things she had learned about the case and pulled the gun. De Sylva started to walk around the table to get the gun, but Pamela pointed it at him and said she would shoot if he didn't sit down. He sat, and she went back to talking to Cuddles. Cuddles was scared and started crying and screamed at Pamela. She admitted sending Crusher over to Skip's house that night to steal the gold but denied ordering him to kill Skip. Pamela said something about telling that to Skip when she got there … and shot her in the chest. We were scared, too, and froze in our seats, wondering if she was going to shoot all of us. I've never seen anyone shot before." Phelps' voice was shaky as he told his account of the shooting.

Seaton turned to De Sylva, "Do you have anything to add to this story, Gene?"

"Nope, that's just how it happened. I'm still shaking."

"How about you Carol? Can you add anything to this?"

"No, I can't, Sergeant. After she pulled out the gun I sneaked a call to 911 and told them we had a gun here. The troopers came right away, but it was too late for Claudia. My ears are still ringing from the shot." Carol, too, was speaking with a shaky voice. All three were in shock.

"Had any of you ever seen a confrontation between Pamela and Claudia in the past?"

"No," answered Carol, "In fact, she was nicer to Pamela than to anyone else. She really liked the girl. She helped her out all the time. I can't figure out what set her off."

"I'll be going to the pretrial facility to talk to her when I leave here," Seaton commented, "I'll see if I can find an answer to that question."

"Is there somewhere the three of you can wait while we gather evidence and take pictures? It is going to take quite a while to finish our work and it would be best if you were not in here during that time," Beeles directed, organizing the investigation.

"Yes," said Phelps, "we can all go up to our room upstairs and wait. Is it alright if we turn out the beer signs and the open sign? We are definitely closed for the rest of the night."

"Yes, that's OK. We don't want anyone walking in here tonight. Thank you." Beeles left the table to instruct the other troopers on what was to happen now.

Seaton directed Beeles to take charge of the investigation and the body while he went to the jail to interview Pamela Williams. The three witnesses went upstairs to wait.

Seaton parked inside the gated area where prisoners were normally admitted. He entered the jail through the rear door where he was greeted by the shift supervisor, Sarah Britton. Pamela was being held in the front holding cell, awaiting his arrival. Two officers led her and the trooper sergeant to the attorney visiting room where Seaton would conduct his interview.

Seaton said nothing until the correctional officers were out of the room and the door closed. He placed a small recorder on the table. "I am going to record this interview, if you have no objections."

"No, that will be fine with me," she commented.

"I am going to read you your rights at this time." Seaton read the statement from a card. "Do you understand your rights as I have read them to you?"

"Yes, I understand," she admitted quietly.

"You have a right to have an attorney present while I question you. Would you like to have a lawyer at this time?"

"No, I'll answer your questions and tell you what happened." Again she spoke softly.

"We have several witnesses who say you are the one who shot Claudia Morris. Did you shoot her?"

"Yes, I shot her, and if she's still alive I'll do it again." This time her voice was hard.

"Our witnesses say Claudia was always kind to you, is that true?"

"Yes, always. She helped me get off drugs and to get new teeth and fix my hair and gave me a place to live. She was good to me." There were tears in her eyes now.

Seaton was making notes quickly. "If she was good to you, why did you shoot her?"

Again her eyes grew cold when she answered. "Grant Cummings explained to me she was the one who sent Carson to kill my brother. Cummings said she had Carson steal a box of gold from him and kill him. She faked some papers and took his property, as well as the property the old prospector left him. The things she gave me were never hers. She stole them from Skip in the first place. I went there and confronted her. She finally admitted the truth to me, and I shot her. She killed my brother, and I killed his killer for him."

"Where did you get the gun, Pamela?"

"I think it was one that belonged to the old prospector who lived in my trailer before," she answered without hesitation.

"Do you mean Otis Fairfax?" the trooper asked.

"Yes, the gun was in the night stand beside the bed. I found it when I was cleaning up after moving into the trailer."

"Were there any other weapons in the house when you moved in?"

"No ... well, a couple of hunting knives, but no guns."

Bob Seaton was amazed at how straight forward and honest she was during the interview. So far she had not tried to hide anything. "Let's go back to the beginning, Pamela. I want to try to put all this in order."

"OK, that will be fine. I don't think I'll be going anywhere," she said.

"Would you like a cup of coffee or a soda? This may take a while." Seaton had done hundreds of interviews like this and wanted her to be relaxed.

"No, not right now, I'm fine. Maybe later." She sat with her shoulders forward and head lowered. She had already accepted her probable fate.

"I'll ask you one more time, do you want to have a lawyer here to advise you?" Seaton gave her the opportunity to change her mind about the lawyer.

"No, Sergeant, I killed Claudia. There's no getting around that. I did it to avenge my brother's death. There is nothing complicated about it. I thought about it a long time before I went to the bar. I don't regret it one bit. She killed my brother and I killed her. I know I'll never get out of jail, but I also know she will never get out of her grave, at least not until Skip gets out of his."

"The district attorney will be asking you all these questions again, but I have to ask everything and get as many answers as possible before you go to arraignment, which will be tomorrow. I advise you to call a lawyer to be there with you when you go before the judge. I want you to understand the seriousness of the charges." The trooper wasn't sure she fully understood how much trouble she was in. She knew she had been arrested for murder, but he didn't know if she entirely understood the consequences.

"Do you know a good lawyer, Sergeant? Mine helped Claudia get away with murder, so I don't think I want him to help me," she smiled sadly as she commented.

"I am not allowed to recommend anyone to you, but the jail has a list of attorneys who can represent you. You will be going to court in the morning, but if you pick a lawyer you don't like, you can change before the next hearing. You have some choices here, Pamela. I advise you to use them wisely. It has to do with the way you will spend the rest of your life." It was kindly advice from a compassionate trooper.

"OK, Sergeant, I'll call someone after you leave, if it makes you feel better."

"Yes, it will make me feel better," said Seaton, smiling back at her. "Now let's start at the beginning again. You say the lawyer, Cummings, called you about some papers. Were these papers the mining claims once belonging to Otis Fairfax?"

"Yes, he gave me a check from a mining company who bought them from Claudia. It was a sizeable check, too. I deposited it in the bank on my way home. And there were some other papers, too. There was a registration for an airplane, a Piper something-or-other. And there were the titles for the old pickup and the two pieces of property Skip owned. The court gave all this to me when Skip died. Those papers are in my trailer in North Kenai, on the kitchen table. My keys are in my purse the jail took from me when they brought me in here."

"I'll need to get those keys from you before I leave." Bob Seaton was furiously making notes in his book. "You said Cummings implicated Claudia in the death of your brother. Exactly what did he tell you?"

"Until then, no one had told me she was arrested with Carson for the murder of my brother. All the time I have been here I couldn't figure out how she got all of Skip's property. Then when you told me about finding the gold—Skip's gold!—it all eventually came together. She was behind it all. She sent Carson to rob Skip. Carson is a big man and Skip would never have had the strength to fight him off. It probably was Carson's idea to set fire to the place, but he brought the gold and the mining certificates to Claudia. She was the one lusting for his property, not Carson." Pamela was sobbing now, not from remorse but from sadness.

The interview lasted another two hours. When he left the jail, he took Pamela's house keys with him. The investigators would have to search her home for any clues she may have hidden there. He drove back to the Forelands Bar where he found Beeles. The body had been removed and Beeles and his helpers were gathering up the final pieces of their equipment when Seaton arrived.

"I've locked the back door and advised the three employees to stay out of the area until we allow them back. The body was flown to the crime lab and the medical examiner notified. We have the gun in evidence. There are photos of the entire scene as well as a video record. I think we have done as much as we can do tonight," Beeles reported to his sergeant. "How about you? Did you get a good interview with Pamela?"

"Yes, I did. She said she did it for revenge. She found out from the lawyer, Cummings, that Cuddles was the one who hired Crusher to rob Skip Williams. A simple motive and a simple solution, according to her."

"I don't know about you, but I think I'll quit for the day," said Beeles.

"Wus!" accused Seaton, with a grin.

Chapter 40

Springtime was in full swing on the Kenai Peninsula. The trees were beginning to leaf out and the grasses, both lawns and roadside, were turning green. Moose were beginning to disappear into the woods, preparing for calving season. It is a magical time in South Central Alaska. It seems that overnight the white of winter changes to the green of spring. Songbirds return, geese land on their way to Siberia, and the whistle from the wings of a snipe can be heard in the morning time. People become more tolerant of one another. Ladies consider tall, rubber breakup boots to be fashionable. The days are longer and warmer.

Troopers Beeles and Seaton had spent most of the early springtime in the office writing reports and preparing legal documents to assist the district attorney in her pending cases. The normal load of investigations continued keeping both men on the run most of each day. The two had developed a close working relationship. Beeles was a willing student and Seaton an apt teacher. Together they were able to produce excellent results.

Crusher Carson had been sent to Spring Creek Correctional Facility in Seward. He was considered a model prisoner and given privileges not usually allotted to new maximum security prisoners.

Pamela Williams remained at Wildwood Correctional Facility in Kenai, pending final disposition of sentencing. Where she would be sent to serve her time had not yet been decided by the Department of Corrections. Meanwhile she was housed in the pre-trial facility, segregated from the other female inmates.

Grant Cummings had filed a stack of motions with the court in order to recover what he had called "payment for legal services rendered to Claudia Morris and her estate." The bottom line of all his legal maneuvering was to claim all the property owned by Claudia Morris for providing his legal expertise. He had worked diligently on this project; it was the retirement plan he wanted. Several months of preparation and filing had gone into his scheme, which was working well. On the surface, the stacks of papers filed by Cummings were a logical end to the estate, and the judge was about to order his ruling when another set of probate documents was entered ... by Jason Quimby, attorney for Claudia Morris. These included a last will and testament signed and notarized by the clerk of the court. The judge gave his clerk the task of determining if and how the two cases were related.

The clerk for the judge called Quimby to ask about his filing of a written will dispersing the property of Claudia Morris. The probate filing by Cummings claimed there was none. It took several weeks to verify all the legal sheets and signatures. In the end, the will submitted by John Quimby was deemed to be the valid legal document.

Further investigation by the court determined that the amounts submitted by Cummings were not verifiable. The discrepancies continued to mount. Cummings continued to call the court and prod the clerk into releasing the property to him.

Unbeknownst to Cummings, the judge had asked the Alaska Bar Association to investigate the claims made in this case. It was this investigation which uncovered all the unethical and illegal acts of Grant Cummings. The Alaska Bar Association disbarred Grant Cummings and repealed his rights as an attorney at law in Alaska and other states. The judge ruled in favor of the petition by Jason Quimby, allowing him to distribute the property of Claudia Morris in accordance with her wishes.

Pamela was now one of the richest inmates in the Alaska prison system. She was sentenced to fifteen years for second degree murder in the death of Claudia Morris. The reduced sentence was a plea deal reached between Pamela and District Attorney Nancy Collins, through Pamela's new lawyer.

<<<.>>>

Sergeant Bob Seaton leaned far back in his desk chair and put his feet up. Jason Beeles was sitting across from him, both men holding hot cups of coffee. The thread of cases which began with an airplane crash in Cook Inlet and ended with the death of Claudia Morris were now finished. They had taken a long time and much effort to finalize. Both men felt good about the results.

Beeles peered over the top of his ceramic cup. "Something has been puzzling me from the start," he began. "There were no true good guys or bad guys in all this. I had a terrible time keeping the suspects and the victims separated. I don't know how you do it, Sarge."

Seaton chuckled knowingly. He remembered when he had had the same problem. "In all our investigations, we have to remember to discount personalities. Remember this, Jason: no one is *always* good and no one is *always* bad. Good people do bad things, and bad people do good things. Take a look at Cuddles. She was a victim in the beginning, during her illegal career. Then she bought the bar and changed her life from prostitute to a more highly reputable businesswoman. Look at Otis Fairfax. He was too poor to buy gas for his plane and ran out of it, causing him to crash and be killed, with $1.75 million in gold on board! Look at Skip Williams. He was a drug dealer with nothing to show for his life. Suddenly he became a millionaire and was killed because of it. Look at Pamela Williams. She was a drug user and a failure at life. She became a millionaire almost overnight, and in the process became embittered and obsessed with vengeance. Now she's going to be in prison for most of the rest of her prime. Look at Crusher Carson. He was a soft-spoken, washed-up wrestler who had enough money to last him the rest of his life, but he loved Cuddles ... and she got him to do things he would never have done on his own. Now he's in prison for the rest of his life. Most of the time, each of these were nice people who did bad things or bad people who did good things. The best advice I can give you is to investigate the facts and leave out the personalities. You are going to have to arrest a lot of people you really like."

"I guess you're right, Sarge. They say that even Jack the Ripper was only a bad person a small percentage of the time. He was probably a well-liked and respected person most of his life," Beeles spoke thoughtfully, through the steam over his coffee cup.

"It sounds like you may have learned something, Partner," smiled Seaton wisely. "Thus ends the lesson for today."

Other Books By Ron Walden

Cinch Knot

Pigs, politics, and Petroleum.

The Multinational Plot to Nuke the Trans Alaska Pipeline

Devil's Heart

Native American Lore and Modern Police Work

Ice Blue Eyes

An Alaska Story of Greed, Live, and Revenge

Blue Sky and Green Grass

Murder, Money Laundering, and Winter Farming in Alaska

Poacher's Paradise

An Alaska Wildlife Trooper Novel